Praise for Jerry Rodriguez and
The Devil's Mambo

"*The Devil's Mambo* blew me away. Wonderful, dark, dark stuff . . . Scared the hell out of me. Noir has a new name."
—Ken Bruen, Shamus Award–winning author of *The Guards* and *American Skin*

"This novel invents a new genre: sex noir. A well-written, gripping travel guide to the seedy underbelly of mankind's mind. I read it in one sitting."
—Jimmy Palmiotti, author of *Beautiful Killer*

"*Bien escandaloso*. Double-barreled, 12-gauge pulp . . . You'll love it!"
—Mario Acevedo, author of *The Nymphos of Rocky Flats* and *X-Rated Bloodsuckers*

"Many novels promise to take us to a dark, dangerous world we've never seen before, yet few deliver the way *The Devil's Mambo* does. Debut novelist Jerry Rodriguez holds no punches, doesn't flinch, and comes through with a knockout performance."
—Jason Starr, Barry Award–winning author of *Twisted City* and *Lights Out*

"Rodriguez's debut is a menagerie of sex, violence, and the hardboiled noir genre fans can't live without . . . A seductive read with a Spanglish accent."
—Kenji Jasper, author of *Dark* and *The House of Childress Street*

"Better fortify yourself with a blast of the hard stuff, check your clip, and keep your radar on 'sweep' when you follow Nick Esperanza on his descent into the artfully portrayed dark and dank and seamy underbelly of the big, bad city."
—Gary Phillips, author of *Bangers* and the *Martha Chainey* series

"A wild ride on the wild side. Rodriguez pulls no punches."
—Rick Mofina, Ellis Award–winning author of *The Dying Hour*

The Devil's Mambo

jerry a. rodriguez

KENSINGTON BOOKS
http://www.kensingtonbooks.com

KENSINGTON BOOKS are published by

Kensington Publishing Corp.
850 Third Avenue
New York, NY 10022

ISBN-13: 978-0-7582-1710-3
ISBN-10: 0-7582-1710-2

First Kensington Trade Paperback Printing: May 2007
10 9 8 7 6 5 4 3 2 1

Printed in the United States of America

To the loving memory of my brother Malik.

Acknowledgments

To my wonderful *familia*: *Gracias* for your unwavering love and support. You always make me proud to be a Rodriguez.

To my lovely editor, Sulay Hernandez: You believed in my novel when no one else would, always fight the good fight and never give up. You've proven to me that angels do exist. When an editor becomes a muse, a writer can't ask for anything more.

To Michael A. Gonzales: For being my best friend for more than twenty-five years, for all the wild drunken nights and for inspiring me to become a writer in the first place.

To Paul Calderon: For being a guiding force in the writing of this novel and a major part of my evolution as a fiction writer.

To all my *amigos* and *amigas*: For your love, inspiration, many years of wonderful friendship and never-ending support. Magie Jordan, Tomislav Novakovic, Phillip Batiato, Benny Nieves, James Shell, Tony Jackson, Justice Banks, Richard Goteri, Ethan Wolvek, David Bellantoni, Cecile Matip, Terez Thorpe, Lissette Espaillat, Cathy Calderon, Gia'na Garel and Sheila Jamison.

To Kate Duffy and everyone at Kensington Publishing: For taking a chance on my novel.

To all the talented artists I worked with over the years: For inspiring the best in me, and always making me look so damn good.

Finally, to all the people I've encountered through this journey called life: Without you none of my stories would exist.

Chapter 1

*"No kind of sensation is keener and more active than
that of pain; its impressions are unmistakable."*
—The Marquis de Sade

Nicholas Esperanza thought he was dead. He couldn't open
his eyes. Couldn't move his body. Last thing he remembered
was the buxom stripper popping the Ecstasy tab in his mouth
while giving him a wild lap dance. The rest was a blur. Fun-
filled and crazy, but still a blur. So, maybe he wasn't dead
after all. Maybe this was simply the worst hangover ever.

He concentrated his thoughts and finally managed to
sluggishly open his eyes. Bright sunlight gushed through the
windows and made his head shriek in pain. He clamped his
eyes shut again, for a moment uncertain where the hell he
was. Esperanza reached into his pocket, whipped out a pair
of Calvin Klein sunglasses and popped them on. Now he
could see without his pupils melting. The room steadily came
into focus.

Oh, okay. He'd awakened from his post-party coma on the
floor of his upstairs office, in his nightclub, Sueño Latino—
Latino Dream.

On the floor beside him were his gold lighter and matching cigarette case. Esperanza reached out, picked up the case
and opened it. Inside were several nicely rolled joints. He
stuffed one into his mouth, sparked it up and toked on it,
enjoying the primo weed. Otherwise, Esperanza didn't move.
His cobalt-blue Hugo Boss suit was covered in dust and carpet fibers, and wrinkled like an old lady's ass. A few feet away,

there was a mustard-yellow, very comfy, Italian leather couch he could've crashed on. His brain was pounding as if a crew of gangsta rappers was locked inside, shooting off monster rhymes to a ceaseless, thumping ghetto beat.

Coño, I shouldn't have polished off that bottle of Bacardi last night.

He smiled to himself as the memories of the bachelor party he and his boy Havelock attended came flooding back in Technicolor images of champagne drinking, cocaine sniffing, pot smoking, porn videos, strippers getting off with dildos, girl-girl sex acts and all kinds of other debauchery. Havelock had thrown the party for his cousin Justice Lightbourne. If Justice's fiancée found out what went down last night, Esperanza wondered if she'd still want to get married.

It took forever for Esperanza to sit up. At least the weed helped soothe his headache a little. As much as he drank these days, he rarely got hangovers anymore, but last night he'd gotten a little *too* carried away. He looked at his Hermès watch. Three PM. Esperanza sat there for a long moment, like a toddler in a playpen anxiously waiting for a grown-up to pick him up and take him out to play. But no one was coming any time soon. It required a ridiculous amount of effort, but Esperanza finally managed to heave himself to his feet. The office spun for a few seconds, then stabilized to a low-key sway.

Okay, Esperanza. You can do this. One step. Two steps. Three.

He dropped into the high-back leather chair behind the expansive glass-and-chrome desk. Behind him, the panoramic windows, which offered a spectacular view of Manhattan's Upper West Side, were letting in too much blinding sunlight. Though he should've gotten up and drawn the blinds, his body refused to obey the "get your ass up" command he repeated to himself several times.

As he continued to puff on the joint, his eyes scanned the

far wall. It was decorated with framed citations, awards and newspaper articles detailing his career from Navy SEAL to N.Y.P.D. homicide detective. A couple of newspaper headlines screamed: LOTTO COP WINS 30M! That was the final chapter of his life in law enforcement. The ghetto kid from El Barrio in East Harlem, the oldest brother of three whose father prayed every day for him not to wind up on drugs, or in jail, or dead, like so many of the other boys in the neighborhood, was now a very wealthy man.

Esperanza retired three years ago at the age of forty. No more crime scenes, decomposing bodies, search warrants, stakeouts or courtroom testimony. All of it wiped away by the very first lottery ticket he ever purchased. He hit the jackpot, and it completely changed his life. Even made him a small-time celebrity for a short while. Esperanza appeared on a couple of talk shows and some local morning news programs, and did a television commercial for the New York State Lottery. Because he cut an imposing figure, with his rugged, dark, *Boricua* good looks, a couple of Hollywood agents believed he had the right stuff to become an action-movie star. A Puerto Rican Steven Seagal. *Can you imagine that?* The talent agents offered to rep him and get him auditions at the major studios, but Esperanza politely declined. He'd seen enough violence in real life and had no interest in playing pretend in some silly movie. Hell, he retired from the force because he was fed up with dealing with liars and criminals, so why would he want to go into the movie business?

Life was *bien chévere*. Esperanza was still madly in love with Legs, his high school sweetheart. She was formerly an investment banker, and now co-owner and manager of his club. She was five ten, with luscious legs that came up to her neck and glorious raven hair that came down to her waist, all topped off by a keen mind and discriminating taste. With Legs's guidance and advice, Esperanza made some wise investments in various stocks, bonds, mutual funds and start-up dot-coms, and they paid off handsomely. Unless he screwed it up in some kind of major way, he'd never have to work another day for the rest of his life.

Esperanza owned the hottest salsa club in New York, a beach house in Isla Verde, Puerto Rico, an apartment with a stunning wraparound view of Central Park and several vintage sports cars, including a 1967 Jaguar XKE coupe, a 1963 red Corvette convertible and a 1971 Ferrari Spider. A total clothes hound, his closets were full of Armani and Hugo Boss suits, Donna Karan dress shirts and Gucci shoes. Esperanza was a man-about-town without a care in the world.

Except for that damn cup of coffee he so desperately needed. He could also use a shower, a workout, a steam and a massage. *Vaya*, his afternoon was already mapped out for him. Esperanza picked up the phone and buzzed Legs at the bar downstairs, where she was most likely doing inventory.

"Hey, angel," he said in a raspy voice.

"Well, well. The dead has risen," she said. Esperanza loved the fact that Legs's voice was always sultry, as if she'd just had multiple orgasms.

"You could've woken me up, you know. Helped me get on the sofa."

"Floor's better for your back."

"Keep it up with the smart mouth, *mami*. I'll deal with you later. Do me a solid and ask Maria to bring me a giant cup of *café negro*."

"I'll think about it," she replied and hung up.

He also hung up the phone, thinking about what a pain in the ass Legs could be sometimes. That's why he adored her so much. She kept him on his toes with that sarcasm of hers. A Puerto Rican Princess, a salsa diva, she was all the woman he'd ever need.

They don't make 'em like her anymore.

He stubbed out the joint in the crystal ashtray, dropped

his head onto his folded arms and impatiently waited for Maria, the assistant manager, to show up with a dose of pure caffeine.

Legs stepped into Esperanza's office and stopped dead in her tracks when she heard the shower running. Esperanza, who was hiding behind the open office door, got excited as he spied on her. Legs dragged her fingers through her waves of shimmering hair and seemed to be debating whether she should come back later.

She ran her tongue over her meaty, eminently kissable lips and yelled, "*Mira*, Nick. Why are you buggin' me to come see you if you're taking a shower?"

Esperanza kicked the door closed, and when it slammed shut, Legs reeled around, startled by the loud noise. Before she could utter a word, he grabbed her and roughly pushed her, face first, against the door.

"Assume the position," Esperanza demanded, and without question, Legs complied.

He was naked except for a towel wrapped around his waist. She bent forward and firmly planted her palms flat against the door, then placed her feet wide apart, like a suspect ready to be patted down.

Legs's body provocatively filled out her white, silk blouse and her tight, black skirt, which came to her knees and was slit high up the back. Before touching her, Esperanza's eyes took a leisurely stroll along her sumptuous *cuerpo*. She was a straight-up *mami*, blessed with the kind of *curvas* that convinced even the most devout atheist that God *does* exist. Esperanza's hands traveled up and down her thick thighs, then vigorously explored every inch of her warm body, caressing, squeezing and fondling.

"What did I do, officer?" she asked in an exaggerated girly voice. Legs admired Esperanza's muscular body. He was six foot one, with copper skin, a square jaw and neatly trimmed, jet-black hair with streaks of silver at the temples. She always said he looked more like a rugged 1940s movie star than a cop.

"You have the right to remain silent," he said as she arched her back and rubbed her impressively round ass against his erection, which eagerly poked through the towel. "But I don't necessarily want you to exercise that right."

He pulled up her skirt, revealing round, smooth cheeks accentuated by the line of a black thong. On her lower back, there was a tattoo of the sun glowing amber. Inside the sun, written in black Chinese calligraphy, was the word "hope," the translation for "esperanza." Legs wriggled her big Puerto Rican butt, urging him on. Esperanza pressed against her, and buried his face in her smooth-as-silk hair, which smelled faintly of coconut. She reached back, grabbed his cock and aggressively stroked it.

"You're not gonna hurt me with your nightstick, are you?"

"Only if you resist." He spun her around and kissed her slow and deep, his hand crawling underneath her skirt, pulling her panties to the side, penetrating her already soaked pussy. Legs recently got a Brazilian bikini wax and was extremely smooth down there. Her musky sex-scent hit him, and nothing turned Esperanza on like the bouquet of a woman ready to be ravished.

"Then resist I will." She gazed at him for a moment, her honey-hued, enigmatic eyes catching fire.

She kissed him with such ferociousness, she made Esperanza's head spin. He loved kissing those voluptuous lips of hers, so incredibly supple, hot tongue darting and spiraling and exploring. From the very first *beso* they shared back in high school, no woman had ever kissed him with such unbridled hunger.

She gave him a hardy shove to the chest, knocking him back, then leaned against the door and leisurely peeled off her clothes. Her breasts weren't too big or too small. They were just right as far as Esperanza was concerned. Still taut and pert, and sprinkled with tiny, reddish freckles, they were beautiful.

"Think you can handle me, *papi*?"

Her resplendent beauty entranced him. The golden afternoon light hit her body in a way that highlighted the arc of her hip and the roundness of her perky breasts. Her finely textured *piel canela*—cinnamon skin—gleamed with tiny beads of sweat, and he could no longer contain himself. Esperanza attacked her and crushed her body against his, sucking on her ear as she moaned. He slipped his cock inside her and was consumed by pure euphoria as he plunged deeper with every thrust.

She nibbled his earlobe and whispered, "This could be constituted as sexual harassment, you know."

"I guess I'll have to report you, then."

Legs and Esperanza melted into each other, mouths and legs and hands and fingers and tongues colliding and then drawing away, investigating and teasing. Sinking, crashing. Breathlessness. *Candela*—heat. Eyes searching, making declarations of love, revealing passionate *secretos*. Arms encircling, thighs clamping, voices clamoring.

"Oh, Legs, *mi amor.* You drive me so crazy."

"Yeah. You like that, *papi chulo*, don'tchu? *Mi macho. Dámelo.*"

Against the wall. On the desk. The floor. The sofa. Everything on fire. Skin, tongue, pussy, mouth, cock. Raw and tender. Loving and nasty. Kisses and caresses so familiar, yet always, always full of surprises.

Legs stretched and groaned. "Hmm, that was fab, you horny beasty boy, you." The office glowed bright orange as the sun lackadaisically retreated to its daily hiding place. Legs and Esperanza cuddled on the sofa, basking in rapturous satisfaction, limbs tangled in a knot of sheer tenderness.

She grabbed his face and mashed it. *"Tan chulo."* She planted a sloppy kiss on his mouth, followed by a hard slap to his ass. "Time to get dressed. Some of us have a business to run."

He grabbed Legs's wrist and looked at her platinum watch. "You can stay a little while longer."

"My boss wouldn't appreciate my slacking off."

His fingers gently painted circles along the small of her back where the tattoo was. "Fuck 'im."

"I already did." Legs rested her head on his broad, hairy chest, and he squeezed the breath out of her.

As far as Esperanza was concerned, to hell with the money, the cars, the clothes. These were the best of times, this soothing intimacy they shared. The tenderness. The laughs. They'd been through it all: Breakups. Reconciliations. Marriages to other people followed by divorces. The bottom line was, through the toughest of times, they were always there for each other, no matter what. If there was ever a couple that should be called best friends, it was Legs and Esperanza. He could always be himself with her. No pretending. Ever. And that was a rare and wonderful thing.

Esperanza smiled thoughtfully and said, "You're my heart."

Even after all these years, Legs beamed every time he said those words. "And you're mine." She gave him a peck on the cheek and chuckled. "By the way, I'm impressed that you managed to survive Justice's bachelor party," she said as she pinched his nipple.

"Barely."

She looked up at him, squinted and scrunched her face. "You look like hell, *papito*. Got suitcases under your eyes, and shit."

"The price one pays for having fun."

"You didn't bang any of those strippers last night, right?"

"Of course not. Why pay for pussy when I have you?"

"Hey. Remember," she said and gave his balls a gentle

squeeze, making him wince. "This is the most expensive pussy you'll ever have."

"And worth every goddamn penny."

"You can give me the sordid party details later." She climbed off of him and began collecting her clothes. "I have to get back to work."

He turned onto his side, rested his head in his hand and admired her as she dressed.

"I'm going home and—"

"You don't have time," Legs said. "You have to meet with Abuela in an hour."

"Shit, I forgot I was supposed to see your grandmother."

Legs wiggled into her skirt and chuckled. "With all the drinking and smoking and who knows what else you did last night, I'm surprised you even remember your name."

Esperanza sat up and realized his headache was gone. No better cure for a hangover than sweet, nasty sex.

"This is about Alina, right?" Not again. Dealing with Legs's buck-wild niece was not something he was in the mood for.

"Don't be coy," she replied as she slipped on her shoes.

Legs's grandmother had been raising Alina and Alina's younger brother, Cookie, ever since Legs's sister Soledad—whose life revolved around cocaine, alcohol and bad boys—abandoned them several years ago. Alina used to be a well-behaved kid, until she entered that warped dimension called puberty, and now she seemed hell-bent on following in her mother's footsteps. She ran away a couple of times, not liking her great-grandmother's strict, traditional rules, and Esperanza was drafted into finding her and bringing her back. He was tired of this whole business with Alina. They needed to send her to an all-girl Catholic school or boot camp or something. He'd gladly pay for it.

"Chasing after runaways isn't one of my favorite pastimes, you know. We went through this last year."

"She didn't run away this time," Legs said, sounding exasperated. "She disappeared."

"What makes you so certain?"

"Abuela said so." Legs picked up a brush from his desk and ran it through her ebony waterfall of hair. "Besides, interrupting your partying for a few days won't kill ya."

"Says you." Esperanza searched her eyes, knowing he didn't have a choice in the matter. "I'll speak with your grandma, then make some inquiries. Okay?"

Legs sat down beside him and casually played with his flaccid penis. "That's all I ask."

"You're lucky I can never say no to you," he said as he became harder with every dreamy stroke of her hand.

"What's luck gotta do with it?" She leaned over and took him in her mouth, sucking and licking with an expertise that was simply exquisite.

He threw his head back and said, "Nothing at all," while losing himself in her magnificent oral performance.

After a couple of minutes, Legs abruptly stopped, licked her lips, jumped to her feet and said, "Too bad we're gonna have to finish this later."

She grinned, waved and strolled out of the office, leaving him erect and wanting more.

Esperanza shook his head and guffawed, rolling on the sofa and clutching his stomach. As much as he didn't want to go hunting for Alina, ultimately he would, because Esperanza loved Legs more than life itself and there was nothing, absolutely nothing he wouldn't do for her.

Chapter 2

Freddy DeNunzio was having a sex party with himself. His eyes were glued to the television screen, admiring the porn star. She was all tits and lips and ass, with skin the color of rich, dark chocolate, and was busy taking on five studs at the same time. Every orifice was being penetrated, and both her hands were also busy. She went by the name of Serena Blue, and Freddy thought she was a genius.

To the pounding beat of a lame-o, hip-hop soundtrack, the luscious ebony slut was feverishly servicing her well-hung co-stars, while the camera swooped from wide shot to close-up and back again, zipping around sinewy, brown-skinned bodies glistening with sweat. All the people on the dingy television screen were happily screwing their brains out.

This was porn the way Freddy liked it. No story, no dialogue. Just raw, nasty fucking.

Sprawled out on the sofa, Freddy worked his hands like a magician. He managed to jerk off, smoke a joint, sniff coke and munch on pork rinds, all in one smooth, continuous motion. There was also a bottle of tequila he'd soon crack open. If Freddy was hanging out at a club or a bar or a party, and wanted to hit on real broads, he became timid and nervous, and ended up sitting in a secluded corner, nursing his drink. What did you expect from a middle-aged fat man with a gnarled face, a military crew cut and crooked teeth?

Aside from breaking bones, there was nothing Freddy loved more than watching porn. All kinds. Interracial, girl-girl, tranny, gang bang, S&M, B&D, you name it. As long as it was good, commercial product. He didn't go for the cheesy amateur crap, which was mostly populated by skanks and losers. He wanted no pissing, no kids, no animals. None of that disgusting, freak-show shit. Although he was Italian, his favorites were the videos starring hot, black bitches. Big, brown and soft. The kind of stacked bodies a man could lose himself in.

Freddy was watching *Black Super Ho Gangbang* #4 on one of the motel's many adult movie channels. Non-stop televised sex was the only redeeming quality this dump of a motel had. Who the hell paints a room the color of puke? No windows. Stale air. Salvation Army furniture. And the gray carpet looked like some shithead's hair transplant gone bad.

The plaid sofa was all lumps and stains, and about to give in under Freddy's massive weight. He brushed crumbs and ashes from his mountainous belly as he took another toke of the joint. Held it in for several seconds, head swimming in sweet intoxication. Then he expelled a huge cloud like fog in some crappy horror flick.

Nemec, who was in the other room, finally quieted down. Sick fucking puppy must've finished getting his cookies off. This was a nasty business Nemec was into. Freddy never imagined himself working for such a low-life degenerate. His kind of muscle was meant for the business of extortion, murder and drug trafficking, not perversion.

Unfortunately, he'd fallen out of favor with some serious drug players back in L.A., and they put the word out on the street that he was a screw-up. Now, no one with a serious bankroll was willing to hire him as a bodyguard, a hitman or a debt collector. Nothin'. So he ended up working for Nemec. At least the gig paid well, and he got to travel to exotic places like Brazil, Thailand, Russia and the Dominican Republic. Every fat payday made up for the disgust Freddy felt cruising through Nemec's sordid and perverse secret world. Freddy understood being involved in trafficking guns and drugs. But trafficking in human beings was beyond his comprehension. He just took the money, looked the other way and prayed that God would forgive him.

The only light illuminating the room was the glow from the television screen. With all the empty beer bottles and Chinese food containers scattered all over the place, you'd think a frat party had gone down. Freddy shuddered as an orgasm unexpectedly crept up. The low angle shot of a perfect double penetration and that huge, bouncing ass was more than he could take. Freddy's hand went into overdrive, and he let out a growl. Just as he shot his load on the towel tucked between his thighs, there was a knock at the door. The interruption pissed him off. It stifled what should've been a powerful climax, his first in many days.

Muttering obscenities, Freddy wiped his hands on the towel and snatched the .357 Magnum from underneath the bag of pork rinds. *Who the fuck would be knocking at this hour?* No one knew they were holed up at the Chastity Motel, which was located way out in butt-fuck Queens.

Freddy struggled to his feet, woozy from the release of sexual tension. He slipped on his boxer shorts with the yellow smiley faces, cocked the hammer of his massive revolver and waddled over to the door. He peered through the glass fish-eye peephole, which distorted his view. It took Freddy a second to figure out what exactly he was staring at. By the time he realized it was the barrel of a silencer-equipped automatic, it was too late.

There was a bright flash, and a hollow-point, 9-millimeter slug blasted through Freddy's right eye and exited through the back of his head, spewing hair, blood and most of his brains.

At least Freddy's final party was one of his best.

Nemec was dreaming of happy little boys, dancing in the streets and singing, "The Candyman can . . .," when he was startled out of his deep slumber by a loud thud. It sounded as if someone dropped a bag of cement off the roof. Nemec jerked awake and rubbed the sleep from his eyes.

"Freddy?" No response. "Freddy!"

In a panic, Nemec lunged out of bed and, with great difficulty, managed to slip into his jeans while not falling flat on his face. From under the lumpy mattress, he snatched his .32-caliber Colt with a sound suppressor attached, and stumbled backward, slamming against the wall. Nemec hated guns, but in his line of business, it was smart to carry one. He heard the moaning and groaning from the porno movie his bodyguard, Freddy, was watching in the other room, and it was accompanied by soft murmurs. Then the sound from the television grew louder.

The doorknob leisurely turned. Nemec shut his eyes and squeezed the trigger over and over until the gun was empty. There were several holes in the door and the wall, through which sharp beams of pale light were projected. The abrupt silence creeped Nemec out. He wondered if he scared them off or, even better, killed them dead.

But the door swung open, and Jason Rybak entered. A hulking, menacing man, Rybak was a statue of flesh, blood and bone who rarely expressed even the slightest hint of emotion. He flicked on the overhead light. Nemec squinted, trying to adjust to the brightness. Rybak's lifeless blue eyes gave Nemec the once-over. Rybak sported an immaculate suede duster, black crewneck shirt, straight-leg jeans and shiny cowboy boots.

"Your bodyguard wasn't worth whatever you were paying him," Rybak said as he stepped into the room.

Nemec dropped the gun, held up his trembling hands and silently prayed that Rybak was alone. At least that way, his death would be immediate and relatively painless.

A voice came from the other room. "Yer a bloody cunt, fer stealin' from me." Nemec immediately recognized the guttural cockney accent and grating voice. Bishop.

Rybak stepped to the side, and instead of Bishop revealed his wife, Mistress Devona Love. Nemec forgot that Devona had a gift for impersonating voices. At that moment, he knew that God intended to punish him for all of his sins.

There was a compact .32 Kel-Tec semiauto in Devona's hand and a mischievous glimmer in her eye. Devona oozed so much raw sex appeal, she even turned Nemec on, and it was rare for an adult woman to have that kind of effect on him. She was of impressive height, with a luxurious, well-proportioned body. Devona's wavy, shoulder-length hair was the color of rust and made her hypnotic hazel eyes stand out like beacons in the night, calling to you. Those sensually copious lips seemed to belong to a black chick.

Devona smiled. It was seductive and radiant, that damn smile of hers. Made you want to fall in love with her. Surrender to her every whim. Let her corrupt your very soul. As much as he tried to fight it, Nemec found himself mesmerized by her.

"'And there will be such intense darkness, one can feel it.'"

Nemec had no idea whom the crazy bitch was quoting, and didn't care. All he knew was, the reaper had come for him disguised as a temptress. Death, in all of its seductive splendor, stood before him, ready to claim him. He clenched his knees tight, tried to hold it in, but a puddle of urine gradually spread around his bare feet. Devona giggled lavishly.

Rybak shook his head and stared at Nemec like he was some starving bum scraping together lunch from a garbage can.

"You thought you'd steal from Bishop and get away with it?" Rybak ran his fingers through his short-cropped, golden hair. "You'd be better off double-crossing the devil himself."

Nemec dropped to his knees. He wasn't a tough guy. He wasn't proud. Begging for his life came natural to him. Nemec, who was nearing sixty, was a wisp of a man with a gray, receding hairline. His bland face was composed of a feeble chin, virtually invisible lips, a petite nose and squinty eyes.

"I just . . . it's the urges. They take control, and I can't help myself." It was true. *The urges.* Any normal person would say it was the blackness in his heart. Nemec saw himself as a drug fiend without any control over his behavior. *A drug fiend who'd stop at nothing to get another fix.* Except his drug was young, innocent flesh.

"The little miscreant decides to be honest," Devona said. "Impressive." She slipped the gun into the pocket of her shiny, ankle-length, latex coat. Underneath, she wore a sapphire-and-violet, form-fitting, latex bodysuit, and thigh-high, platform boots. Such bright colors for so dark and sadistic a creature.

"C'mon, guys. I've been doing business with Bishop for nearly twenty years."

Rybak ignored Nemec, sauntered to the closet door and opened it.

On the floor was Bobby, an unconscious, ten-year-old boy with blond hair. His nude, bruised body was half-covered with a towel. He was bound with duct tape. Beside him was the wild Hispanic girl, Alina, whom Nemec had derived great pleasure from. She wore only a T-shirt and was tied up with thick rope, her panties stuffed in her mouth. Alina was awake. Her eyes should've been wide with fear. Instead, they blazed with raw hatred and defiance.

Rybak didn't even blink. He turned his attention back to Nemec, who began to weep. "Bishop is very disappointed in you," Rybak said.

"I'm sorry, Rybak. I made a huge mistake. Please don't kill me."

"I'm not gonna kill you."

Nemec's body went limp, and he suddenly was able to breathe normally again. He couldn't believe his luck. They were going to spare his life.

Then Rybak added, "I'll leave that to Mistress Love."

Nemec couldn't move. Or speak. There was only this hum. It was incessant and growing in intensity. It was like his head was trapped in a jar filled with a thousand bees.

Devona said, "Ready to party, Nemec?" She was twirling a gleaming scalpel between her slender fingers. In her left hand, she casually bounced a red, rubber ball.

She strutted over to Nemec, her body movement confident, aggressive. Almost feral.

Devona smashed her knee into Nemec's throat. He toppled over, gagging, coughing and spitting up blood. She crouched, grabbed him by his thinning hair, jerked his head back and shoved the ball in his mouth. Nemec heard his jaw crack. The pain was so intense, he wished he was already dead.

Devona produced a pair of handcuffs, and though Nemec struggled to get away from her, his body squirming and limbs flailing, she easily cuffed his hands behind his back. Then Devona rose and languidly stretched her arms up in the air like a ballet dancer getting ready for a performance. She approached Nemec and cackled as she stomped on his stomach three times. Those heavy, six-inch platform heels shattered his ribs on impact. She grabbed Nemec by his arm, hauled him up as if he weighed nothing and hurled him to the bed. Nemec's head slammed against the flimsy headboard, splitting the cheap, imitation wood. His eyes rolled back and he seemed as if he was about to lose consciousness.

Devona stepped away, and in a most chivalrous fashion, Jason took off her coat and neatly folded it over his arm.

"See why I adore my husband so much?" Devona said to Nemec. "He treats me like a lady."

She turned to Jason, gaze singing with adoration. Jason's face transformed with a roguish smile. Devona gave him a soft kiss on the mouth, then sat on the edge of the bed and carefully examined Nemec's desperate eyes. She could never remember what he looked like. His face was like a blank page. But now it was filled with words. Phrases like "Please, stop. I beg of you." She savored the ammonia-like stench of urine. It was the smell of fear.

This was the part Devona enjoyed most. The fear she created. The way any artist has a muse, fear was Devona's. She relished having such power over others, and her senses tingled.

She could feel herself getting wet.

Devona waved the scalpel back and forth as if conducting an orchestra. "I'm a pain artist," she said. "And you'll be my latest canvas." Devona pulled down Nemec's pants, and then straddled his legs. "Oh, goody. You haven't been circumcised. Let's start there."

Rybak joined them on the bed and placed Nemec in a tight headlock. The little man frenetically attempted to flip Devona off him, but wasn't strong enough. Rybak watched Devona with stoic eyes as she adjusted her latex gloves, took Nemec's limp penis in her hand and eagerly began to work the blade, slicing with surgical precision as droplets of blood spattered on her.

Nemec tried to scream, but the rubber ball stuffed in his mouth had unhinged his jaw. Devona could hear him, though. She heard the screeches of pain emanating from each and every pore of his body.

And to Devona, it was the loveliest sound in the world.

Chapter 3

La vieja—the old lady—sat before him, with Cookie standing by her side, his hand gently resting on her stooped shoulder. Esperanza lounged behind his desk, wearing jeans and a black T-shirt with the Puerto Rican flag on it. There was a small notepad in one hand and a pen in the other.

"The police will do nothing," Abuela said in Spanish, her usually spirited voice a whisper. Her face was a complicated map of deep grooves and wrinkles. Her white hair was tied in a neat bun and stood out against her nearly jet-black skin. She reeked of lavender water.

"This isn't a new situation, Abuela," Esperanza said, trying not to sound disrespectful.

"This is different, *m'ijo.*" Abuela clutched rosary beads in her frail, calloused hands. Her fingernails were thick, yellowish and chipped. "Alina's in great danger."

"What gives you that idea?"

"I've had visions." She made the sign of the cross and gently kissed her fingertips. "Dark and disturbing ones."

Then call the Psychic Network, Esperanza thought. "And what do those 'visions' tell you?" he asked her

"That Alina's being held by evil men." Abuela leaned forward, her gaze confident. "Men who do the work of the devil."

Esperanza stared down at the notepad where he was supposedly taking notes. Instead, he was doodling on it. An assortment of exaggerated tits and asses. He was still horny from earlier in the afternoon. Esperanza took a deep breath, tried to remain patient. *Premonitions and visions. Evil men and the devil. Bullshit.* The lady was supposed to be an *espiritista*, but Esperanza never believed in any of that pseudo-psychic stuff. He'd been a homicide detective for five years. It was all about facts and forensics.

He returned his attention to the *vieja* and the kid. Abuela couldn't weigh more than ninety pounds. Cookie accompanied his grandmother because she sometimes needed help walking and still refused to use a cane. The ruby dress Abuela wore was ill fitting and faded from too many washes. But there was clarity in those emerald eyes of hers, a wisdom that Esperanza had to admire, despite her flights of fancy.

"Anything else besides these . . . 'visions' that will help me find her?"

"She's been spending time with a very bad element lately." Abuela turned her attention to her grandson.

Cookie was thirteen. He got that nickname because when he was a baby, it was the first word to come out of his mouth. *Thank God he didn't say "ca-ca."*

The kid's oily, pudgy face was sprouting an impressive crop of pimples, and there were a few curly hairs decorating his strong, cleft chin. Cookie possessed that awkward goofiness boys can't avoid as they struggle to make the transition into manhood. His head was shaved, and he wore the ultra-baggy, jailhouse-influenced, hip-hop style outfit Esperanza detested.

"She's been runnin' wif a freak," Cookie said, bobbing his head as if the words were stuck in his throat or something.

"What do you mean by 'freak'?"

"Ya know . . . one o' dem faggits that looks like a girl. Tit . . . breasts and everythin'."

"Pre-op transsexual." Esperanza assumed Alina was testing new waters when it came to her sexuality. A tranny sure was a different way to go.

"Whatevah. All I know is, lass time I seen Alina, 'bout two weeks ago, she was bouncin' wif the freak on her way to a party. Ain't come back since."

"You have a name for the transsexual?"

"Midnight Desire."

"Cute," Esperanza said and closed the notepad. Then he proceeded to reassure Abuela that he'd do his best to find Alina and bring her back, and everything would be just swell. *Yeah, right.*

Truth was, Esperanza didn't really give a damn. Esperanza genuinely cared about Abuela. That wasn't the issue. Alina was. Baby girl was a selfish, out-of-control, fourteen-year-old, little tramp who was disrespectful and ungrateful, and was going to shove the poor old lady headfirst into an early grave. Last time Esperanza went searching for her, Alina was shacked up with a small-time coke dealer ten years her senior. The punk pulled a machete, and Esperanza gave him the beat-down of his life and then forcefully dragged Alina home kicking and screaming. While in his car, Esperanza almost knocked Alina's teeth out when she had the nerve to curse him out and spit in his face. As far as he was concerned, the little 'hood rat was bad news. But he'd go searching for her again for only one reason: Legs had asked him to.

Esperanza swaggered through the club as his staff cleaned, mopped and polished, preparing for another big Friday night at Sueño Latino. He smiled to himself, loved the sensual feeling the joint evoked. The decor was influenced by the old mambo clubs from the fifties, with a dash of the avant-garde. Spattered colors, huge arched booths, a winding wraparound balcony and twisting columns. Kind of like Frank Lloyd Wright meets Jackson Pollock meets Tito Puente.

Legs stood at the end of the sinuous bar, berating some

busboy for his poor attendance. Legs was a tough boss to work for. She was a perfectionist who demanded better than the best of everyone. But she inspired loyalty because she didn't hesitate to pick up a mop and get down and dirty, if it was called for. And if any of her employees needed help—whether it was with an immigration problem, or co-signing a loan for a new car, or paying for a relative's funeral—they always felt free going to Legs, because she usually came through for them.

As for Esperanza, besides signing checks and okaying the occasional delivery, he spent his time at the club playing a rice 'n' beans version of Rick Blaine in *Casablanca*. He didn't get lucky and strike it rich so that he *actually had to work*.

Esperanza buttoned up his heavy cashmere overcoat as he approached Legs.

"Just make sure you do it right next time," Legs said to the busboy. The Mexican kid appeared so ashamed, Esperanza thought he might drop to his knees and beg forgiveness.

"*Si, señora,*" he said and quickly scurried off.

Legs turned to Esperanza, a reticent expression on her face. "How'd it go?"

He shrugged. "Okay. She's been having . . . nightmares, so she's concerned something bad has happened to Alina."

"Premonitions. Something I'm sure you don't take very seriously."

"I'm an ex-cop, baby. I go by facts."

"What about hunches?"

"That's different."

"If you say so." Legs bumped up against him. "So, what's next?"

He stared deep into her eyes, and beneath the tough facade, he could sense something was bothering her. "What's wrong?"

She wagged her head. "Sometimes I feel really guilty that I didn't take responsibility for Cookie and Alina. Abuela's too old to handle two teenagers."

"You were young, dealing with your career, building a life for yourself. Just because your sister Soledad's a fuckup doesn't make it *your* responsibility."

"Still, there's no excuse for not being more actively involved in those kids' lives. Maybe if I'd spent more time with Alina, like I should've, maybe—"

"'Maybe' isn't going to get us anywhere right now. First, I'll track down Alina and bring her back, and then you can deal with whatever issues you have." Her burgundy, leather coat was folded over the seat back of a bar stool. He picked it up and held it open for her.

"Where are we going?" she asked as she slid into the coat.

"To give Abuela a ride home. Then we'll search Alina's room to see if there's anything that might give us an indication as to her current whereabouts."

Legs grinned. "I love it when you talk that detective speak of yours."

Esperanza meticulously sifted through the drawers of Alina's decrepit bureau as sweat snaked down his face. The bedroom wasn't much larger than a jail cell. The radiator clanked and whistled and spit out thick steam, making the air difficult to breathe. He pulled out a crisp handkerchief from his back pocket and wiped the perspiration from his burning eyes.

For a moment, he checked out the posters of rappers haphazardly taped to the stucco walls: The Notorious B.I.G., Snoop Dogg, and Ice Cube. There were also a couple of reggaeton stars, like Daddy Yankee. This made Esperanza understand Alina's attraction to thugs.

Outside, the Lower East Side—or Loisada, as the Ricans still called it—was alive with reggaeton music and the occasional screaming and cursing and name-calling in Spanish.

Esperanza sifted through colorful panties and bras, and found a Polaroid snapshot of Alina posing in front of Nathan's at Coney Island. He studied it. She was a tiny girl, more bone than flesh. Practically looked like she was ten. No tits, no hips, no nothing. She was composed mostly of hair—dark ringlets falling across a child-like face.

Legs was sitting on the flimsy single bed. She looked like she might be swallowed into the deep crater at the center of the worn-out mattress.

Esperanza showed her the picture. "How long ago you think this was taken?"

Legs swatted at a fly and scrutinized the photo, then frowned and said, "A couple of years ago."

"She doesn't seem to develop much. Still looks pre-pubescent."

"Some perverts like that."

He opened a black lacquered music box sitting among the bottles of nail polish and the knockoff versions of Lauren, Obsession and Shalimar perfumes on the top of the bureau and found a stack of letters and papers. He leafed through them, and a particular letter caught his eye. The letterhead was that of an organization called The Sanctuary. It was a referral for Alina to get a medical checkup and was signed by Rupert Alladice, Program Director. Dated two months ago.

"Alina ever mention a place called The Sanctuary?"

"No," Legs said and took the letter, quickly reading it. "Maybe they deal with troubled youth?"

"Sounds like it. I'll check it out." He took the letter back, folded it and stuffed it in his pant pocket. Legs stared into space, and her shoulders slumped. Esperanza took her hand and affectionately squeezed it. "Look, I'll find her, I promise."

"Thank you, *papito*. This is the last time, I swear. She's not gonna run away again. Not if I can help it."

"What're you going to do, chain her to the bed?"

"No. I'm going to be there for her," Legs said and stood up. "Be a part of her life. Send her to therapy. Do whatever it takes to help Abuela, and make sure Cookie and Alina stay on the straight and narrow."

"A good start would be moving them out of these projects."

She snorted and rolled her eyes. "*Olvidate.* I've tried that plenty of times. You know Abuela. She's thickheaded. Lived here all her life and refuses to make a change."

"Well, do whatever you gotta do, *nena*," Esperanza said, trying to sound encouraging. "Just don't go on a full-fledged guilt trip."

He swept her up in his arms and held her tightly, feeling her take deep, extended breaths. She shuddered slightly, and he gave her a reassuring kiss on the cheek.

Chapter 4

Wearing a big grin, Esperanza confidently made his way through the Midtown North station house. It was like being home again. This was the place where he'd spent five years working narcotics and ten years working homicide cases. His head was filled with memories of intense interrogations. Endless stakeouts. Bloody crime scenes.

He was heading to the detectives' squad room to see his ex-partner Anibal Santos. Esperanza knew many of the cops at the house, and most of them greeted him enthusiastically, offering him warm bear hugs and handshakes and big smiles. But there were a few who gave him the cold shoulder and shot him looks like he was a common perp. Esperanza couldn't blame them. They were probably envious of the fact that while they slaved away sixteen hours a day, putting their lives on the line, hoping to retire and receive a measly pension, he was living it up like Donald fucking Trump. What they failed to realize was, no matter how much money was in Esperanza's bank account, in his heart he'd always be one of them.

The detectives' squad room was one huge room. High ceilings. White pillars running down the center. Rows of hulking, gray, metal desks, which hadn't been replaced since the 1990s. Phones rang and beepers beeped incessantly. The squad room was alive with frantic energy as an army of detectives interviewed various witnesses and suspects, consulted with each other about leads, talked into cell phones and poured over reports. It was organized chaos. The enormous, arched windows looked out over 54th Street, but were covered with so much dust and soot that barely any sunlight was able to shine through. Most of the beige, peeling, water-stained walls were decorated with giant bulletin boards featuring memos, wanted posters and leaflets stapled to them. Some of the overhead fluorescent light fixtures flickered on and off.

Santos was at his desk, thick reading glasses low on the bridge of his wide nose as he stared at his computer monitor. His desk was a mess, as always. Surrounded by stacks of files, reports and forms, plus a few empty Styrofoam cups, Santos seemed utterly perplexed by the screen, which kept flickering. He hated computers, believed they'd be the death of all culture and society. He also believed cops relied on them too much, rather than on what he called "good ol' fashion footwork." Santos muttered something in Spanish and impatiently slapped the side of the monitor a couple of times, until it went completely dead.

"S'matter, partner? Can't figure out how to turn it on?"

Santos looked up, his face relaxing into a mischievous smirk. "Had the same problem with my third wife." He rose, gave Esperanza a vigorous hug, patted him hard on the back.

"How are you, *compai*?"

"Screwed," Santos said. "All the overtime in the world ain't gonna keep up with my alimony payments."

"Maybe you should stop getting married."

Fifty-two years old, and Santos had been married and divorced three times. "I'm a hopeless romantic," Santos said, then stepped back and checked Esperanza out, impressed by his single-breasted, charcoal-gray, thousand-dollar suit. Ralph Lauren Purple Label, tailored to perfection. "You look like a million bucks."

"Thirty, to be exact."

"Rub it in, asshole." He pointed to the battered, aluminum chair beside his desk, and Esperanza took a seat. Anibal leaned back in his creaky office chair. Put his feet up on the desk and rested the back of his clean-shaven head against his interlocked fingers. The soles of his cheap shoes were worn, his five-dollar tie had a small grease stain on it. His white shirt and black pants were in desperate need of an ironing. When Santos didn't have a wife around to dress him, he always looked like he'd just rolled out of bed fully dressed. He'd lost plenty of weight since Esperanza last saw him, and Santos was fairly slender to begin with. Even his copper-colored skin was looking somewhat pale. His heavy-lidded brown eyes were bloodshot and didn't seem focused. The man could use a long vacation. But Santos never took vacations. He was one of those rare cops who believed the city would crumble if he wasn't around to fight crime.

Santos and his constant rants about the terrible state of world politics, about the terrible state of contemporary literature, about the terrible state of humankind in general. Every time they started a new murder investigation, Santos would stop in front of a church and say a quick prayer for the victim. Yet he never actually stepped into the church. Esperanza missed his old partner and all his idiosyncrasies more than he cared to admit, even to himself.

He'd clocked more time with Santos than with anybody else on the job and had trusted him with his life every time they went through a door to bust a murder suspect. Santos felt a compelling sense of duty, of conviction, always saying their mission was to bring justice to the dead, no matter who they were, no matter what the victim's ethnicity or social standing was, because every corpse lying on a slab at the M.E.'s deserved equal justice.

Santos's dedication had rubbed off on Esperanza. Searching for the truth, bringing down the bad guys, there was honor in that. Santos made Esperanza proud to be a homicide detective. In Narcotics, Esperanza had been a cowboy. In under-cover work, the line between the good guys and the bad guys is often blurred, and Esperanza crossed the line way too many times. But Homicide was clear-cut: Comb the crime scene for evidence. Canvas the neighborhood. Interview witnesses. Track down the killer.

Esperanza noticed that there was a hardcover copy of Flaubert's *Madame Bovary* on the desk, dozens of yellow Post-it notes sticking out from between the dog-eared pages.

"How's your novel going?" Esperanza asked, the same way he'd asked him once a month, every month, for five years.

Santos had been writing, and re-writing and re-writing, his novel for over ten years. He read everything from John Cheever to Isabel Allende to James Baldwin. Latin American magical realism. Harlem renaissance. Techno-spy thrillers. Greek mythology. He was voracious when it came to literature. You couldn't find a television in Santos's apartment, but there were enough books to fill a library. Every time Santos got divorced, he'd lose furniture, money, his dignity (and who knows what else), but he didn't care, he said, "Not as long as those *putas* don't take my books." Or his ancient, electric typewriter. No matter how crazy his schedule got, Santos always found time to write. Esperanza expected Santos to be working on a crime novel or police procedural, some Ed McBain kind of stuff. Instead, he'd written a passionate period romance about an African slave and a Taino Indian, set in Puerto Rico during the early 1800s. It was eloquently written and filled with magic, history and culture. Esperanza was quite impressed by his partner's talent. The only problem was, as soon as Santos completed a draft, he'd start all over again, and Esperanza wondered if he'd ever be satisfied. He was that way about the job, too. Even when they solved a murder and gathered enough evidence to secure a grand jury indictment, Santos always felt there was more they could've done.

"Still working on it," Santos said.

"Ever think of writing something else for a change?"

"Once in a while. But until I can get this novel exactly where I want it. . . . You know James Joyce worked on a single sentence from *Finnegans Wake* for fourteen years?"

"That's about how long it took me to finish reading *Ulysses*, and I still don't get it."

"Nobody does. But you didn't come up here to talk about literature. What brings you 'round, big man?"

Esperanza quickly filled Santos in on the situation with Alina. Just as quickly, Santos checked out the alias Midnight Desire and came up with a rap sheet for a skell named José Soto. He was a small-time hustler who'd been pinched for soliciting, possession with intent to sell and public lewdness. Alina sure kept fine company.

Santos picked up a Styrofoam cup, took a sip of bitter black coffee and grimaced. "Soto spent a lot of digits turning himself into a girl," he said. "But hasn't gone all the way yet. I don't get that. You wanna be a girl, then cut your shit off and get on with your life."

In his miniature notebook, Esperanza jotted down Soto's last-known address, place of employment and known associates.

"So you'll talk to Missing Persons about Alina?"

"For what it's worth. But you know they're not going to put much effort into finding some spic girl from the projects. But I'll see what I can do."

"Ever hear of a place called The Sanctuary?"

"It's on Tenth and Forty-Third. Runaway facility," Santos said as he stroked his smooth, shiny head. "Cops drop off kids there all the time."

"Seems like Alina stayed there a couple months ago. Know anyone there I can reach out to?"

"No, but we can talk to Vice." Santos wagged his head and grinned. "Nicholas Esperanza, back on the job."

Esperanza liked the sound of that. For a moment, he felt like a detective again. It was more exciting to him than he would've ever anticipated. Maybe this thing with Alina wouldn't be so bad after all. He'd spend a few days tracking her down, following up leads and interviewing a couple of lowlifes. Just like old times. Legs would be very appreciative of all his help, and that was never a bad thing. So Esperanza decided he'd make the best of it, turn the search for Alina into a game and have a little fun in the process.

Chapter 5

The Sanctuary's recreation room was a cavernous space. Even though it contained a pool table, two ping-pong tables, a couple of pinball machines and a big-screen television, there was still enough room to play a game of touch football. It had been recently painted tangerine orange. There were overhead florescent lights. No windows. The half dozen maroon, vinyl love seats, whose tears and rips had been bandaged with gray duct tape, needed to be replaced. Esperanza leaned against the wall, behind a group of black, Latino and white teenagers. They sat in a semi-circle on the buffed hardwood floor, enraptured by Rupert Alladice as he acted out a soliloquy from *King Lear*. The teens were a combination of rough-and-tumble ghetto kids and fresh-off-the-bus victims of suburban family dysfunction.

Esperanza was pleasantly surprised by Alladice's polished performance. The man certainly possesed a riveting presence. With subtle physical expression, resonant voice and eloquent British accent, he could've easily been delivering this speech at the New York Shakespeare Festival. Esperanza guessed Alladice's age to be around fifty-five. His white, starched Oxford shirt and khakis were offset by a pair of ratty running shoes. He wore round, wire-rim glasses, and his receding, silver-blond hair was freshly trimmed. Alladice's deft performance kept Esperanza and the runaways engrossed for fifteen minutes.

Esperanza glanced over at Mrs. Rosario, the plump case manager who'd escorted him in to meet Alladice. She beamed and nodded, proud of her supervisor's enormous talent.

Alladice finished, and the runaways applauded and whistled and whooped and rose to their feet. He graciously bowed, and the teens suddenly swarmed around him, giving him high fives and hugs, like he was some kind of big-time celebrity.

"That is the power of Shakespeare," he declared. "The power of words."

Esperanza watched Alladice interact with the kids and couldn't help admiring the man's passion. In his old neighborhood, up in El Barrio in East Harlem, Esperanza occasionally worked with what the social workers called disenfranchised youth. He volunteered his time, teaching martial arts classes. He gave away a couple of college scholarships every year. Esperanza never made a big deal out of it, because he knew there were men like Alladice who dedicated their careers— *their lives*—to bringing hope to the less fortunate.

Esperanza could ponder his sense of guilt later. Right now, his job was to find Alina and bring a little hope and happiness home to Legs.

In Alladice's cramped office, overflowing, oak bookshelves and file cabinets lined the walls, barely leaving any space to walk, or to sit for that matter. Other than that, the place was spotless, and the gentle scent of potpourri laced the air. Alladice rocked back and forth in his ancient, wooden swivel chair as he carefully studied the Polaroid snapshot of Alina. Then he removed his glasses and stared back at Esperanza with alert, deep-blue eyes.

"She looks vaguely familiar," he said. "But you must understand, Mr. Esperanza. Dozens of children come through this facility every month, and I don't have the opportunity to interact with each of them personally."

From the single open widow, frosty air and the jarring noise of Midtown traffic streamed in. Esperanza shifted, trying to make himself comfortable in the wobbly metal folding chair. "Maybe this will jog your memory," he said politely. His knees were jammed against the front of Alladice's desk. Esperanza handed Alladice the referral letter he found in Alina's room, which he'd personally signed.

"I sign off on every report and referral for The Sanctuary," Alladice said, remaining reticent. "The counselors handle the individual cases." He finished reading the letter and handed it back with the snapshot. "Also, I'm sure you realize you're requesting confidential information."

"I'm aware of that. You can call Detective Anibal Santos at Midtown North to verify that Alina *is* missing and I'm trying to help find her." Alladice's expression relaxed just a little. Esperanza slipped the letter and photo back in his pocket and added, "I'm a retired homicide detective, and my girlfriend is Alina's aunt."

"I must say, I have to admire you for taking on something like this," Alladice said with a lackadaisical nod of the head. "Runaways don't usually want to be found."

"Yeah, well, I've been down this road before," Esperanza said. "So I know what I'm dealing with."

"And what are you going to do once you do find her?"

"That's not my area of expertise. I'll leave that up to her grandma and aunt."

"Do you have any children, Mr. Esperanza?"

"No."

"Why not?"

"Too much energy. Too much time," Esperanza said. "I'd rather have a pet. They don't talk back."

Alladice let out a hearty laugh. "You're quite a candid chap," he said. "Refreshing."

"I'm like a walking breath mint." Esperanza was glad that Alladice seemed to be loosening up somewhat. "By the way, that performance of yours was impressive."

"Thank you." Alladice grinned regally, the harsh lines of his face melting. Like any other performer, he wasn't immune to flattery. "I find that the arts help stimulate my young charges' imaginations."

"This must be a very tough job."

"Teenagers are growing up faster than ever. Not raised in the best of environments. The runaway population is growing every year. Living on the street, drugs, prostitution, then A.I.D.S." He shook his head, his eyes turning vaguely despondent. "Even after all the years I've been the director at The Sanctuary, seeing what these kids go through, it still breaks my heart."

"'So wise so young, they say, do never live long,'" Esperanza said, quoting from *King Richard III*. He'd taken a Shakespeare course in college and got hooked. Never thought old Billy boy might actually come in handy one day.

Impressed, Alladice raised his furry eyebrows and clapped. "Bravo. I see there is more to you than meets the eye."

"Yeah. I'm not as dumb as I look." Esperanza leaned forward, resting the palms of his hands on his knees. "About Alina's file," he said. "I'm not asking to see it. I just want to know if there is anything in it that will help me figure out her current whereabouts. You read the file and tell me."

Alladice pursed his sparse lips for a moment, then stood up, went to one of the beige, slightly dented, metal filing cabinets and pulled a thick file. He leafed through it and then put it back.

"She was here for two weeks," Alladice said, "but was discharged for engaging in . . . inappropriate behavior with some of the male residents."

"She ever come back?"

"No. Sorry I can't help more."

Esperanza was certain there was more information in that file than Alladice was willing to share, but by the letter of the law, the dedicated program director already said more than he was allowed. Besides, Esperanza wasn't a cop anymore. He wasn't going to get the kind of cooperation you experience when you flashed a badge.

"Don't sweat it," Esperanza said.

"Do you think something bad has happened to her?"

"Nah. She's probably staying with a boyfriend or something." Esperanza stood up and shook the stiffness out of his knees. He reached into his jacket pocket and produced a business card, which he handed to Alladice. "If Alina comes around, please give me a call."

Alladice also rose. "I'm supposed to contact only her legal guardian." Alladice put the card on his desk and graciously extended his hand. "But being that you're an ex-policeman, I might be willing to bend the rules."

Esperanza shook Alladice's hand. It was smooth and nicely manicured. "Thank you, Sir Rupert, for taking out time from your matinee performance to speak with me."

"Anything for one of my loyal fans," Alladice said with a sly wink.

Later that evening, as he cruised west on 42nd Street, Esperanza pulled up the collar of his overcoat in a failed attempt to protect himself from the ass-kicking February wind blasting in from the Hudson River. Esperanza cursed under his breath as he aggressively pushed his way through the throngs of out-of-towners jamming the street.

After talking to Alladice, Esperanza stopped off at Ollie's Chinese Restaurant on 44th and Broadway for some succulent roast duck, mei fun noodles and plenty of hot tea. Now he was on his way to Eighth Avenue to see if he could track down Alina's tranny friend, Midnight Desire. He was always amazed every time he returned to the neighborhood once called the Deuce.

He was on the frontline in the late-eighties, and as an undercover narc, he saw more action and made more collars in those few years than in his entire career as a cop. Back in those days, Times Square was Sodom and Gomorrah, Dante's Inferno and Mardi Gras all wrapped into one. Peep shows, live sex shows, strip joints, massage parlors, topless bars and porno theaters lined a ten-block radius. The call of "Girls! Girls! Girls!" ceaselessly blasted over P.A. systems from inside the peep shows. There was a steady symphony of blaring car horns as heavy traffic moved at a snail's pace. The streets teemed with possees of high-strung black and Puerto Rican ghetto kids emerging from triple kung fu features, throwing kicks and punches and starting fights with anyone who looked at them the wrong way. Businessmen in three-piece suits cruised the neon-drenched boulevard searching for a quick hand job in one of the massage parlors or peep shows. There were window displays filled with sex toys, videotapes, porn mags, martial arts weapons, knives and drug paraphernalia. Con men played three-card monty on top of cardboard boxes, eagerly ripping off any sucker willing to bet a twenty. Fresh-faced, teenaged, white-boy hustlers in cut-off jeans, black tank tops and leather sandals shared slices of gooey pizza while hoping to find a quick trick so they could get high and go clubbing downtown at Danceteria. Stoned, big-haired hookers in red, Lycra microminis, tube tops and six-inch platform boots aggressively flashed their tits and asses to potential customers. The foul odors of urine, spilled beer and rotting food in overflowing garbage cans competed with the scents of freshly popped popcorn, grilled hot dogs and cotton candy sold at open-air fast-food stands. Stone-cold junkies and crackheads hobbled around, looking to snatch a gold chain or a purse from some meek tourist. Blinding, flashing lights from the dozens of theater marquees and porn shops turned night into day. Broken glass, used condoms and empty crack vials littered dirty, sticky, often blood-stained sidewalks. Drug dealers in velour sweat suits, blasting rap music from suitcase-size boom boxes, munching on Nedick's hot dogs, aggressively hawked crack, coke, skag, weed and acid.

Times Square was like the Wild West back then, bustling with tense, prurient energy. There was a tremendous sense of danger lurking at every turn. You felt that at any given moment, a fight, a stabbing or a shoot-out might go down. Esperanza had seen and experienced it all and was fascinated by the never-ending cycle of decadence. He rolled with the dregs of society and was right at home.

Over the years, 42nd Street had been transformed into an antiseptic, open-air shopping mall featuring the face of a very familiar animated mouse. In the early nineties, Mayor Giuliani rode into town like a modern-day Wyatt Earp and slowly but surely cleaned up the streets, all in the name of his specific brand of neo-fascist morality. But the truth be told, the makeover had more to do with powerful real estate developers, multinational corporations and, most of all, billions in potential tourism dollars. By that time, Esperanza was off the mean street and working homicide. He was glad, because the police became an urban gestapo, searching suspects (usually people of color) and arresting them for even the most minor of offenses. What was the point of throwing people in Rikers for the weekend because they were drinking a beer or smoking a joint while walking down the street?

The new Times Square was sterile, safe, pleasant and soulless, and by the late nineties, it was an amalgam of giant glittery logos. *The American Airlines Theater? Legions of dead playwrights gotta be spinning in their graves. Madame*

Tussaud's wax museum? That's some corny L.A. shit. If you want to see a wax version of Arnold Schwarzenegger, go see one of his performances in a movie.

There was the flagship Disney store, where you could buy ancillary merchandise from all the company's movies, television shows and Broadway productions. *Talk about synergy.* The Hello Kitty store was a lemon-yellow paradise selling an assortment of bags, pillows, shirts and purses adorned with Japan's famous greeting-card character, a cute kitten with a missing mouth and a bow on its head. The sidewalks were spotless and actually sparkled. The entrance to the high-tech Broadway City Arcade was a huge arch of green, yellow and pink blinking neon lights. Too bad kids from the 'hood couldn't afford to play the two-dollar-a-pop video games. The streets were packed with wide-eyed, annoying tourists who stumbled around just like the old-school *tecatos*—junkies—Giuliani sent packing. Pedestrian traffic ground to a halt as tourists stopped and stared in awe at giant video screens and eye-catching advertisements of glowing rainbow lights.

In some perverse way, Esperanza missed the old Times Square. He'd rather be mesmerized by a seedy world of violence, drugs and sex instead of huge signs hawking an endless variety of brand-name products.

Esperanza arrived in front of one of the only remaining peep-show emporiums in Times Square. The Pleasure Palace on Eighth Avenue was the last-known address of employment for José Soto, a.k.a. Midnight Desire. He entered and glanced around. The front part of the peep-show emporium had been converted into a candy store and newspaper stand, and there were shelves of videotapes and D.V.D.'s of B movies starring washed-up TV stars. All the legit stuff was part of the recent 60/40 law for sex-oriented establishments to remain open in the city. Sixty percent "regular" stuff, forty percent porn. *Kind of takes the thrill out of it.*

He headed to the back, to check out the fun forty percent. He wished he'd gone home and changed. Wearing a Lauren suit in a peep shop drew too much attention. Besides that, it was hot as hell in there. He removed his overcoat and folded it over his arm. He cruised the aisles, checking out the assortment of X-rated tapes made for every conceivable sexual taste. He stopped and checked out the box for *Buttman's Bend Over Brazilian Babes 18*. The brown-skinned Brazilian girls on the box were fine as hell and had enormous, bubble butts. He'd seen all the other tapes in the series, and they were his favorites because they always featured attractive, eager performers and really steamy sex scenes. Esperanza was an avid collector of porn. He and Legs often watched videos together. Some of them were really bad, so it became a goof, as they laughed and made fun of the lame sex scenes. Other times, they'd watch some really hot video and become turned on, and they'd screw their brains out afterwards.

Esperanza moved on to the toy section. There was a variety of dildos, vibrators, rubber versions of porn stars' pussies (with lifelike pubic hair!) and blow-up dolls. *How desperate do you have to be to fuck a doll? Might as well get yourself a hooker.* He thought about buying Legs a new vibrator. It drove him crazy with lust when he watched her masturbate with one of her toys. Maybe after he asked around about Midnight Desire, he'd do a little shopping. Esperanza checked out a vibrating rubber butterfly. It came with straps, which meant it was hands-free. The woman wore the harness, and the butterfly stimulated her clit while her partner fucked her. Nice. *Legs might dig this. I'll get a couple of D.V.D.s, some toys, some flavored lubricants, a bottle of champagne, some weed, and we can have a little party.*

"Upstairs—live girls and private booths," a man's staticky voice declared over the P.A. system. He sounded like he needed a nap.

Esperanza accepted the invitation and climbed a spiral

staircase. On the second floor, there were rows of booths. Red, yellow and blue Formica. Hovering in front of the booths, a crew of bikini-clad, bored-looking peep-show girls perked up when they saw Esperanza. *Not a very appealing bunch.* A couple of scurvy white chicks, some overripe and over-the-hill black mamas, a few emaciated Mexican *chiquillas*—little ones—and a spattering of butt-ugly trannys thrown in for good measure. Esperanza sauntered over to one of the trannys. The rest of the girls seemed disappointed by his choice.

The tranny cheesed it up, did a flamboyant head toss. The cheap platinum-blond wig almost fell off his head. Esperanza bit down on his tongue so he wouldn't laugh. *You gotta be kiddin' me. He really thinks he can pass for a girl? I want some of what he's been smokin'. So this is what Alina's into these days? Baby girl's more screwed up than I thought. Legs believes that with the proper guidance, Alina's gonna go on the straight and narrow? Well, at least my honey's still idealistic.*

"*Papi chulo,*" the tranny said in a gravelly voice. "I'm Lola. Let's party."

Esperanza squeezed into the booth, and the harsh stench of cheap pine disinfectant made his nostrils burn. He stuffed a couple of dollar bills into the change slot, and the metal divider leisurely rose in fits and starts while making clacking, mechanical sounds. The Plexiglas dividing the booth was smudged with fingerprints and cum stains. Esperanza kept his hands at his sides, making sure he didn't touch anything. Lola's body was decent enough. It was well-proportioned and smooth, especially for a dude. But that face would never fool anyone into believing he was a female. On Lola's face was a worse five o'clock shadow than Esperanza's, and his skin was pockmarked and plastered with pancake makeup. Looked like a clown in drag.

Lola picked up the phone on his side, and Esperanza did

the same, except he used a handkerchief to make sure no skin made contact with the phone, which he held an inch away from his ear and mouth.

Lola smiled in amusement. "Take out your cock," he said and batted his long, fake eyelashes.

"Don't you wanna cuddle first?"

Lola became suspicious and backed away a step. "You vice?"

"Nah, I'm looking for an old friend." Esperanza pulled out a twenty-dollar bill and cautiously slipped it in the half-inch gap between the Plexiglas and the side wall of the booth. "Midnight Desire."

Lola rolled his eyes. "Whachu want with that bitch? I'm more fun."

"I'm sure you are, sweetheart," Esperanza said. "But Desire and I have some unfinished personal matters to talk about."

Lola stuffed the twenty in his massive, silicone-enhanced cleavage, and then scratched his stubbly chin. "You evah hear of a club called Calista's Hideaway?"

Chapter 6

Esperanza was having a grande Macchiato coffee at Starbucks. He managed to secure one of the plush, teal armchairs
in the back. At the circular, wooden tables, there were a couple of young dudes wearing glasses, turtlenecks and khakis,
typing into laptops like their lives depended on it. In the
only other armchair, a plump lady with bad skin and curly
hair held a big drawing pad on her lap. Transfixed and waiting for inspiration, she purposefully stared at the blank
paper, her hand held up in midair, stumpy fingers clutching
a piece of charcoal. Esperanza needed to kill some time before heading to Calista's Hideaway, so he'd gotten himself a
New York Times and a coffee. Turned out to be a much busier
day than he anticipated. Hopefully, in a couple of hours, he'd
find Midnight Desire, who'd tell him where Alina was, and
that would be that. Before coming to Starbucks, Esperanza
made a quick stop at the parking garage and left his bag of
Pleasure Palace goodies in the trunk of his Jaguar. He was
on his cell phone with Legs, filling her in on his progress. She
was at the Sueño Latino. It was noisy in the background, since
the crew was getting ready to open for the evening. Esperanza
could hear the sounds of tables being moved, liquor bottles
clinking, employees laughing, glasses getting washed.

"Alladice didn't give me too much info," he said as he
stirred the caramel-flavored coffee and then took a sip. "I

might have to go back with Abuela, since she's the legal guardian."

"Now what?"

A few bars from a salsa song played as the D.J. tested the sound system. Sounded like conga maestro Ray Barretto. "I have to go to the tranny club where Midnight Desire works."

"You're enjoying all this, aren't you?"

Esperanza sniffed the air, relishing the mellow aroma of steamed milk as the espresso machine hissed while tourists, all bundled up in heavy coats and hats, patiently waited on line for their orders of flavored coffees.

"What do you mean?"

"Being back on the street," Legs said. "Playing detective."

"Who's playing?" He admired a cute blonde in tight jeans and cowboy boots who strolled by. Willowy figure. Appealing, marine-blue eyes. Fresh-faced, midwestern babe. Her red, leather motorcycle jacket stood out against the forest-green walls. She looked over her shoulder and smiled at him. He smiled back. She blushed. "By the way, peep shows ain't what they used to be."

Legs snorted. "Not seedy enough for you?"

"Nope."

Legs suddenly sounded terse. "It would be nice if you actually pretended to take this seriously."

Esperanza rolled his eyes. Legs was making too much of a big deal out of this. Alina was off partying somewhere. End of story. "Okay," he said. "I'm sorry."

"I don't mean to snap at you," she said, her tone gentler. "Abuela called." Legs sighed nervously. "Had some other premonitions."

He didn't want to hear about the old lady's visions. "Tell her to chill. I'm on the case. But it might take a few days," he said firmly, so Legs wouldn't further elaborate on her conversation with Abuela. She didn't. "Everything straight at the club?"

"Don't worry. We'll survive without the big cheese in the house."

"Remember, angel, I'm the one who brings that special touch of class to the joint." He threw her a loud kiss. "I'll try not to be back too late."

"I know what a pervert you are." Legs giggled. "Don't fall in love with one of those transsexuals."

"I'll try my best not to. Bye," Esperanza said and hung up. He opened the *New York Times* and proceeded to lose himself in the arts section.

Calista's Hideaway was a private club not too far from Times Square. It was located on 45th Street and Eleventh Avenue, in the neighborhood formerly known as Hell's Kitchen. Calista's catered to pre-op transsexuals, transvestites and their admirers. For an extra fifty bucks, Lola told Esperanza the week's secret password. Otherwise, he wouldn't be able to get in.

After cruising around for a while and checking out the joint, he lounged at a cocktail table near the stage, curiously observing the visual menagerie of sexual ambiguity. Thumping, repetitive techno music blasted through the jam-packed club. On the dance floor, bathed in surreal strobe lighting, there were several striking transsexuals bumping and grinding with middle-aged, white men in expensive business suits and wearing diamond jewelry. There were also plenty of enormous, beastly transvestites crammed into tight sequined gowns and leather miniskirts. Bad wigs, missing teeth, facial hair galore. They staggered around in high heels, trying to hustle drinks from some of the more desperate losers hanging around the horseshoe-shaped, mahogany bar.

The male clientele was a mix of hardened ex-cons, curious suburban boys from Jersey and Long Island, and the ballas who flashed enough cash to have the loveliest she-males on their arms. These were the ones with hourglass figures, unblemished skin, bountiful lips and flowing, luxurious hair. They appeared extremely feminine. Esperanza dealt with plenty of transgenders when he worked the Deuce all those years ago and thought that there was something strangely sexy about the idea of a beautiful woman brandishing a penis. He didn't think of it as a gay thing. Just something completely out of the norm. A remarkable, kinky fusion of genders.

Calista's was fairly dim, decorated in red and black. There was a profusion of shadowy cubbyholes. Silhouettes of drugs being taken and sex acts being performed. This wasn't the first time Esperanza hung out in a tranny club. What he found most appealing about them was the tremendously relaxed atmosphere. Unlike a club with heterosexual men and women, these were *all* guys and they *all* wanted to get laid. Most trannys were there to trade sex for cash or a little blow, and the dudes were there to get an exotic piece of ass. Put a bunch of men in a room together, and all the intentions are very clear. Nobody was searching for romance or a relationship.

Esperanza sipped his rum and coke, and politely turned away a half dozen trannies who asked to join him at his table. A couple of them were stunners and could easily pass for babes. That was, until they spoke. Then they sounded *muy macho*. The voice was always a major clue. Of course, the over-the-top female behavior was another dead giveaway. The operatic flick of the hair, hand-waving and hip-swishing were much more homo than femme and an insult to real women, like Legs, who were subtle with their seductive powers. That's why any *pendejo* who claims he didn't know a tranny was a man until he discovered a hard-on was full of shit. It was a matter of self-deception. No matter how beautiful a transsexual was, Esperanza could always tell it was a man.

The music faded, and everyone surged around the tiny

platform stage as the voice of an effeminate emcee filled the room. "Ladies and gentlemen and freaks of the night," he said. The emcee wore a tux, a purple-bob wig, heavy makeup and a pencil-thin mustache. *Welcome to the cabaret, old chum. Bob Fosse woulda loved this joint.* "Are you ready for the finest piece of ass New York has to offer?" There were screams of approval from the crowd. "Please welcome the diva of decadence: Midnight Desire!"

The stage lights dimmed, and Donna Summer's "Love to Love You Baby" thundered from the impressive sound system. A hush fell across the room as everyone's attention was drawn to the stage. When the lights came up, Esperanza's jaw dropped like a wolf in one of those Tex Avery cartoons. Desire stepped on to the stage in a white satin gown. His voluptuous body would make a *Playboy* centerfold seethe with jealousy.

My, my José, how you've changed.

Donna Summer moaned and groaned, and Desire danced—strutted and gyrated and undulated—and Esperanza found it difficult to accept the fact that the sensual creature performing on stage was actually a man. He leaned forward, attentively watching Desire do his thing. *Damn, he's fine.* This was the ultimate illusion. Desire stripped down to a G-string, revealing flawless, sun-kissed skin, tits and hips that said *pow!* Topped off by a comely face framed by waist-length, shimmering, auburn hair.

Desire leisurely made her way down the stage's steps, and the club swelled with randy anticipation. Desire did his thing, and everyone enthusiastically stuffed bills in his G-string, copping a squeeze here and a squeeze there. Desire would rub up against one man, then hop on another's lap, doing a wild, carnal lap dance as the crowd urged him on.

From the corner of his eye, Desire noticed Esperanza, and gave him such a rapacious look, Esperanza's heart beat a little faster. Desire immediately sashayed over and began to dance for him. Even up close, Esperanza couldn't tell it was a fucking guy. Oval, dazzling eyes the color of shadows. Petite, elegant nose. Fleshy, inviting lips painted scarlet.

He stuffed a twenty into Desire's G-string, and Desire rubbed his impressive, heart-shaped ass against his chest, then jumped on his lap and worked that incredibly sexy body of his. Esperanza became dizzy. He was getting turned on by the lap dance. It scared him a little. *This is a guy, remember? Jesus. Look at his face. Gorgeous. Body. To die for. That ass is better than Legs's. This is too fucking weird. I'm getting hot over a dude. Damn, Nick, you gotta be kidding. Clear your freakin' head. You're here for one reason. To find Alina.*

"How would you like to get together later?" Esperanza whispered in Desire's ear. He figured he'd pretend he was trying to pick up Desire. If he started asking questions straight out, he might scare the tranny away. And Calista's wasn't the place to get Desire to give up info about Alina, particularly if it took more forceful convincing. He needed to talk to Desire somewhere private.

Desire gave him the once-over and grinned excitedly. He ran his tongue along his enticing mouth and said, "Oh. My night just got real interesting." Even his voice sounded like a woman's.

"It sure has."

"I got one more set. You'll wait for me?" Desire kneaded Esperanza's muscular arms. "I sure hope so."

"I'll be right here."

Desire reached down in between Esperanza's legs and gently squeezed his crotch. Esperanza practically jumped out of his chair. He had never been touched sexually by a man. He was embarrassed but couldn't show it. At the same time, deep down, he was extremely attracted to Desire. It was the ultimate sexual taboo. Male and female wrapped into one.

He became flustered and felt his face get hot as he watched Desire strut away, swaying that amazing ass as he went off to entertain the rest of his fans.

Between sets, Desire drank pale, green apple martinis, while Esperanza kept on downing rum and cokes. To his surprise, Desire was quite funny and sexy and engaging, and had Esperanza's mind reeling with confusion. The plastic surgeon that did the work on him was a genius. Hell, Desire even got the female behavior down to an art form. If Esperanza had encountered Desire somewhere else, he would've been easily fooled, and he never thought that was possible. It was a major blow to his male ego that Desire sure proved him wrong. He could be suckered like any other chump.

"You like the way I move?" Desire asked.

"Like a goddess," Esperanza replied with a grin.

"You ain't seen nothin'," he said. "When I get you later, you're gonna know what heaven is like."

"Wanna go to a hotel?"

"Nah. You're special. We can go to my crib. I live a couple of blocks away."

"That works for me."

"By the way, *papi*. Your gear is the bomb. You got taste."

"Thanks."

"One thing, though. I don't come cheap." He waved around a wad of hundreds held together by a gold money clip. Desire's eyes lit up and he grinned. "*Vaya*. A man with class and cash. Boy, are we gonna party."

Esperanza wasn't sure why, but he felt a tinge of excitement at the prospect of being alone with Desire. How curious was he? How far would he go? Those questions deeply troubled him. Soon enough, he was going to get the answers.

In front of Calista's Hideaway, Esperanza hailed a cab. One pulled up, and he held the door open for Desire, who strutted out of the club wearing a full-length mink coat and demurely climbed into the cab.

"Tenth Avenue between fifty-fifth and fifty-sixth," Desire said to the cab driver as Esperanza followed her in and slammed the door shut. As the cab drove away, Desire slid close to Esperanza and hooked her arm around his. "You seem a little tense," Desire said. "Have you ever been with a special girl like me before?"

"Honestly?" Esperanza cleared his throat. "No."

"Wow. I'm flattered to the max." She gave him a peck on the cheek. "Don't worry, honey. We'll take it nice and slow. I'll be your tour guide to a night of endless pleasure."

Desire leaned her head on his shoulder. Her hair gave off the fragrance of vanilla. Esperanza noticed that he started thinking of Desire as a she. It didn't surprise him, since there was nothing male about her. *Except for the cock between her legs. Be careful, Nicky boy. Don't let yourself get seduced here. Don't do something you'll regret.*

Desire took Esperanza's hand and kissed it, then began sensuously sucking his index finger. Esperanza didn't pull his hand away. He closed his eyes and leaned his head back, and enjoyed himself, lost in the soft, wet heat of Desire's lush mouth.

Esperanza chilled out on Desire's antique sofa, which was newly upholstered with wine-red crushed velvet. He sipped a scotch on the rocks and took a deep breath. This was his sixth drink, and he was beginning to get a serious buzz. Desire's apartment was done up in tropical pastel colors, with lots of velvet, lace, silk and satin. She'd lit several candles and sweet-smelling, coco-mango incense. On the smoked-glass coffee table, which was shaped like an artist's palette, there was a champagne flute filled with bubbly, a single-edge razor, a rolled-up twenty-dollar bill and several perfectly cut lines of coke. Esperanza was waiting for Desire to change into something more "comfortable." He should've started questioning her as soon as they walked into the immaculate apartment, but something stopped him. He was intrigued and somewhat perplexed by feelings he never experienced before. Sure, he'd met tranny's sexy enough to turn him on, but he never actually thought about fucking one.

Is that what you're planning to do? No, no, no. We're just gonna have a little fun, that's all.

Desire finally appeared, attired in a beguiling, light-blue, satin teddy and sheer, matching robe. She stopped for a moment, as if giving Esperanza the opportunity to relish her beauty, and he did so wholeheartedly. Desire came over, her stride graceful and confident, and sat close to him.

"God, you're a real fine *papi*," she whispered in his ear. Her hot, apple-martini-scented breath caressed his neck and gave him goose bumps.

Desire leaned over and sniffed a couple of lines of coke. She handed Esperanza the bill and he did the same. The *perico* was quite good. Singed his sinuses. Brain came alive. The alcohol-induced fog instantly vanished and his senses heightened.

"Nice," he said. *Nothing better than blow to get your mind truly flying.* They snorted and smoked weed and drank, and Esperanza got fairly wasted. He was having a blast partying with Desire. Like he was on a date or something.

"Let me ask you something," he said. "Just curious. If you wanna be a female, how come you haven't gone all the way, done the complete surgery?"

Desire tilted her head slightly and arched an eyebrow. "'Cause if I cut my *pipi* off and then changed my mind, I'd end up a very unhappy girl."

Esperanza clutched his stomach as he cracked up, and leaned his head on Desire's shoulder. He snorted another line of coke so he would stop laughing. He caught his breath, then found himself silently staring at Desire, as if hypnotized by her presence.

Desire dipped her index finger into a line of white and provocatively sucked on it while gazing at Esperanza with smoldering eyes. "I can tell by the look in your eye that you wanna fuck the shit out of me, daddy."

That statement brought Esperanza back to reality. He was there for information, not to indulge in some weird fantasy. *Enough. Time to take care of business.*

"That's not gonna happen," he said gruffly.

Desire flinched, caught off guard by Esperanza's sudden change in attitude. "Whatchu mean?"

Esperanza reached into his suit jacket and tossed Alina's Polaroid snapshot on the coffee table. Desire didn't react to the photo.

"Let me cut to the chase," Esperanza said. "I'm looking for Alina Perez, a missing teenager who's been running around town with you, José."

Desire kept her composure and lit a Newport, while sniffing back coke. "Shit, I hadda feelin' you weren't a trick. How you know my real name?"

"Don't worry about that. Just tell me where to find the girl."

"What's it worth to you?"

He reached into his wallet and tossed a couple of hundred-dollar bills on the coffee table. *"E'ta bien?"*

"That's not what I had in mind." Desire leaned back, crossed her lengthy, sinuous legs and blew out a cloud of cigarette smoke. "There are mens who'd pay a lot more than that to spend the night with me. I'll make you a deal," she said. "You're fine as shit, and I got it bad for you. We get naked, get in my bed and play for a few hours, and I'll tell you anything you wanna know. Truss me, it'll rock your world, *papi.* 'Cause there ain't no female who can compare to Desire."

What a proposition. Esperanza straightened up and folded his arms across his chest. He was equally repulsed and titillated by the idea. And he didn't appreciate the fact that Desire was playing games with him. He thought about punching her in the mouth to get her to talk.

But you're not gonna do that, are you? Face it, Esperanza. You got it bad for her, too. She's smokin'. Desire wants to play. So why not give her a little action, just to see what it's like? Just a taste. See, see. This is why you shouldn't get so fucked up. You throw caution to the wind. That's not a good thing. Gets you into trouble.

He shrugged. "Sure, why not?" Leaned back and spread his arms out, resting them on the edge of the sofa's back, his index finger drawing soft circles on her shoulder. "There's a first time for everything, right?"

Desire's eyes widened in surprise, then narrowed in anticipation. This wasn't the answer she expected. "I knew you couldn't resist me."

She sat up and, with well-rehearsed dramatic flair, let the robe fall from her delicate shoulders. Esperanza admired her for a moment, then leaned over and began kissing her neck. He liked the scent of the perfume she was wearing. Kind of fruity, yet quite subtle. His hand slithered from her ankle, up her silky leg, to her supple thigh, which he kneaded and caressed. He moved to her breasts, which felt exceptionally real. Esperanza eagerly played with them, pinching her erect, dark brown nipples. Desire began to moan. *This is wrong, Nicholas. What about Legs? She's the reason you're here in the first place. She puts up with a lot of your shit, but how far you think you can go and think it's OK?* Desire reached down between Esperanza's thighs and massaged him, making him hard. Esperanza began to surrender to her sensuous touch, his hips jerking to the movement of her hand.

Wait a minute. What the fuck are you doing? Besides the

fact that you got the best woman in the world at home, Desire's a guy, remember? A bootie bandit. Even if Legs wasn't in the picture, even though Desire's got you all hot and bothered, this is a line you ain't never gonna cross. You ain't gonna let her manipulate you into this. She thinks she can play you?

Stop calling him she.

The fact that Desire was seducing him so effortlessly sent Esperanza into a rage. He clamped his hand around Desire's throat and choked him. Desire's eyes bulged in terror, and he started to thrash in a vain attempt to break away as Esperanza strangled the breath out of him.

You think I'm a maricón? Flash those nice titties, and I'm gonna bend over for you? How do you like me now, José? Still want to be my special girl?

"Either you tell me where Alina is, or I'm gonna beat it out of you."

Tears streamed down Desire's cheeks. Esperanza finally released him. Desire gagged and coughed and gasped for air.

"You muthafucka. Shit."

Esperanza handed him a glass of champagne, and Desire gulped it down.

"I ain't got all night," Esperanza said.

Desire glowered, and for a moment, Esperanza thought the tranny might try to hit him, but he was smarter than that. Instead, Desire sniffed another couple of lines of *perico*. Esperanza gave him his handkerchief, and Desire dabbed his face, which was smeared with black eyeliner. Then he seemed to quickly regain his poise.

"Lass I seen her, she ran off with a pimp named Star. He got a stable of hos in the Bronx. Most of the pimps been pushed to the outta boroughs."

"Maybe they should unionize," Esperanza said. "What does Star look like?"

"Not hard to find. Ain't too many white-boy pimps on the street. Even though that nigga swears he's black."

"You know how Alina hooked up with him?"

"Met 'im at a party I took her to. Star's got the bank, and the smooth rap, so she broke out with 'im," Desire said as he brought his legs up and wrapped his arms around them, then rested his chin on his knees. "Made me look like a sucka. Ain't heard from her since. Little *puta*."

So Alina's graduated from crack dealers to trannies to pimps. Baby girl is certainly open-minded.

"What was your relationship with her?"

"I like females, too."

"Why not stick to the ones at least old enough to vote?"

Desire hopped to his feet, started pacing while hammering his hips with his fists. He stopped. "Look," he said, suddenly calm, "I tole you whachu wanted to know. The rest ain't none of your fuckin' business. Now get outta my house, *cabrón*."

Esperanza stood up on wobbly legs and stared at Desire with a condescending smirk on his face. "It was fun while it lasted," he said, then grabbed his coat and took off.

When Esperanza emerged from the building, the bitter cold air cleared his head. Slightly. He was going to hail a cab, but decided to walk instead and gather his faculties. He could barely walk straight. The coke. The alcohol. The pot. All mixed together, they sent massive waves of euphoria straight to his brain. He tripped and almost fell. Luckily, his reflexes were still good. He put his hands out and prevented himself from slamming face-first into the hood of a parked S.U.V. He stood there for a moment, trying to get his vision in focus. Esperanza realized he still had an erection. Partly because Desire made him horny, and also because of his propensity for violence. Bloodlust. The sense of

power he experienced while strangling Desire was as intoxicating as the drugs.

*You're way out of control, Nick. What the fuck is going
on with you? Now you're getting off on hurting someone?*

Esperanza was so disgusted with himself he ferociously
kicked the S.U.V.'s door over and over, releasing all his
pent-up fury. The car alarm went off in an annoying series
of whoops and beeps and screeches. Esperanza doubled over
and took several deep breaths. Nausea swept over him.
Better get outta here before someone calls the cops. He trotted down the street. The freezing air was like icy slaps to the
face. He used to live life on the edge, and he'd left that all
behind. Now he seemed to easily return to that dark place
deep inside him.

*Why are you letting yourself get caught up in this weird
shit? It's okay to have a little fun, but you take things too
far. What did you used to call it? Dancing the devil's
mambo. Crossing the line. Sometimes you had that same
problem when you worked undercover narcotics. Beat con-
fessions out of suspects. Pulled the trigger at least once
when it wasn't completely necessary. That's not you anymore. You have a new life now. Which is why you have to
find Alina quick and get everything back to normal. Otherwise, you might get in too deep and not be able to find your
way back.*

Chapter 7

Viernes Social—Social Friday—at Sueño Latino, and the club was jam-packed and hopping. Dancers swarmed the dance floor and got busy to the live salsa band, Decargando, on the stage. Congas, bongos and timbales shouting out and responding to each other. Esperanza was an accomplished singer and conga player who often sat in and jammed with the bands that played at the club.

The Spanish Harlem Orchestra was performing at the moment, playing a cover of one of Esperanza's favorite mambo songs, Tito Puente's "Cuando Te Vea." Led by piano virtuoso Oscar Hernandez, the thirteen-piece orchestra had single-handedly brought old-school, Nuyorican salsa *dura*—hard salsa—back in style. Esperanza loved the fact that when S.H.O. hit the stage, the dancers on the floor went nuts. Esperanza was at the edge of the floor, stepping and shaking his shoulders and lost in the swinging horn section's fiery interplay. You couldn't slap the big grin off his face, no matter how hard you tried.

It was a big party night. Besides Oscar and his boys tearing it up, Esperanza's idol, Eddie Palmieri, and his band would be performing later on.

One of the things Esperanza loved about the salsa scene at Sueño Latino was the eclectic mix: ancient, hip, chubby, busty, wiry, conservative, caramel, white, black, comely, homely. Puerto Ricans, Dominicans, Japanese, Trinidadians, Mexicans, you name it. The music transcended generations, race and class. Didn't matter what you looked like or how much loot you made. If you were a good *salsero* or *salsera*, there'd always be plenty of dance partners available. Esperanza knew some old-school mambo cats who still sported cheesy leisure suits and pomade in their hair. But with their electrifying dance moves, there were *mamis* literally lined up to boogie with them.

There was a warm, palpable, deeply cultural energy that infused the club. When you entered Sueño Latino, it was like being transported to another time and place. People greeted each other with hugs and kisses, and smiled and were well-mannered. In all his years going to salsa clubs, Esperanza could remember only one time that he ever saw a fight break out. Because of an unspoken sense of tradition. *Respeto*. If a man was at a table surrounded by a bunch of girls and a guy came over to ask one of the girls to dance, he had to ask the man's permission first. Sure, some feminists might disregard the whole thing as *machista* posturing, but Esperanza appreciated the old-fashioned sense of respect between men. Salsa clubs seemed to be one of the last havens. Legs always said that what she loved about salsa dancing was the fact that for a few hours, she could just be a "girl" in high heels and a dress, and let the man lead her and let her feel feminine.

Ironically, Esperanza's director of security was Havelock Walker. Six foot five. Waist length dreds. Black as a conservative Republican's heart. All muscle. Former Navy SEAL. Proficient with a machine pistol or a throwing knife or C-4 explosive or whatever might be handy at the time. Esperanza obviously didn't need someone of Havelock's awesome combat expertise running club security. He just liked having his boy around to hang out with. Though Havelock could easily be working as a personal bodyguard for some Middle

Eastern oil baron, or the head of a Fortune-500 company, or some crazed Scientologist movie star, he preferred working at Sueño Latino. Esperanza paid him handsomely, and Havelock liked nothing more than wearing a designer tux and sipping mojitos while flirting with the endless parade of comely *señoritas* that came through the club every night.

Legs told Esperanza that she'd be hanging in the kitchen for a while, making sure the new head chef was handling his business. The night before, he returned from Desire's apartment extremely late, never even made it to the club. Legs got home at dawn, so they spoke only briefly. He filled her in on the fact that he found a new lead to follow up on. The pimp. Didn't say much about Desire. Wasn't ready to tell Legs about what really went down. He would at some point. Last night was way crazy. He wondered if he should discuss any of it with Havelock.

Esperanza spotted Havelock at the end of the bar, kicking it with a couple of buxom *mulatas*. The pretty, cinnamon-skinned girls were squeezed into revealing minidresses and had the kind of magnificent legs, hips, boobs and butts that made you want to weep with joy. Havelock, sharp in a black Armani tux, black shirt, no bow tie, looked up, and when he saw Esperanza approaching, he smiled that thousand-watt smile of his.

"*Mira!* The *papi chulo* himself has decided to grace us with his presence," Havelock said.

Esperanza gave him a bear hug. "Don't get catty on me now."

They turned their attention to the two *señoritas*. "Sandra, Ariana, this is the infamous Nicholas Esperanza."

They perked up and beamed as Esperanza gallantly kissed each of their hands and then ordered them a round of drinks. Havelock and Esperanza hung out with the girls for a while, flirted and laughed, then went off to Esperanza's private booth to catch up.

* * *

Havelock held up a highball glass filled with thick, dark liquid, and swirled it, trying to figure out what the smelly concoction was made of.

"What's in it?"

"Some herbs, one-fifty-one rum and who knows what else. Just drink it, motherfucker." Esperanza held up his glass, and they downed the drinks.

Havelock grimaced and gagged. "Rass, that shit's nasty," Havelock said, his Jamaican accent kicking in. His mom was from the former Jamaican capital, Spanish Town, and his pop was from New Orleans. "What's it called?"

"*Mama Juana*. Dominican aphrodisiac. After you have a few, you'll either fuck, faint or fight."

Havelock chuckled, his penetrating, champagne eyes brightening in mild amusement. "Well, you know fainting's outta the question for me."

"I still can't believe Giana's gonna marry your crazy ass."

Havelock and Giana planned to be married in Jamaica in the spring. Giana was an old college girlfriend of Legs. She and Havelock had met a couple of years ago, when she came by the club to spend some time with Legs. There was an instant rapport between Hav and Giana, and things got hot and heavy really fast. A few months ago, to Esperanza's complete surprise, Havelock, the self-proclaimed "forever bachelor," actually decided to settle down. He asked Giana to marry him while they were on vacation in Italy. Esperanza was thrilled for both of them, and Legs was beside herself. She believed she was Cupid, taking all the credit for getting Havelock and Giana together, even though she never even thought about setting them up on a date.

"Well, the girl has great taste," Havelock said, stuffing a big Romeo & Julietta cigar between his teeth. "You and Legs need to get hitched next."

"Please. You know Legs and I wouldn't want to spoil a

wonderful relationship by doing something stupid like getting married."

"Thanks for the vote of confidence."

"It's not about you, bro'. It's about Legs and me, and how we feel about marriage, *for us*."

Legs and Esperanza had been previously married to other people. Marriages that started off with great promise (as they often do), then eventually degenerated into vicious, emotional battlefields, which left enduring scars. They were both stalked by their ex-mates. Ended up in nasty court fights. When Esperanza and Legs got back together after so many years, they made a deal that they'd be brutally honest with each other. Would always say what was bothering them. They wanted to stay away from the typical kind of suffocating, controlling marriages they'd previously experienced, so they established an "open" relationship. Didn't mean they slept around or anything like that. They simply kept things loose and fast and fun, just as if they were back in high school. Which was why, after so many years, they still had a playful chemistry between them. They were supportive of each other's needs and desires, were extremely close, loved each other's company and still had wildly fabulous sex, so they both knew a piece of paper ultimately really didn't matter.

"Legs told me you're searching for her niece."

"I don't think the girl wants to be found." Esperanza surveyed the dance floor. Everyone was dancing and drinking and laughing. They all looked so elegant, dressed to the nines. The club was all class and style. Owning a salsa club was a lifelong dream, and every time he held court in his private booth, overlooking the club, he felt incredibly blessed.

"Not the kind of girl that still plays with Barbie, huh?"

"She prefers trannies and pimps. She's a little ho runnin' wild, and she doesn't want to be found. This is a complete waste of my time. I'm doin' this only because of Legs."

"Are you going to hang it up?"

"Hell no. Not just yet, anyway. I gotta put a little time and effort into this, otherwise I won't be gettin' any for weeks." Esperanza chuckled. Though he was kidding around, he knew there was some truth to his statement.

"Nigga, you might not be married, but you sure are whipped."

"Don't be talkin' shit. You're a card-carrying member of the whipped crew, too."

They simultaneously wagged their heads and let out a belly laugh. Long gone were their youthful days, when they ran late nights together, on missions chasing *mamis* and a good time, and no matter what, their mission was always accomplished. In the back of his mind, Esperanza knew, despite his feelings, he'd complete this mission to find Alina, too. It was what he'd been trained to do, it was what his whole career was based upon, so there was no way he'd give up.

"How things change," Havelock said and then took a puff of his Havana. "Damn shame, ain't it?"

"Yeah," Esperanza said and lit his own cigar. "You know, I was hanging out with this tranny last night. Midnight Desire. As beautiful and sexy as any babe in this club right now."

Havelock raised an eyebrow. "You didn't—"

"No. Of course not," Esperanza said. If he could talk to anyone about this, it was his best friend. "But I gotta tell you, bro'. I got smashed, and for a minute there, I was tempted."

"I know that had to be one fine-lookin' tranny for you to even consider the idea."

"Though I hate to admit it, I did cop a couple of feels."

"You're crazy." Havelock leaned closer. "What was it like?"

"Felt just like a woman. Perfect tits."

"You still a freak, huh?"

"I guess so."

"Too bad Giana's comin' tonight. Otherwise I might head uptown with you and check out that lap-dance party."

"I'll tell you all the gory details tomorrow night. If "Rump-shakers" is the bomb, we'll go hang out there next week."

"Sounds good to me."

Legs was in the kitchen taking a break, keeping herself busy with a large plate of *arroz con gandules y pernil*. She was waiting for Esperanza to come in and tell her if he was leaving early to go find that pimp her niece managed to hook up with. *What's gotten into Alina? Why is she turning out just like her mother? Abuela's been so good to her, and still she's running the streets.* The whole thing was making Legs depressed. *Don't think about this right now. You have a long night ahead of you.*

Legs asked her assistant, Maria, to join her. The kitchen was noisy. The chefs created a variety of traditional Puerto Rican dishes, such as *mofongo*. Legs loved the mouth-watering taste of the mashed plantains with chunks of pork and garlic. But her favorites were *bacalaitos fritos*. Codfish fritters were a rare treat in any restaurant in New York. There were plenty of other delish dishes that were staples at Sueño Latino. *La cocina*—the kitchen—was a sanctuary for Legs; the scents of garlic and onions and *sofrito*, the sizzle of hot oil, the sound of knife chopping, the bright lights reflecting off the immaculately clean stainless steel surfaces, the commotion, all were soothing to her.

Maria was ecstatic. She recently discovered that she was pregnant, and she asked Legs to be *la madrina*—the god-mother.

Wow. I can't believe Maria's having a baby. She's ten years younger than me. She looks so happy. I wonder what it would be like if I got pregnant. Slow down, nena. Don't start thinking crazy now.

"Of course I'll do it," Legs said joyfully and embraced Maria.

When Maria began working at the club, it didn't take long for her to become Legs's protégé. Legs had a gut feeling about the young Dominican girl and took a chance on her. Under Legs's guidance and tutelage, the shy waitress gradually transformed into a crack assistant manager. Legs didn't hesitate to trust her to run the club if she was away on vacation or business. Best of all, they became close friends, almost like *hermanas*. To top it off, Legs also hired Maria's husband, Lucho, as the head bartender. That's why there was such a sense of family at Sueño Latino.

"I'm so glad, *ma*," Maria said, her eyes watering. She was a tiny thing, barely five feet tall. Because of her indigenous features, petite figure and waist-length, straight, jet-black hair, people often confused her for Native American.

Ecstatic, Legs bounced up and down in her chair. "You're gonna be a mom. I can't believe it." They screeched in mutual delight, drawing the attention of the cooks, the dishwashers and the busboys zipping back and forth around *la cocina*.

Esperanza cruised over to the table. "You guys are having way too much fun. Aren't you supposed to be working?"

Legs beamed. "Maria and Lucho are having a baby. And they want me to be the godmother."

"Fantastic!" Esperanza gave Maria a warm hug and a kiss. "Anything you guys need, let me know."

"*Gracias*, Nicholas."

"When is it due?" Esperanza asked.

"October."

"We'll throw you a monster baby shower right here at the club," Esperanza said, suddenly excited. "I'll get a *merengue* band, traditional Dominican food, the whole nine yards."

Maria grinned. "Really? Wow. I really appreciate that." She gave Esperanza an even bigger hug, and he lifted her off her feet and easily twirled her around.

"Congratulations," Esperanza said.

Legs wasn't surprised Esperanza made such a generous offer. It was his style. Under all the street-smart, tough-guy smarminess, under all the gruffness, he was very sweet and loving and giving and sensitive. Her Nicky Bear. That side of him was mostly reserved only for her.

"I'm gonna go tell Lucho," Maria said sprightly and rushed off to give her husband the good news.

Esperanza pulled up a chair and sat next to Legs, then reached over and grabbed a hunk of roast pork from her plate, wolfed it down and licked his greasy fingers. "Don't be gettin' any ideas now," he mumbled.

"My boyfriend's smart, handsome *and rich*. God forbid he might actually want to start a family."

"And spoil all the fun?" He paused for a moment, realizing that Legs wasn't making a joke. "Seriously, you suddenly interested in having kids?"

"Nah," she said, playing it off. "I'm just messin' with you, baby."

She was fibbing, of course. Legs rarely ever lied to Esperanza, but at the moment, she did it without hesitation. Over the years, she repeatedly said she wasn't interested in having children. But during the past few months, for some reason, the idea of being a mom kept popping into her head. Every time she walked down the street and saw a mother pushing a stroller, she felt this gnawing sense of longing, and she wasn't sure why. Why now? *Is it because you're about to turn forty? Your biological clock is ticking.* Legs didn't like to think of herself in such obvious terms. She needed to discuss these issues with her therapist so she might figure out what was going on with her.

"Are you going out to track down that pimp?"

"Yeah. I'm scopin' out the lap-dance party he hangs at and see if I can have a little chat with him."

"You should be right in your element."

Earlier in the morning, when Legs had returned home from work, she found Esperanza passed out on the sofa. She woke him, and he briefly updated her on what was going on with Alina. She couldn't imagine Alina in a relationship with a transsexual and then a pimp. Was she hooked on drugs and simply saw her body as a transaction for her next fix? As far as Esperanza was concerned, drugs didn't seem to be in the picture. She asked him how it went with the transsexual, but he shrugged it off, said it was no big deal. Legs got the feeling there was more to it than he was willing to say at the moment, but she didn't push it. He'd tell her sooner or later. Now her man was headed off to a lap-dance party probably filled with bootilicious *morena* strippers. At least Esperanza never hid anything from her; that was the beauty of their relationship. But it wasn't always easy to deal with. Though she trusted Esperanza, she knew he had a thing for the freaky. She didn't expect him to cross any lines, but she was aware he enjoyed straddling the edge, because that's who he was. She accepted that wild streak in him, because it was in her, too, just slightly more subdued, more feminine.

"You're gonna owe me big time, you know," Esperanza said.

"Yeah, yeah, yeah," Legs replied as she wiped her hands with a napkin, then stood up and smoothed down her turquoise dress. It was an elegant, form-fitting linen, with a high, regal collar and a sexy slit on the side all the way up to her hip. Low-heeled suede shoes with open toes. An understated diamond necklace hung around her neck. Legs was popular with many of the female clientele because she was a fashion diva. They admired her confident sense of style. The men admired her, period. Legs wasn't going to lie; she enjoyed the attention she got as much as Esperanza did.

"Have one of the cooks fix you a plate. You look like you can use a warm meal . . . among other things."

As she passed him, she bumped his shoulder with her ample hip and strutted off.

Esperanza craned his neck and delighted in her sultry sway. Before disappearing through the double doors, she turned, gazed at him over her shoulder, her alluring eyes coquettishly squinting. She loved to flirt with him, to tease him, so that he always desired her. Legs smiled to herself, because she was elated that Esperanza was her man, and knew he always would be.

Spins and dips, twirls and shoulder shakes, smiles and flirtatious caresses, a feverish release of sexual tension. *Caballeros* in stylish suits and ties dabbed at sweat-covered faces with scented handkerchiefs. *Damas* in bright-colored, skin-tight dresses swayed wide hips and gave flicks of their hair. Bodies joyfully beckoned their partners as the club's rainbow of lights washed over them.

Esperanza, with Legs by his side, was back at his booth, enjoying the music of piano man Eddie Palmieri and his orchestra. They burned up the stage. When Palmieri tore into a solo, it was orgiastic, complex, mournful and tumultuous. He grimaced and moaned and groaned and pounded the ivories as if he was going through *un despojo*. Exorcising bad spirits. His eight-piece ensemble delivered layer upon layer of screaming trumpets, saxes and trombones, backed by explosive Afro-Rican percussion. Sweeping, tribal-influenced symphonies possessed the dancers on the floor. Shockwaves of contagious tropical rhythms that always got your feet moving. "Nada De Ti"—"Nothing From You"—was the name of the song. It was one of Esperanza's favorites.

The orchestra finished, and the place broke out in deafening applause, as dancers fanned themselves and surged to the bar to grab a cold beer or a *piña colada*. Palmieri grinned and leaned into the mike. "Ladies and gentlemen, for our next number," he said, "I'd like to invite our fabulous host, Nicholas Esperanza, to the stage to sing for us."

The crowd whistled and chanted, "Nick! Nick!"

But Esperanza was about to head uptown to look for Alina's pimp friend, Star, and didn't have the time to do his thing.

Legs elbowed him in the ribs. "Go ahead, *papi*. Show 'em whachu can do."

The chanting grew louder.

To hell with Star. This was an opportunity Esperanza couldn't pass up. He flashed an exuberant smile and trotted to the stage. He hugged and kissed Palmieri, then went to center stage and grabbed the mike.

"Okay. Here we go . . . *uno, dos, tres*."

Esperanza crooned over a fiery rendition of the salsa classic "Adoracion." His voice was sensual and lush. He oozed a seductive confidence as he shook his hips and rolled his shoulders and did a series of elaborate salsa steps. The audience got revved up by his performance and poured out onto the floor, swept up all over again by the spirit of *la música*.

Chapter 8

The Millennium Ballroom's "Rumpshakers" party was a big-butt lover's wet dream come to life. After getting through the heavy security, which involved pat downs and metal detectors, Esperanza shelled out twenty-five bucks and sauntered into the joint. The cavernous Harlem ballroom, which usually hosted weddings and sweet sixteens, was packed with about three hundred homies and a hundred strippers. Helium-filled balloons floated over the tables, and colorful streamers hung from the ceiling. It was like a prom-night party. Except the antics going on at "Rumpshakers" every week were pure debauchery. A straight-up booty fest. Esperanza grinned while bopping his head to Jay-Z's "Take-over." Jay was rapping about runnin' this rap shit and something about bringing a knife to a gunfight.

Legs was right. I'm right in my element.

To the room-shaking hip-hop soundtrack, an assortment of b-boys, playas, ballas, pimps, drug dealers and hustlers were getting lap dances, table dances and wall dances from the variety of buxom, chocolate strippers dressed in next to nothing or nothing at all. Except for six-inch stilettos. Esperanza thought the way the brown-skinned, ghetto-fabulous honeys moved was astonishing. Big *culos* shaking and swaying and bouncing. Some of the women were light-skinned, others dark chocolate, and there were a few *Dominicanas* and *Boricuas* thrown in the mix. All of them stacked, stacked, stacked. *Coño, I ain't never seen anything like this. I may end up goin' home real late tonight.*

It was nothing like the so-called gentlemen's club, where you sipped overpriced cocktails and watched platinum-blonde, hip-challenged, silicone-enhanced Pamela Anderson clones lethargically stroll up and down a stage or work a pole. The sistas didn't play that. They were a hurricane of sexual energy.

Esperanza squirmed through the dense crowd, unable to lose the grin he was wearing. He definitely had to bring Havelock to this place. Esperanza hoped it took a while to find Alina's friend Star. He sure wouldn't mind hanging for a while. *Like I need an excuse.*

The city can close down all the legal topless joints they want. They just go underground—and underground's much raunchier.

Esperanza passed a circle of men who were whistling and clapping. They were so excited, Esperanza backtracked and peeked over a couple of the revelers' shoulders. On the floor was a stripper with thick legs and huge tits. She fervently worked a massive black rubber dildo in and out of her wet pussy while crumpled dollar bills rained on her. Esperanza laughed. *That's a bad bitch.* He tossed her a twenty. She earned it. *This place is nasty. Obviously, anything goes at "Rumpshakers." Reminds me of the bad old days in Times Square. When sex and decadence used to be fun. Before it got all politically correct and moral.*

Esperanza craned his neck. Connected to the stage was a twenty-five-foot runway that cut through the center of the room. At the end of the runway, a pudgy, light-skinned brother was lying on his back while a stripper with a panoramic butt squatted over his head, her crotch jammed into his face, seeing how long he could hold his breath. Each ass cheek separately moved up and down as if they had a mind of their own. His boys laughed, hooted and hollered, and counted out, "Fifty-two, fifty-three . . ." They were taking bets.

Mira eso. Culo for days. Imagine that on your face, Esperanza. My man must be havin' a blast.

Esperanza finally made it to the bar. He ordered a rum and coke. He'd changed into a rust-colored, cashmere, V-neck sweater, a calfskin ski jacket and brown corduroys. He should've worn baggy jeans and a baseball cap if he really wanted to fit in, but it wasn't his style, and he wasn't going undercover, anyway.

A statuesque stripper, a shimmering onyx goddess, approached him. He dug the shiny red, latex, thigh-high boots and matching underwear she was wearing. *Wow. Look at her. Quite yummy.*

"Hey, handsome. Name's Goodie," she said in a heavy Jamaican accent. Dense, lengthy braids dangled past her shoulders, and those abundant, crimson lips smiled warmly. "Want a dance?"

Esperanza said, "Well . . . I don't know . . ."

Hardcore, dance-hall reggae played as Goodie straddled Esperanza, who was sitting on a padded folding chair, his hands dangling by his sides. She did a searing bump and grind, to the music's heavy, rolling bass line, her body slithering and rubbing against him. At first, Esperanza was hesitant to touch her. He was used to the legal clubs, where such behavior got you tossed out to the street. But as his eyes surveyed the room, he saw nipples getting sucked, butts getting spanked, pussies getting fingered, he figured he'd get into the spirit of the party, and he let his hands go to work. Goodie's skin was smooth and warm and pliable. She gave off the scent of sweat and musky perfume. Esperanza's fingers explored the inviting curves of her body. *God, I love the texture of her skin. The way she moves her body is too much. This is my idea of a lap dance. Candela. Makes me wanna fuck her right here, right now. Searching for Alina has sure brought a lot of extra temptation. Quite some fun, too. I hope she runs away more often. Damn, Nick, what a fucked-up thing to say. Yeah, Legs is upset and all that, but Alina ain't no saint. If not, you wouldn't be at "Rump-shakers" right now having such a blast.*

"Ooh, baby . . . I like the way you touch me," Goodie said as she pressed and rubbed her pelvis against his erection and shoved her shapely *tetas* in his face. He sucked her luscious nipples, and she reached down between his legs and adeptly stroked him.

"Damn, girl," he said. "You're hot."

This was the best ten bucks he ever spent. Between Goodie being so sultry and the rambunctiously hedonistic energy permeating the party, Esperanza was vigorously aroused. *This is too much. She got me hard like a mother-fucker. What would it be like to taste that pussy? To have those big lips suck me dry? Easy boy. Don't get crazy now.*

The song ended, and he had to catch his breath as sweat snaked down his face, stinging his eyes. Goodie gave him a peck on the lips and said, "Want another one?"

Esperanza was tempted. Maybe later, after he found the pimp and asked him about Alina. "Not right now." Esperanza tipped her an extra twenty dollars. "I have some business to take care of."

"Generous," Goodie said as she shoved her boobs back into her latex bra. "My kind of man."

"Trust me, *mami*," he said as he pulled a handkerchief from his pocket. "You're worth it." Goodie took it from him and smiled sweetly while she gently patted the perspiration from his face. "By the way, have you seen my boy Star around?"

She scrunched her nose. "Sure," she said, then let out a

sigh. "He's in the V.I.P. lounge." She climbed off Esperanza's lap and jerked up her boots. "Now what would a class act like you want with a blood-clot, asshole, white boy like 'im?"

"Owes me money."

"Well, if ya decide to bust his head open," Goodie said and then winked, "next dance is on me."

The V.I.P. lounge at the back of the ballroom was dark. It was L-shaped, and the stucco walls were painted aqua. There were a half dozen pleather love seats the color of daisies. Beside them were cheap aluminum-and-glass end tables, decorated with votive candles, which supplied most of the light, except for a couple of brass floor lamps with red light bulbs. Silhouettes and shadows of a variety of nasty sex acts undulated in different areas of the lounge. Seemed like one big orgy was going on. Esperanza stood at the entrance for a moment, squinting, waiting for his eyes to adapt to the darkness. Then he carefully inspected the room. At least it was quiet in the V.I.P. lounge. Quiet enough to hear the moans and murmurs. In the far corner, he spotted a white dude, wearing a red "Godfather" hat, a loud, multi-colored Versace shirt, black-and-green alligator-skin shoes and red, baggy silk pants. Bulky, platinum-gold chains dangled from his neck, and candlelight glinted off his collection of gaudy diamond rings. Bling to the tenth degree.

This asshole sure goes for the stereotypical mack-daddy look. Seemed much more like a hick in his mug shots.

Star was thoroughly enjoying a raw, wanton lap dance from a fleshy hoochie with elaborately sculpted hair streaked blond and red that twirled upward in complicated, stiff swirls and curls as if someone went nuts on her head with a Mister Softee ice cream machine. Heavy gold-hoop earrings dangled from her ears. Aside from the four-inch-long nails, gold stiletto heels and some gold glitter, she was completely naked, and puffed on a blunt while working that Rubenesque body of hers. Star aggressively squeezed that opulent backside and buried his face in her deep cleavage.

Esperanza strolled over to Star's table and plopped into the chair opposite the couple. He was quite amused watching the honey girl do her thing while Star lost himself in endless folds of ebony flesh. *I see White Star likes 'em real thick. Not my cup of tea, but this babe is certainly tempting.*

Courtesy of Santos, Esperanza had read Star's rap sheet. Thirty-two years old. Real name was Ralph Beatty. Born and raised in a black ghetto near the notorious Cabrini-Green housing projects in Chicago. Inspired and encouraged by a pimp who lived next door, Star got into the game at the age of sixteen. *Everybody needs a mentor.* Moved to New York when he was twenty-three. Over the years, Star had been pinched several times for promoting prostitution, but like most pimps, all he got was a slap on the wrist. Did a few overnight stints at Rikers now and then, but never any genuine hard time. Despite the blue eyes and white skin, it seemed that his African American brethren accepted him as a genuine mack. He was one of the rare white boys allowed into the club because he was pimpin' old school. Wore the right clothes. Had the right hos. Lots of flash. Lots of cash. Why he was messing with Alina, Esperanza couldn't figure out, since he had no priors involving minors.

On a nearby end table, there was champagne on ice and two flutes. Esperanza noticed it was Veuve Cliquot and was impressed that Star actually had a taste for fine bubbly.

"Work that ass, bitch. Lawd have mercy," Star said. Though he sounded like a genuine Baltimore thug, Esperanza got the sense that Star's tough-guy posturing and rugged features veiled the fact that the pimp had no *cojones*. Slappin' some bitch around is one thing. Throwin' down with the fellas is a whole other story. It even took Star way too long to realize that he was being sized up. He turned to Esperanza, who flashed a smug smile. "You better bounce, yo," Star said, and the stripper paused for a moment. "Seat's taken."

"I know. I'm sittin' in it." Esperanza had debated how he was going to play it with Star. At first, he thought about going for a whole undercover thing: *I wanna fuck a young P.R. girl . . . willin' to pay a gee . . . blah, blah, blah.* But looking into Star's beady eyes, which were set too wide apart, Esperanza could see there was no need to playact. A couple of slaps across the face, and it would probably be impossible to get the pimp to *stop* talkin'.

"You invade my privacy, then you dis me. You got them kinda balls, son, you must have some serious bidness to discuss." Star's tone was tough, and his expression remained confidently calm. "Or you just like to watch?"

"A little of both."

The stripper made herself comfortable on Star's lap, arm dangling around his neck. She puffed on her blunt and happily stared at Esperanza like he was a welcome break from dealing with the pimp.

"Gimme a reason why I shouldn't kick yo ass right now."

"You could try. But it might be kinda hard pimpin' from a wheelchair." The stripper chuckled, and Star shot her a nasty look. "Besides," Esperanza continued, "I'm lookin' for a girl named Alina. Remember her? She's a minor, she's missing and she was last seen with *you.*"

Star casually patted the stripper on the ass and said, "Freshen up, boo." The stripper walked off, broad hips swaying as if they might demolish anything in their path. "You po'lise?"

"Ex."

"Then youse a damn fool. Done lost yo mind, steppin' to *me.* You know who you fuckin' wit?"

"Let's keep this simple, asshole. Tell me where to find the girl, and I let you keep your teeth."

Star grinned. It was a wide, condescending grin, encased

in platinum fronts that made you think the pimp could bite through steel. "Here I am, an International Man of Leisure, on his night out. And you gotta come in here runnin' yo mouf and harassin' me. Poppin' shit 'bout some bitch I ain't nevah heard of."

Esperanza chuckled. *Pimps are fools no matter what their skin color.* "International Man of Leisure, huh? And here I thought you were just a low-life scumbag."

Star stopped grinning, and his cheeks turned beet red. *Look at 'im blush. He ain't as black as he thinks he is.* In a flash, Star snatched the champagne bottle from the ice bucket and swung it at Esperanza's head. Star was fast, but not fast enough. Esperanza blocked him with his forearm, grabbed Star's wrist and twisted his arm, forcing him to drop the bottle. Then Esperanza slapped him twice, and grabbed Star by the back of his neck and slammed him face-first into the table. Using Star's shirt collar, Esperanza flipped the pimp over, and jammed his forearm into Star's throat, keeping him immobile. Blood was oozing from Star's nostrils. Esperanza leaned down, his face close to the pimp's.

"You gonna tell me where the girl is, *cabrón*? Or do I have to bitch slap you again?"

Esperanza suddenly felt the cold steel of a muzzle jammed behind his ear, followed by the unnerving click of a gun's hammer being pulled back. Finally, a resonant voice demanded, "Back the fuck up."

Esperanza backed off and slowly turned to see a massive, middle-aged, bald-headed bouncer with a goatee and Ray-Ban sunglasses aiming a 9-millimeter Smith & Wesson at him. The man sported a sky-blue velvet suit that seemed to have barely survived the seventies. Esperanza had to keep his anger in check. He didn't appreciate a gun being pointed at him. But at the moment, there was nothing he could do.

Star got up, grabbed a napkin and wiped the blood from his face. Without warning, he smashed his fist across Esperanza's jaw. Esperanza shook it off. Star punched like a school-girl.

"Whachu gonna do now, bitch?"

"I'm gonna walk outta here, B. I know Ike Hayes over here ain't gonna shoot me, 'cause that would be bad for business, and business is obviously good."

Chest puffed up, Star got in Esperanza's face. "Lucky you." Esperanza didn't budge an inch. "Lucky's my middle name."

"You got a smart mouf, yo. I'm lettin' you walk outta here in one piece tonight. But if I evah see you 'round here again?" He patted Esperanza on the cheek. Esperanza wanted to bite a piece of Star's nose off. "I'm gonna have the place decorated with yo brains. Now step, muthafucka."

"I'll catch up with you at another time, when you ain't got all the muscle backin' you."

"Is that so?"

With all the force he could muster, Star kicked Esperanza in the groin. Esperanza collapsed to his knees and groaned as waves of nausea swept over him. He thought he might faint. In the movies, a guy gets kicked in the nuts, he stumbles for a second, then keeps running. In real life, the pain is so excruciating, you double over, you get dizzy, you throw up, and it takes a while to get your legs back. In severe pain and coughing, Esperanza glared at Star, and his eyes declared, "I'm gonna rip your heart out."

Fuck, it hurts. Legs thinks I'm not taking this thing with her niece seriously enough. Now it's gotten really serious. Gun to my head. Punched in the face. Kicked in the nuts. This ain't what I signed up for. I ain't as tough as I used to be. Maybe I lost some of that street sense over the past few years livin' the leisurely life. Is Alina worth this kind of trouble? Maybe I need to think about when she was a little girl and she'd come over for Christmas with Abuela and Cookie. How happy she was with all the presents Legs and

82 / Jerry A. Rodriguez

I gave her. How sweet and respectful and charming she was. Always called me Tio Nick while giving me big hugs and kisses. A little angel with an endearing smile. If I'm gonna be puttin' my ass on the line for Alina, I better remember that smile. Star knows where she is. Maybe he's turned her out, maybe she's his piece, but I could see it in the pimp's eyes, he knows where Alina is. One way or another, Star's gonna tell me.

Two other muscle-bound bouncers rushed over. "Get this piece of shit outta here," Star ordered while dismissing Esperanza with a wave. The bouncer with the blue suit put his gun away and nodded at his boys. The two bouncers got on each side of Esperanza, grabbed his arms, hauled him to his feet, dragged him out the back exit to the street and tossed him to the pavement like he was some two-bit drunk. As Esperanza lay on his back in the icy gutter between parked cars, he was already thinking about what he'd do to the pimp once he got his hands on him.

Payback *was* a bitch, and for Star, it would come very, very soon.

Chapter 9

"Why do you have to be such a tough guy?" Santos said sardonically. "You could've come to me first." Then he took a final bite from his *sandweech Cubano* and washed it down with *café con leche*.

Esperanza shrugged. "I was feeling adventurous." He was hunched over Santos's desk and just finished telling Santos about his encounter with Star the night before. About how careless he'd been, and ended up with black-and-blue balls to prove it.

"Adventurous can get you killed, big guy." With a wag of his head, Santos popped a breath mint into his mouth and methodically chewed on it. "Next time, it might be a bullet to the chest."

Bread crumbs peppered the corners of Santos's mouth, and his lips shimmered with pork grease. Anibal could be such a slob sometimes. Esperanza politely handed him a paper napkin. Since the windows had been recently washed, late afternoon sun streamed into the busy squad room, and Esperanza could see thick dust swirling in the beams of brilliant light. The phones rang endlessly, and it was difficult to hear over the chatter of detectives and uniformed officers busy working cases. "I know you always thought I was too much of a cowboy."

"You are," Santos said and wiped his mouth. "When you

left Narcotics and became a murder cop, it took you a long-ass time to get accustomed to the slow beat of homicide investigation. And still, you got that narco-cop bravado shit goin' on."

"When bullets are whizzin' by your fuckin' head every other day, it's kind of a hard thing to let go of." Esperanza wasn't sure why he felt the need to explain himself to his ex-partner. Maybe it was because he felt big-time respect for Santos, who'd been instrumental in Esperanza's transformation from street cop to detective. "I was dealing with drug posses carrying MAC-10s and Uzis. Scumbags weren't scared of the police and didn't care how many bystanders were gunned down in the process."

"I understand that. It was the crack epidemic of the eighties." Santos was trying to get his desk organized. As he spoke to Esperanza, he sifted through messy stacks of papers and started forming neater piles, while tossing useless documents into the plastic wastebasket already overflowing with garbage. "But that was a long, long time ago."

"I was involved in a dozen shoot-outs during my career, and you've never even had to discharge your weapon." Esperanza was a little offended by Santos's flip attitude. He'd been a damn good homicide detective and cleared plenty of cases. The only thing Esperanza hated about the job was showing up at the door of a victim's family to tell them the grim news of their loved one's violent demise. That was something he never got used to. Otherwise, he loved the job. "We're different kinds of cops, with different styles. Still, wasn't I the best partner you ever had?"

"Yeah, you sure were." Santos smiled and loosened his wrinkled paisley tie, which was frayed at the edges. "*Mira*, I'm not tryin' to bust your balls or anything, Nick. I just think you should keep your nose clean. 'Specially since you're a civilian now."

"Your concern is noted."

"What the hell are you getting yourself into, *compai*? Consorting with pimps, chicks-with-dicks and strippers. Trying to recapture your youth?"

Esperanza picked up a pencil and impatiently tapped it against the edge of the desk. "I've stepped into Alina's world."

"Ah, the things we do for love." Santos snickered as he tugged on his scraggly goatee. "I mean, I understand why you'd go to any lengths to please a *mami* like Legs. What man wouldn't? She's exceptionally beautiful and exceptionally smart. Exceptional, period. But I also know you like the adrenaline kick you're getting out of hittin' the streets once again."

"Man's gotta have a hobby."

"I just don't want to see you get hurt. I know you can handle yourself in any situation, but let's face it, you're a little soft 'round the edges."

"Yeah, but at least the edges are still there," Esperanza said. "I gotta tell you . . . if Abuela had any idea what her sweet Alina was into? She'd drop dead of shame."

"I'm glad my kids are grown."

"Did Missing Persons come up with anything?"

"No. Old lady filed a report. You're doin' much better than they are. But then again, you got a lot more free time on your hands."

"I need you to do me one more solid," Esperanza said and dropped the pencil on the desk. "Get the pimp's current address for me."

"Okay. Just don't do anything crazy."

"Me? Never."

Three o'clock in the morning. Tenth Avenue and 44th Street. West side of Manhattan. Hardly a soul on the street. Yet the Malibu Diner was open 24-7. And this late at night, it was populated mostly by gamy homeless men, exhausted graveyard-shift maintenance workers and fashionable club kids still reeling from blissfull Ecstasy highs. Fumes from day-old grease wafted through the air, and Elvis crooning "Love Me Tender" spilled from the aging jukebox.

Devona would usually never be caught dead in such a dump. The blinding fluorescent lights and the loud, loquacious Greek waiters were giving her a headache. But she was with Rybak at one of the large, curved booths in the back of the diner, sipping acrid black coffee. Devona and Rybak had just left a private S & M swing party at a downtown loft because Star paged them several times with some kind of an emergency. Needed to meet them immediately. Devona's sable and mink coat was draped over her bare shoulders, and her hair was tied in a tight ponytail. She wore a burgundy, strapless, leather gown, which laced up the sides from top to bottom, showing off about three inches of bare skin. Her spanking-new, patent-leather ankle boots had metal spikes running up the six-inch, ultra-thin heels. Though Devona adored her latest footwear purchase, the boots were starting to make her feet ache.

"Star, that asshole," Rybak said. "He better have a good reason for dragging us here." Rybak wore a black, leather vest underneath his leather duster. He was starting to sweat, so he removed his duster and neatly folded it on his lap.

Devona didn't reply. She continued to stare out the diner's grimy window. A dusting of snow was falling, and there was barely any traffic on the usually bustling Midtown street. She found herself in a deeply contemplative mood. The life she and her husband were leading recently began to leave her feeling unfulfilled. *This is it?* It had been nearly five years since she met Rybak, and he swept her off her feet. He showed her a whole new world and made her his queen. Their marriage was an endless, hedonic holiday. They obeyed no rules and did whatever gave them pleasure. It had been the most exciting time of her life.

Then why are you hanging out in some crappy diner waiting for a skuzzy pimp? What's going on here?

Rybak noticed Devona's aloofness. "Everything okay, baby?"

"I'm bored," she replied. Her tone was flat. She didn't bother to look at him.

"What do you mean 'bored'?"

"Working exclusively for Bishop."

She still didn't look at him, because Devona knew that when she didn't give Rybak her full attention, it annoyed the hell out of him.

"Spit it out, Devona."

"I need a change of scenery," she said and finally turned to her husband. "Let's freelance again. Do some traveling. Go to Miami. Brazil. Amsterdam. Get the fuck out of New York. The city's become as conservative as the Bible Belt, and I despise it."

He waited a moment before responding, and judiciously surveyed her face, probably wondering if this was one of her frequent temper tantrums or something more serious.

"Bishop won't be happy."

Finally, Devona's eyes bore into Rybak like a stake into a vampire's heart. She abhorred it when her husband took their employer's side. She was his wife. There was no other "side." Devona's glare was so caustic, it made him flinch, and Jason Rybak *never* flinched. She wanted him to know she was dead serious. He got the point.

"What is he? Your boyfriend? Who gives a shit what Bishop thinks?" She leaned back and folded her arms across her chest, the silver bracelets on her wrists clattering melodically. "Tell the truth. Are you happy with your life right now?"

"Except for being with you? Not in particular."

Even though he hadn't said anything, she knew that deep down inside, Rybak was feeling as restless as she was. That was the beauty of their relationship—it was symbiotic. They thought and felt exactly alike. That's why he was the perfect man for her. Few would ever be able to keep up with her or her voracious appetites. What was this misguided loyalty to Bishop? Though he'd never admit to it, Devona believed it was because Rybak had some strange need for a father figure, and Bishop seemed to eagerly provide that.

Devona softened her tone. "You're my world, Jason. We belong together. But it's time to make a change."

Rybak smiled spectacularly. It was the same smile he wore on the day he proposed to her and she wholeheartedly replied, "Yes."

"Okay. Anything you want, baby." He could never refuse her. What Mistress Love desired, Mistress Love got. "Have I told you today how much I love you?"

Without her eyes ever leaving his, Devona leisurely reached out, clasped his rugged hand in hers and left a trail of delicate kisses along his fingertips. She felt herself gush, butterflies fluttering wildly in her stomach. Even her mouth watered as she filled with desire for him. She was consistently amazed by this great love she felt for Jason.

"Yes. But tell me again."

Rybak leaned in to kiss her when Star slipped into the booth beside him.

"My, my," Star said. "How lovey-fuckin'-dovey." His eyes swept over Devona's smooth bosom, which was dotted with tiny black beauty marks, and he flashed those ridiculous platinum teeth of his.

"Well, well," Rybak said with disdain. "If it ain't Super Fly hisself." That was the only way he ever spoke to Star.

Devona hated the little prick. Star was weak. She could crush him in her hand and not even break a sweat. Why the hell did she even have to be in the same room with such a vile, useless creature?

"We might have a little problem, son," Star said, pulling up the thick collar of his outrageous aqua blue faux-fur coat.

"Don't call me son."

"Some ex-po'lise came lookin' for me, sweatin' me about the little Rican bitch ya'll had me track down."

"What do you want from us?" Devona asked as her eyes drifted, showing little interest in the conversation. At the counter, there were a couple of club kids with spiky blue hair and standard-issue black clothes. They were feverishly making out, lost in a drug-infused bliss. It was more fascinating to watch kids suck face than to listen to Star babble on.

"I want you to handle the problem." Star grabbed a packet of sugar, ripped it open and emptied the contents into his mouth.

Devona turned to him and asked, "What the fuck do we look like? Pimp protection?" She slipped her hand into her little ruby Prada handbag and eagerly caressed the pearl handle of her balisong. A Filipino butterfly knife. She was seriously considering pulling it out and slashing the pimp's face. For the fun of it. "Handle it yourself."

"I'm a playa, baby, not a fighter."

"You're an asshole is what you are," she shot back, hand tightly gripping the balisong. *If we were outside, I'd waste Star in a second. I'm tired of his bullshit. I don't like the way he talks. Or looks. Or smells. All I want is to see him bleed. I'm gonna make that happen soon enough.*

Rybak gently placed his hand on the back of the pimp's neck. Star tried to move away, but Rybak applied intense, pinpoint pressure to the nerves, and Star yelped in pain. "How did this guy find you in the first place?"

Esperanza's 1967 Jaguar XKE muscled its way up the West Side Highway. A silver, gleaming predator made of steel and glass. Shaped like a cruise missile. With its smooth lines, extended front section (Legs called the Jag the ultimate phallic symbol) and powerful engine, it was Nick's favorite car. It was in mint condition and set him back seventy grand. The only new addition to the Jag was a powerful, two-hundred-watt Bose stereo. The car had been cleaned recently, and the leather smelled brand new. As Esperanza listened to a Marvin Gaye C.D., he thought about his younger brother, Mark. He was headed home after having broken bread with Mark. They tried to get together at least once a month to catch up on what was going on in their lives.

Mark Esperanza was an F.B.I. agent. Part of the bureau's Joint Terrorism Task Force. Very busy man these days. They ate dinner at Nick's favorite restaurant, the Gramercy Tavern. Warm and vibrant, the Gramercy Tavern had splashy, food-themed murals, engaging lighting and deep-hued, oval-shaped, wooden tables. Mark and Esperanza sipped eighteen-year-old Glenmorangie single-malt scotch whisky and sampled from the impressive cheese selection, which included everything from Valley Camembert, a gentle fresh-flavored sheep's-milk cheese, to the earthy, Italian robiolina.

"You have to be careful working all those long hours, *hermanito*," Esperanza said as he stuffed a piece of fennel bread into his mouth. "You can easily burn yourself out."

Mark cackled. Though slightly smaller in stature than Esperanza, he exuded just as much presence. His hair was trimmed conservatively short, and he wore a blue, pinstriped suit, probably purchased from someplace where business types shopped. "That's silly advice coming from you, Nicky-boy." Mark carefully sliced several pieces of cheese and neatly lined them up on his plate. "When you were on the force, you were relentless with the amount of overtime you put in. Now you're telling *me* to slow down."

"I guess I shouldn't talk."

"Nope." Mark closed his eyes for a moment, savoring a piece of robiolina. "And it kills me that you're playing private detective."

"Crazy, ain't it?"

"I don't think it's cool you working without a badge. Might get yourself into trouble."

"It's no big deal. Just having a little fun."

"Uh-huh. Your idea of fun scares me. Be careful, anyway. You never know."

The Esperanza brothers thoroughly enjoyed their elaborate three-hour meal. Chilled cucumber soup. Tuna tartar. Roasted sirloin of beef. All topped off by Mexican coffee and coconut tapioca. By the end of dinner, they were both ready for a nap. Too bad Mark had to go to work.

Esperanza was always happy to spend time with his *hermanito*. Family was important to both brothers. That's why they always did their best not to miss their monthly dinners together, no matter how crazy Mark's schedule got.

As Esperanza paid the check, he promised Mark he'd take his sons, Gabriel and Joaquin, to the movies in a couple of weeks.

Esperanza bopped his head to Marvin Gaye crooning "Trouble Man" as traffic on the West Side Highway slowed down to a crawl, then a walk. It sucked driving a sports car in New York City unless it was late at night and there was zero traffic. His cell phone rang. He lowered the music and put on the speakerphone.

"*Buenas.*"

"It's me, Desire. I gotta talk to you right away," he said with a nervous stutter. "*In person.* I know where Alina is. She's in trouble."

Oh, great. All I want to do is lie down, and now I gotta get this phone call.

"Why can't you just tell me over the phone?"

"If you don't get your ass over here, Alina's gonna be hurt." Desire abruptly hung up. Esperanza dialed back. The phone rang and rang. *Why does Desire have to see me in person? Why did he sound so nervous?* Esperanza knew something was not on the up-and-up. For a moment, he thought about going home first and picking up his piece, just in case. He usually carried a semiautomatic, but in his rush to meet Mark, who was annoyingly obsessive about punctuality, he'd left it at the office. Esperanza decided it would take too much time to go all the way uptown and back. So he'd go straight to Desire's place instead. *Just be careful.* It probably was no big deal, anyway. Desire probably wanted to play games and get some more cash out of him. Tranny might end up getting a beat-down if he was lying about knowing where Alina was.

Esperanza parked his Jag in a lot down the block from Desire's tenement building. He stood in the tiny foyer and rang the bell several times, but got no answer. One of the tenants came out. She was a petite Dominican lady in a bright purple coat, walking a chubby cocker spaniel with shifty eyes. Esperanza smiled boyishly and sweet talked her, and the lady gave him a quick once-over and let him in. He climbed the four flights of stairs. A single dim bulb lit the hallway, which was painted mauve and had graffiti scrawled all over. Thumping merengue music blared from one of the apartments, and from the other, the evening news. Esperanza wondered if the tenants were deaf. The hallway smelled like it had recently been mopped with bleach. Esperanza knocked on Desire's door several times. Still no answer. He reached down and turned the doorknob. The door was unlocked. His internal alarms suddenly went off. Something suspicious definitely was going down here. Was this an ambush? Now he seriously regretted not returning to the club to retrieve a firearm.

What a punk ass. You've gone soft. You've entered much more dangerous situations—with nothing but your wits.

He took a deep breath and silently slipped into the apartment.

He cautiously made his way through the darkness, down the long hall. The floor creaked with the weight of his every step. His heart beat a little faster. Esperanza was nervous and excited at the same time. *What are you getting yourself into? Maybe you should turn around and call 911. C'mon, don't be such a pussy. You're a Navy SEAL for chrissake. No fear.* It was freezing inside, and he could hear the sounds of traffic and a dog howling as if he was out in the street. All the windows must be open. *That's great fuckin' detective work, Nick.*

Esperanza finally made it into the living room, and the overwhelming stench of urine and feces assaulted his nostrils. *You know the drill. Breathe through your mouth.*

Desire was standing by the window. All Esperanza could see was his silhouette. "What took you so long, *papi?*" Desire said.

"I ain't got time for fucking games."

There was a brass floor lamp with a beaded, red shade, and Esperanza switched it on. The room glowed with eerie crimson light. It wasn't Desire sitting by the window. It was a woman. A beautiful woman.

Before Esperanza could say anything, he was whacked across the back of the head with a blunt object, and there was sharp, searing pain.

When he hit the floor, Esperanza saw Desire a few feet away from him. Facedown. Naked. Hog-tied with an extension cord. All along his body, there were perfectly symmetrical lacerations and cigarette burns. Desire's face was lying in a fresh pool of blood. The transsexual's throat had been slashed from ear to ear.

Esperanza's vision got blurry, and he tried to get up, but was hit across the back of the head again.

Then his world went black.

Chapter 10

Esperanza gradually regained consciousness. His eyelids felt nailed shut. He was unable to breathe through his mouth. Overwhelmed by tingles of sexual pleasure coursing through his body, he struggled to move, but neither his arms nor legs would respond to mental commands.

Finally, he managed to open his eyes, and though it took a few seconds, the room finally came into focus. The walls were stainless steel, like he was in a meat locker. Except there were no sides of beef hanging. Instead, an elaborate assortment of whips, chains, cuffs and restraining equipment covered the walls. An aluminum cage large enough to hold an adult male dangled from sharp hooks connected to the concrete ceiling. The provocative scents of leather, rubber and latex were overwhelming. Soothing classical music played softly. Sounded like a Mozart violin concerto.

Where the fuck am I? Some S & M nut's paradise. Damn, it's cold in here. Why can't I move? Focus, Esperanza. Figure out what's going on.

Esperanza realized his teeth were clenched. He was biting down on a thick metal bit that was firmly held in place by leather straps crisscrossing his head and face. Drool ran down from the corners of his mouth. His jaw ached.

He was naked, standing upright. Except he wasn't exactly standing. Esperanza was bound to some kind of steel torture wheel. His body was in the center of the wheel, spread-eagle, wrists and ankles fastened with leather manacles. It was as if he'd been crucified. The sides of the wheel were secured with massive, metal elbow joints connected to hydraulic pipes jutting from a bulky apparatus on the floor. Esperanza assumed this device allowed the wheel to move up and down and to spin forward and backward.

Esperanza moaned. It was a guttural, carnal moan, emitting from deep inside his body. Amazingly, he was shaking in lustful gratification. The acute rush enveloping him was the result of someone performing oral sex on him. The soft mouth expertly sucked and nibbled and lapped, and slender fingers gently danced, squeezed and stroked. It was as if the person knew, to the most minute detail, how he liked getting head.

Wait a minute, asshole. You were knocked unconscious. Now you wake up gagged, strapped to a wheel, and someone's giving you the blow job of the millennium. You can't lose your erection—which, under these circumstances, you shouldn't have in the first place—and all you're concerned about is how good it feels? Most of all, you're praying it ain't a man.

Esperanza's erotic benefactor kept taking him to the brink of orgasm, and then would stop and fondle his testicles with nimble fingers. He wasn't sure how long this had been going on, but in some ways, he didn't want it to end.

Get a grip, Nick. Your life's on the line here. You're not supposed to be having fun.

The talented lips began to move upward. Esperanza wasn't even aware of the pain coming from his nipples, which had some kind of metal clamps on them, until his new friend tugged on the thin chain linking the clamps, while lavishly licking his chest. Deep throat wore shiny latex gloves, and with a free hand continued to skillfully jerk him off. She finally came into view. Esperanza thanked God *it was* a woman.

Her face was concealed by a black rubber mask decorated with metal spikes. It had zippered slots for her eyes and mouth. From her nostrils, two thin tubes snaked out, arched up like antennae and connected to the back of her head. A ponytail of wavy, reddish brown hair stuck out from the top. Despite the scary-looking mask, there was no doubt that she was an incredibly stunning creature. She grinned, and her moist lips showcased pearly, perfect teeth. Some were sharp, as if they'd been filed down. When Esperanza gazed deep into her intense hazel eyes, he saw through doorways to something so disturbing that, for the first time in his life, he felt genuine terror.

"Hello there, lover. I'm Mistress Devona Love," she said, as puffs of steam floated from out of her mouth. "I'll be teaching you how pleasure and pain are one." Even her whisky-soaked voice oozed sex. Lauren Bacall had nothing on this broad.

Mistress Love stepped away. In her futuristic costume, she looked like the kind of evil supervillain conjured up by a very demented and horny comic-book illustrator. She wore a ruby, latex catsuit, which seemed painted on. Short metal spikes ran down the sides from her shoulders to her forearms and from her waist to her knees. The black, thigh-high boots sported several straps and buckles, seven-inch spiked heels, two-inch platforms and toes that came to sharp points. Mistress Love's firm, impressive breasts protruded from the circular openings of her black, rubber corset, and there were metal clamps on her nipples, too. The outfit was crotchless, revealing pubic hair shaved into the shape of a lightning bolt. Cute.

She grabbed the torture wheel's handheld controls. It was a small box with a series of knobs and switches on it.

Mistress Love turned one of the knobs, and the hydraulics whirred audibly. The wheel flipped so that Esperanza was on his back, staring up at the ceiling. Mistress Love immediately slipped a condom on, mounted him, and inside her was a drenched, searing paradise of velvety flesh. At the same time, the added weight pulled the straps of his wrists and ankles so tight, his hands and feet went numb from the lack of circulation. Mistress Love's taut body undulated against him like a machine built for the wanton exchange of ecstasy. She smelled of expensive, fruity perfume and musk.

Mistress Love worked that sexy body of hers, and man-oh-man, was she gifted. Esperanza tried to fight it, but this *puta* had taken total control and was giving him the fuck of a lifetime. Esperanza was drenched in sweat, despite the frigid temperature in the high-tech dungeon.

She bucked and jerked and rotated her hips, her inner muscles tightening and loosening, tightening and loosening. At the same time, she pulled on his nipple clamps. It hurt like hell, but it was also delicious.

To be possessed, to be manipulated, it was liberating. His senses were completely on fire. He wanted her to hurt him more. To degrade him. Always had to be the man. *El macho.* Always had to be the one in charge. Being her slave was to be free of responsibility, of thought, of control. Mistress Love fiercely slapped his face. Again. And again. It was as if he was floating over his own body, stoned on some powerful lust drug, liberating him from himself.

You like this, don't you? No rules. No love. No intimacy. Simply rawness.

Esperanza thought he was slipping into madness.

"Oh, you fuck sooo good," Mistress Love said between her own moans. She looked away and spoke to someone else in the room. "He's incredibly hot, honey. He can fuck me like you can't." It took an incredible amount of effort, but Esperanza managed to turn his head sideways. "That's my husband," she added.

Across the room, there was a man in a leather straight jacket, hanging from a thick chain, which was tied around his waist. His mask was white latex, and the only opening was for the mouth. The man couldn't speak because there was a rubber ball stuffed between his teeth. *How the fuck can he breathe?* Besides polished combat boots, he was naked from the waist down. Esperanza shuddered. Attached to the man's penis and testicles were several metal alligator clips with chains and small weights at the ends. His genitals were stretched to the point that they seemed as if they might be torn from his body.

Jesus Christ. What kind of freak show have I gotten myself into? How can that asshole take that kind of pain? Who are these people?

Esperanza turned his eyes away in disgust. He noticed that there were spotlights on flimsy light stands throwing harsh, eerie, blue and red light. A tiny digital camera sat on a tripod in the corner of the room, red light blinking as it recorded the bizarre sexual proceedings.

"That's my useless husband, Jason Rybak," Mistress Love said as she continued to ride Esperanza, moving faster and faster. "All he's good for is groveling at my feet like the lapdog that he is. Can't get his little dick up. Dares to call himself a man." She spewed the words with such viciousness, it even made Esperanza want to punch her in the mouth.

Her husband went berserk. Body flailing and bouncing wildly. The chain rattled as if it was going to snap. It was unadulterated rage.

I don't want to be in here when she cuts that crazy motherfucker loose.

Esperanza got the feeling he was going to be the main course. Mistress Love spit in his face. Her breath gave off the sweet, orangey scent of Grand Marnier. "I want your full attention, you low-life piece of shit." He gazed deep into her tempestuous eyes. She plunged into a sexual frenzy, her pelvis slamming against him with enough power to shake the sturdy metal wheel. She tightly pinched his nostrils closed so he was unable to take in air. Esperanza had heard about this practice. S & M devotees called it edge play. He closed his eyes. He could hold his breath longer than most people. Sixty seconds passed. As a BUD/S (Basic Underwater Demolition SEAL) student, Esperanza was put through a psychological test called drown-proofing. Your feet were tied at the ankles and your hands behind your back at the wrists, then you threw yourself into the deep end of an Olympic-size pool and had to swim to the other end. Ninety seconds. Esperanza experienced drown-proofing several times.

"Impressive," she said. "But you can't hold your breath forever."

Esperanza opened his eyes. One hundred and twenty seconds. She furiously fucked him, and her body tensed up and trembled, and he could sense she was on the verge of coming. The classical music seemed to grow louder. Nearly three minutes passed. His mind began to spin because of the lack of oxygen, and the color drained from the room as his lungs seemed like they might explode. Esperanza began to hallucinate. Visions of blood-soaked crosses and burning churches and armies of decapitated babies crawling down deserted Manhattan streets. The world was fading, fading into nothingness. All he could see was pure whiteness, blinding whiteness, then shadows, thick and heavy, oozing like black lava, engulfing him, cooking the skin off his bones. An icy finger of death tapped him on his shoulder, and Esperanza became hysterical, wanted to weep and cry out for his mother to hold him in her arms. Weakness. Weakness. Esperanza swelled with rage. He hated himself. Despised Legs and Alina and Abuela. He watched them as they stood at his grave-side, all of them dressed in black lace veils covering their faces as they commented what a shame it was for him to die so young. *Fucking cunt. You did this to me. For what? For what?*

Mistress Love screamed from the unrestrained intensity of her orgasm. Blasts of exhilaration shot from her body to Esperanza's, and the visions dissipated, swept away by a firestorm of pain and pleasure. He also climaxed as Mistress Love finally let go of his nose, right before he would have lost consciousness. The rush of blood and oxygen coupled with the feverish, primal gratification of their simultaneous orgasms made Esperanza feel as if he was exploding from the inside out. Air. Precious air. Breathing was never so good. He never felt so totally alive, absolutely alive, and ex-hausted at the same time. Like free-falling into a bottomless pit.

Mistress Love painted his face with gentle, sensuous kisses and said, "Oh look, we have created enchantment." The line sounded familiar to Esperanza. It was from a movie. Or maybe a play? He wasn't sure. "What a good boy you are," she added then slapped him so hard, it snapped him out of his haze. "I'm not finished with you just yet, fucker."

She climbed off Esperanza, leaving behind the pungent fragrance of her sex juices. He didn't know when this twisted game was going to end, but his gut told him it was only going to get worse.

But after all is said and done, you relished it, Nick, didn't you? Your mind's so twisted that you enjoyed what she did to you. Mistress Love was taking him to places he only dared fantasize about. Places of ultimate dark sexual fan-tasies. *But let's get back to reality. You're gonna die here. This is the end of the road unless you can come up with a way out of this mess.*

He gazed at the ceiling, trying to gather his faculties. *Think, motherfucker, think. What the hell do these two have to do with Alina? What's the connection?*

With its creepy whirring noise, the wheel flipped Esperanza into a vertical position again. Mistress Love's back was to him. She was adjusting straps to some kind of leather harness. Her body was both athletic and curvaceous. Quite the looker. Havelock always said the devil was a woman in disguise. Now Esperanza had proof of it.

Mistress Love spun around, and Esperanza cringed at the sight of her wearing an enormous, black, strap-on dildo. She stroked it, covering it with a gooey lubricant.

The dominatrix peeled off the mask, revealing a gorgeous, sweat-covered face. She was the same woman from Desire's apartment. Her exotically ethnic features appeared Eastern European. Maybe Russian.

She tossed the mask and fanned herself. "There, that's much better."

The fact that she removed the mask was bad news. Mistress Love was telling Esperanza that when she was finished with him, they were definitely going to kill him, since he could now I.D. her. He thought about it. Maybe death wouldn't be so bad. At least he wouldn't have to face Legs. How could he? How could he go back to his normal life when he'd seen such a decadent, repulsive part of himself? How could he ever look in the mirror again and feel okay about who he was?

The dominatrix patiently searched through her assortment of whips and finally selected a bullwhip. Flashing a devious smile, she strutted over to him, adroitly swinging and twirling the whip. Then Esperanza chomped down on the metal bit as she brutally whipped his legs, his chest, his arms, his privates. Whack. Whack. Whack.

But he didn't make a sound. Not a whimper. *Nada.*

At first, the pain was pretty severe, like fire on his skin, but after a while, he actually began to enjoy it. He wondered what the hell was wrong with him. Did he like pain? Did he enjoy being humiliated and manipulated? *They must've given me some kind of drug. This is not me. This is not me. Please, stop.*

Mistress Love continued whipping him, and Esperanza wanted to say: *Is that the best you can do, you crazy bitch? I can handle a lot more than that. You ain't shit.* She must have read it in his eyes, because she suddenly stopped.

"You have a very high tolerance. God, I love Latin men. Sooo macho," Mistress Love said. "Esperanza's your name, right? Isn't that a girl's name? Means 'hope,' doesn't it?" She tossed the whip and once again grabbed the torture wheel's controls. Esperanza was rotated forward until he was staring at the tiled floor, where there was a huge amount of dried blood splattered all over, as if someone had been disemboweled. Esperanza obviously wasn't their first vic and wouldn't, unless he escaped, be their last. "Well, I *hope* you're having as much fun as I am." She climbed on his back, spread his buttocks wide apart and inserted the tip of the dildo in his rectum. She wiggled a bit, making herself comfortable, then rested her chin in the crook of his neck and whispered, "Now you get to be *my bitch.*"

To his surprise, she was extremely gentle, only pushing in the tip. She held it for a second, then began to thrust it in and out ever so slowly. Her hands reached down, and she fondled him. It took her a while, and though Esperanza tried to fight it, Mistress Love managed to get him hard again. She worked him for a few minutes, and as much as he hated to admit it, this hot bitch fucking *him* was an incredible turn-on.

I'm more of a freak than I realized. Am I a closet faggot and didn't know it? I wonder what Legs would think of me now. Whipped, fucked and takin' it up the ass, and not complaining about it. Esperanza thought he knew himself.

Thought he knew how far he would go. He was dead wrong.

"You're ready," Mistress Love said in an ominous tone.

Without warning, she crushed his testicles in her hand and ruthlessly rammed the dildo deep inside.

This time, the pain was so unbearable, Esperanza screamed, and sour-tasting bile filled his throat. *Jesus, Jesus. Stop. Stop it*! He thought he was going to vomit from the relentless anguish as she raped him, the dildo tearing up his insides. Shock waves blasted through his body as if he'd tongue kissed a light socket. Devona's insidious, child-like laugh reverberated in Esperanza's head as she joyfully took his manhood and any dignity he had left. She bit down on his shoulder, sharp teeth drawing blood. The more muffled screams Esperanza let out, the harder Mistress Love sodomized him. His body finally went limp, and he hoped he'd pass out, but he didn't. His suffering was going to go on for a long time. For as long as Mistress Love wanted it to.

Mistress Love savagely continued to violate him, and if the metal bit wasn't in his mouth, Esperanza would have done something he'd never thought he'd do: He would have begged her for mercy.

Chapter 11

Rybak and Devona casually hovered over a nude, unconscious Esperanza, who was curled up on the dungeon's floor
in the fetal position, his hands and ankles bound with rope.
He appeared to be barely breathing. A series of welts, bite
marks and black-and-blue bruises adorned his powerfully
built body. Devona noticed a couple of old scars. One from
a gunshot wound to his chest. Two from a knife.

"After we dispose of our friend here," Jason said, "want
to go to that new after-hours club in Soho?" Rybak and
Devona had changed into their street clothes.

Devona liked the way Rybak looked in the olive green,
fleece pullover. His corduroys and suede Beatles boots
matched nicely. Sophisticated yet casual.

"Sure," Devona said, even though she intended to go
home first and change out of the brown leather pants and
lavender, velvet crewneck sweater she wore. She wanted a
more provocative outfit. A hot bubble bath would be nice
too. "We should toast Esperanza for all the fun he provided."
Devona tilted her head, pompously admiring her sadistic
artistry. She inspected the tattoo on Esperanza's right shoulder. It was a detailed illustration of an aggressive-looking
bald eagle clutching a trident, an anchor and a rifle. Underneath, in flowing letters, it read: SEAL TEAM 6. "What does
that tattoo mean?"

"He was a Navy SEAL," Rybak said.

"What's a seal?"

"Acronym for Sea, Air and Land," Rybak said. "Special warfare unit. Toughest bastards in the world. Their training's more grueling than what most soldiers experience in actual combat. Only ten percent of the recruits who try out for the Navy SEALs actually make it."

"He don't look so tough now." Devona grinned, filled with pride. She'd transformed an ex-soldier, ex-cop—a tough guy who probably took down plenty of killers—into a harmless, whimpering child. The whole experience with Esperanza had thrilled her and left her more sexually fulfilled than she'd been in a very long time.

God, he turned me on. In this day and age of weak, socalled sensitive males, it's refreshing to encounter a true man's man. Made it much more fun to break him.

Rybak crouched, waved smelling salts under Esperanza's nose, and the hunky ex-detective came violently awake. Before Esperanza could even catch his breath, Rybak grabbed him by the throat and choked him. Devona smiled, titillated by her husband's smoldering jealousy.

"Did you enjoy fucking my wife? Nah. You're a faggot. You loved it when she rammed that big cock up your ass." Rybak laughed and released Esperanza, who appeared utterly bewildered as he desperately gasped for air and coughed. "Let me tell you one thing, slick," he continued. "Since you decided to play the knight in shining armor, I'm going to make sure your little whore Alina dies a slow, agonizing death." Rybak threw him a kiss, rose to his feet and turned his attention to Devona. "Gotta give 'im credit. Man can sure take a workin'-over. Lasted much longer than most."

"That's why I want to keep him for a few days," Devona said, her eyes glued to Esperanza.

"Have you lost your mind?"

She looked up at her husband, determined to have her way, no matter what.

"I want to keep him. Train him. Break him again and again. Make him my slave."

Rybak wagged his head. "Sorry, but you're going to have to forget about this one. More trouble than he's worth."

"Where else am I going to find such a perfect male specimen?" She roughly squeezed her husband's groin. "Since I can't get a rise out you." Rybak slapped her hard across the face. She slapped him right back. Both smiled extravagantly.

"Don't push it. I let you have your fun. Time to get down to business. I'm going to get the car. Finish him." Rybak passionately kissed her, then left.

Rybak's impotence—a physical condition courtesy of a gunshot wound he'd suffered many years before while working as a merc in Central America—didn't bother her, since there were plenty of other ways Rybak satisfied her sexual needs like no one else ever could.

She wondered why she was so uncontrollably drawn to Esperanza. She felt intensely connected to him. Never even heard him speak, yet when she looked into his eyes, she recognized a part of herself in him. How odd. And exciting.

She squatted, and caressed her slave's scrumptiously muscular body, then affectionately stroked his hair. He gazed at her with confused, pleading eyes.

Oh, I've crushed him all right. I own him.

"As you heard, I've been ordered to kill you," Devona said. "But I'd rather let you go, because I know a single night will not pass in which you won't think about me." She was serene, almost nurturing in her attitude. She drew a tiny, nickel-plated Derringer from her coat pocket and jammed it against Esperanza's temple. "I want you to say, 'I'm forever your bitch, Mistress Love.'" Esperanza was being either hard-headed or just plain stupid because he didn't immediately obey her command. Devona cocked the hammer of the Derringer to let him know she wouldn't hesitate blowing his brains out. "Say it."

He struggled to speak. In a hoarse whisper, he finally declared, "I'm forever your bitch, Mistress Love."

Hearing him utter those words sent tingles up her spine, making her shudder. "Good slave. Now kiss me nice, and I'll untie you."

He hesitated again, and stared at her for a long moment with confused eyes. Devona knew he wanted her to possess him again. But he'd have to wait. Esperanza suddenly surged forward and kissed her. The hunger, the ferocity of the kiss made her giddy with lust. At that moment, she was certain she would haunt him for the rest of his life. That's why she chose to let him go rather than kill him. "Hmm. Delish." She untied him and quickly backed away, keeping the Derringer leveled at his forehead. Esperanza struggled to get to his feet, and it took him a minute to find his balance. He stood there, in all his naked glory, swaying like a building ready to topple over.

Look at that. An average man wouldn't have been able to even stand up, not after what she put him through. *Regardless, I better get him moving before he passes out again. I hope he gets away. As wrecked as he is, if he manages to escape when Jason goes after him, he deserves to live.*

"Head out that door, then make a left. At the end of the hall, there's a window with a fire escape." Esperanza remained fixed, almost as if he couldn't break out of the spell she'd put on him. "Go, before my husband gets back and finishes you. Go!"

He turned, staggered out the door and disappeared into the darkness of the warehouse.

Devona hopped into the leather sex swing hanging from the dungeon's ceiling, gave herself a push with the heels of her cowboy boots and swung back and forth. She unzipped her pants, slipped her hand in between her thighs and began playing with herself, eagerly awaiting her husband's reaction to her latest naughty deed.

Esperanza climbed out the window onto the fire escape. He was two stories up from an alley and could see a pile of boxes and black garbage bags right below him. The fire escape was one of those enormous, industrial ones that ominously zigzagged down the back walls of factories and warehouses like twisted metal spines. He tumbled down the steps to the first landing, then found himself about twelve feet off the ground. Esperanza tried to unhook the ladder release, but it was stuck. *Come on, come on.* He gave the pile of boxes and garbage bags the once-over. *I've jumped out of planes plenty of times. This ain't nothing. So what if I'm naked and freezing and my body feels like it's been torn from the inside out? Just like BUD/S training. So move it.* Esperanza climbed over the rail and dangled for a couple of seconds, then let go and landed on top of the boxes with a loud, unceremonious thud. After what he'd been through with Mistress Love, the pain wasn't so bad, and it didn't feel like anything was broken. He scrambled to his feet and managed to break into a sluggish, unbalanced trot.

Why did that psycho bitch cut me loose? I need to stop thinking about her right now. I need to get the fuck outta Dodge before Rybak comes for me. Breathe. Take the pain. You can do this.

Esperanza realized he was in the Meatpacking District, near 14th Street, on the West Side. The neighborhood consisted mostly of ugly, ancient industrial buildings and meat-processing plants. It must have been a couple of hours before dawn because there were also several trendy nightclubs and bars in the area, yet at the moment, there wasn't a soul in sight. Esperanza could hear the low rumble of traffic coming from the nearby West Side Highway. His bare feet hurt, and it was difficult to run on the slick cobblestone streets, but he ambled forward in the direction of the traffic—and salvation.

Rybak returned to the dungeon with a plastic tarp folded under his arm. He knew there was a problem when he saw Devona in the swing, moaning as she fingered herself into an orgasmic frenzy. The ex-cop was gone. She let him go. That made Rybak mad. Really mad. She was the mistress when it came to their personal relationship, but he was boss when it came to business. Like a spoiled brat, Devona smiled whimsically, and giggled as she licked her wet fingers.

"I don't fucking believe you," he growled.

He'd deal with her later. Rybak threw the tarp down to the ground, pulled out his 9-millimeter and raced out the door.

Esperanza was moving as fast as possible while fighting excruciating pain. As he stumbled down the deserted street, he kept glancing back over his shoulder, praying that Rybak wasn't on his heels. For the first time in his life, he understood what it was like to be the prey, and he didn't like it one bit.

He made a sharp turn and found himself in another alley. Near a bunch of garbage bins, several emaciated cats eagerly feasted on raw meat. They hissed, meowed and scattered. Esperanza couldn't go on. There was no way he was going to make it to the West Side Highway. Any minute now, he'd pass out in agony. He opened one of the bins, hauled himself in and quietly closed the lid.

Though the putrid stench was overwhelming, Esperanza didn't even gag. He'd been around so many decomposing bodies during his career in Homicide, he was accustomed to the rankness. He covered himself with scraps of rancid meat, bones and other garbage, and prayed Rybak wouldn't find him.

Rybak galloped down the street in the direction of the West Side Highway. Then something instinctive told him to stop. He turned into an alley. Nothing. Saw a row of garbage bins. Four of them. He knew the spic cop, in his condition, couldn't have made it very far. He smiled. The garbage bins would be a good place to hide. Not wishing to draw any attention to himself, Rybak took a sound suppressor from his pocket and screwed it in onto the barrel of his gun.

Rybak stepped over to the first bin and flung it open, then fired several shots into piles of rotting meat and bones. As his arm dug into the muck to make sure Esperanza was either dead or not in there at all, he wished he had gloves on. The disgusting smell was unbearable. Made him retch. He flipped open the next bin, fired several rounds and then inspected the bin's contents. This dirty work was more annoying than the stunt Devona pulled.

He was about to hit the last two bins when he heard a car's engine coming closer. In the distance, he could see a police car headed in his direction.

Damn you, Devona.

He slipped the gun under his coat, turned and hurriedly made his way back to the dungeon, wondering how he'd deal with his undisciplined, sometimes selfish wife.

An earth-shaking roar of thunder woke Esperanza. The sound of heavy rain splattering against the metal bin was almost deafening. He didn't have a clue as to how long he'd been hiding in the garbage bin. There was a squeak, followed by the sound of rummaging. Esperanza adjusted his eyes to the darkness and saw a couple of monster-size rats devouring maggot-infested meat. He turned on his back, propped the soles of his feet against the top of the bin and kicked the lid open. He stood up. There was another roar of thunder followed by a dazzling flash of lightning. Esperanza slipped, and nose-dived over the edge of the bin and slammed to the pavement, landing on his side. The alley floor was flooded, and Esperanza was in a deep pool of muddy, icy water.

Okay, soldier. Time to see what you're really made of. Get on your feet.

His mind drifted back to his BUD/S training. He remembered the cold-water conditioning, or "surf torture," as the instructors liked to called it. BUD/S trainees spent months in water preparing to be frogmen. The class had to sit up to their necks in 58-degree Pacific Ocean water as massive, brutal waves crashed over their heads. They'd stay like that for an hour, to learn to mentally fend off the effects of hypothermia. It was all coming back to Esperanza now. His mind was his ultimate weapon.

He'd been beaten, raped and humiliated. Been pushed to the brink of death. Mistress Love and her husband believed they broke him, but they had no idea who they were dealing with. Esperanza had been a fighter since day one. A warrior. This wasn't over yet. Still, his life would never be the same. The money, the club, the clothes and the cars didn't mean shit anymore. He'd been to the edge and back. Saw a part of himself—a degenerate part of himself—he didn't even know existed. *I can run away in shame and hide. But I won't. No one's ever gonna know about what went down tonight. The hardest thing will be looking Legs in the eye and lying to her. But I can never tell her the truth.* Esperanza wanted to blame her for what happened, but he knew it was all his fault. If he'd handled himself like a pro from the beginning, he would've never gotten himself into such a jam. If Mistress Love . . . No. He wasn't calling her Mistress Love or Mistress anything anymore. *Devona.* If Devona and Rybak did this to him, he didn't even want to imagine what they'd done to Alina. *No matter what, I've got to find her. I'm gonna wreak havoc on Star, Rybak and most of all, Devona. Searching for Alina was just a game to me. Now it's a mission. And I'll do whatever it takes.*

Whatever it takes.

He clumsily labored to stand up, moving like a recently born fawn. All Esperanza managed was to get to his knees. He vomited, and then fell forward and landed on his elbows. This was going to be much, much tougher than he thought. He gathered all the strength he could manage, gritted his teeth and began to crawl.

An ordinary human being would've given up. Not Esperanza. Though extremely weak and in mind-numbing agony, he was pumped full of adrenaline, because all he thought about was survival.

And revenge.

Chapter 12

Crawling, crawling, crawling. Knees and palms and elbows and stomach scraping along the wet sidewalk, over shattered beer bottles, skin peeling off like wet paper. Keep moving. Through the icy puddles, along the gutter, between cars, to the street. Mind reeling out of control. Vision blurred. Madness. Mistress Love's giggles reverberating. Revenge. Beams of light. Car horns blaring. Screams for help. Sirens.

Salvation.

He didn't know what kept him going, and he barely remembered any of his journey, but Esperanza managed to crawl three blocks to the intersection of 14th Street and Tenth Avenue, where he was almost run over by a cab. The cabbie called 911, the police arrived (thankfully the officers didn't know him), and he was put in an ambulance and rushed to Saint Vincent's Midtown Hospital. He recalled bits and pieces of the emergency room doctors and nurses treating him, stitching him, bandaging him, poking him and prodding him. Then nothingness.

Several hours later, Esperanza finally woke up. In a hospital room. Fading in and out of consciousness, drowsy from the wonderful morphine drip dulling much of the pain.

He was on his side, his head propped up on pillows, and his body was so stiff, he was hardly able to move. *Am I par-*

alyzed? And every time he did move, it was as if razor wire was being twisted and tightened around his muscles.

Stay still. Breathe deeply. Control the pain.

When Esperanza opened his eyes, the first person he saw was Legs, like some beautiful mirage, standing next to his bed, holding his hand, her face serene as she bent over and kissed him on the cheek and said, "It's okay, *papito*. I'm here."

Even in the most difficult of circumstances, Legs always managed to remain strong and handle the problem in the most calm and efficient way possible.

He needed her, and she'd be strong for him now.

Legs asked him what happened. Through his morphine haze, he told her he was knocked out, dragged to a warehouse and beaten, and through a sheer stroke of luck, managed to escape. He kept the details to a minimum. Couldn't bear the idea of her knowing the whole, sordid truth.

"Nick, we've never kept secrets from each other," she said. "I know there's more to this."

He assumed Legs spoke to the doctors and had at least a general idea regarding the nature of his injuries (like the stitches in his rectum), so he wasn't fooling her. He didn't care.

"This is different." Esperanza said, "I'll tell you when I'm ready."

It probably took an incredible amount of self-discipline, but she did what he requested and asked no more questions.

"This is all my fault," she said. A long, sleepless night of worrying had stamped purple crescents under her eyes. Legs's pallid face was void of any makeup, her hair was tied in a ponytail, and she wore a New York Yankees baseball cap and a faded, gray sweat suit that erased all the lovely curves of her body. Esperanza thought she never looked lovelier.

"I'm sorry," she said, "for what happened."

"Don't be," he said, his voice like sandpaper, throat aching every time he spoke. "I'm the one who screwed up. I gotta be straight with you, *negra*. Alina's in serious trouble. Her life's on the line."

"Now what?"

"I'm going to have to handle things in a very aggressive way from now on," he said. "It's gonna involve guns, and it's gonna get ugly." *As if it already hasn't.* At least he now realized that Abuela was right. Alina hadn't run away. This wasn't some silly game. This was life-and-death. "Don't be scared. I'm gonna do what I'm best at. Trust me."

"I trust you with my life," Legs said.

The conversation made him tired. He was fading in and out. Everything his eyes saw seemed to be in black and white and muddled. Legs's voice was far away and fading. Esperanza once again plunged into a morphine-induced slumber.

Esperanza was glad he could afford a private hospital room. The last thing he'd want was some nosy, babbling, annoying roommate, since he already had enough shit to deal with. Like the two Special Victims Squad detectives who spent the past hour patiently questioning him about his assault. He knew Detective Fortes from his days in Narcotics.

"I can't remember much of what happened. I was going for a drink, and a group of thugs jumped me, dragged me somewhere and . . . beat the shit out of me."

"You sure 'bout that?" Fortes said. He was still gangly, with a bad crew cut and a cheap suit. His partner, Detective Rovins, was a plain Jane with short reddish hair and freckles and a relaxed attitude. She didn't say much. Just stood there in her sweater and khakis and tweed jacket, trench coat folded over her arm, pad in hand, scribbling notes.

"Maybe I have memory loss due to the shock of the blunt-force trauma to the head. I think they nailed me with a pipe." Esperanza was sweating, and his eyes burned. The room was too hot. He'd have to tell the nurse to lower the temperature. Otherwise, for a hospital, it was a nice room. Walls recently painted teal, decorated with vibrant watercolor paintings of country landscapes. Matching yellow furniture and sheer curtains. On the windowsill, a simple glass vase filled with fresh, white carnations.

Fortes handed him a paper napkin, and Esperanza dabbed his face. Fortes then turned to his partner and said, "Detective Rovins, can you please give us a minute?" She shrugged and immediately left the room, making it obvious that he was the senior detective. Or maybe she was so accustomed to dealing with female rape victims, the idea of a hardened ex-cop like Esperanza getting sexually assaulted was a joke. Fortes pulled up a chair and sat close to the bed. "What the fuck is goin' on, Nick?"

"Leave it alone. I don't want you to pursue this."

"I don't know if I can do that."

"You owe me."

When they were partners, they'd gone into a crack den in Hell's Kitchen to bust a dealer named Little Cuz. They'd been looking for him for weeks and finally got a tip from an informant. Little Cuz was wanted for three murders and was known to be quite trigger happy, particularly when it involved cops. Guns drawn, they searched the empty apartment. Fortes thought he'd cleared the back bedroom, but he failed to check the fire escape. When Fortes turned around to say something to Esperanza, Little Cuz, dark as night, with cornrows, gold-capped teeth and a bubble coat, popped up from outside the window and aimed a MAC-10. Luckily, Esperanza was an expert marksman. He nailed Little Cuz with a single shot to the forehead before the crack dealer was able to cut Fortes in half with that high-powered machine pistol.

"Yeah, I ain't never gonna forget you saved my life,"

Fortes said. It was obvious by his pained expression that he wasn't pleased that Esperanza was collecting on a favor. Too bad he didn't have much choice in the matter. "So what do you want me to do?"

"Talk to your partner. Tell her whatever you want. Just get her to back off and not write a report," Esperanza said. "I'm sure S.V.S. has plenty of more-serious cases to deal with."

Fortes gave Esperanza his business card, told him that if he changed his mind or just wanted to talk, to call him. He left, and Esperanza tore up the card.

Santos showed up later on and was a whole other headache. A major fucking migraine. Didn't even wait two minutes before he started grilling Esperanza like any other crime victim, wanting to know *everything*. He wasn't buying any stories about memory loss. Though Santos was persistent, Esperanza didn't cave in and coughed up only the Cliff's Notes version of the events of the previous night.

"Are you sure you can't remember anything more specific about the location of this warehouse?"

"No." Esperanza lied, of course. He had a general idea about the location of the warehouse, but stayed mute.

"Why is it that I get the feeling you're lyin' through your teeth?" Santos was a master when it came to sensing dishonesty. Came in quite handy when interrogating suspects.

"What? I'm a fucking perp now. My word's not good enough?"

From the hall, Esperanza could hear the murmurs and footsteps of the cafeteria crew as they prepared to drop off trays of lunch. *Why does everything sound like I'm in an echo chamber? Like it's coming from inside my head?* The savory aroma of steamed broccoli and baked chicken snuck its way into the room, making his stomach growl. But he wasn't about to eat hospital food. He knew that no matter how good it might smell, when it came to taste, it would be like eating sautéed cardboard. Legs was coming back with dinner from Sueño Latino.

"I'm here to help, you know," Santos said. "Gotta be so damned *cabesi duro.*" He didn't bother to disguise how disillusioned he was at his ex-partner's reticence. "Hard-headed bastard."

Upright posture, expressionless visage, determined gaze, Santos was the picture-perfect image of the hardworking police detective. Except that the cuffs of his dark brown suit pants and his shoes were soaked from rain and sleet.

"Devona and Rybak are pros. Except they like to add a little spice to their work."

"Time to let the police handle this."

"I'm my own police."

"When you were a cop, you frequently bent the rules. Now that you don't have a badge, you think you can break them?"

Those two psychos were going to murder Alina if Esperanza didn't go after them right away. The only reason they might keep her alive was to use her as bait. Rybak wanted Esperanza dead. He'd make every attempt to finish the job. If Esperanza handed the investigation over to the cops, it would take too long, because the cops had to play by the rules, and in Devona's world, there were none, except hers.

"You really think I'm gonna just walk away after what those motherfuckers did to me?" Esperanza adjusted his hospital gown. Hated how it left his back completely exposed. He pulled the stiff sheet up above his waist. "To top it off, I may have gotten Alina killed, so I have to move quick and *my way.*"

Santos's jaw clenched tight. He peered out the window and stroked his goatee. It was a gloomy, soggy afternoon. Wind was furiously whipping rain and sleet and snow flurries around as pedestrians clutched the collars of their

coats, held on to their hats and struggled with broken umbrellas as they rushed to escape the merciless winter storm.

Anibal turned back to him and curtly said, "You do this
your way, Nick, and there might be hell to pay."

"Believe me," Esperanza said. "I already paid . . . in full."

Santos studied Esperanza's face and seemed to finally realize it was a lost cause. He shrugged it off and said, "You
want to come to the squad, check out some mug shots?"

Esperanza had a gut feeling that Rybak and Devona
weren't in the system. "I'll give it a shot," he said. "But I
have a quicker way of finding them."

Find Star, find Rybak and Devona.

Santos struggled into his damp trench coat and then
pulled his signature black, felt fedora onto his head. "Then
what are you going to do?"

"Whatever it takes."

"How dense are you?" Santos shouted, his face turning
red as he finally lost his patience. "You're going to ruin
your life. End up in jail, or end up a stiff, just because you
want to play hero?"

Esperanza raised the head of the bed a little and squirmed,
trying to find a more comfortable position, as if that was
possible when your asshole's been torn up. "I'm done playing, *compadre*. The gloves are off."

"No use trying to talk sense into you," Santos said, and
cleared his throat and pulled the wide brim of his hat low
over his disenchanted eyes. "I'm going back to work. You
know where to reach me."

How delicious it was fucking Esperanza. Dehumanizing
and degrading him. Like a powerful sorceress, she transformed a streetwise tough guy into her "bottom," her slave.
His eyes radiating confusion and shame, the drool running
down the side of his mouth, were wonderful. Fucking him
in the ass was the best, though. Controlling him like that. It

made Devona feel incredibly powerful hearing Esperanza whimper and grunt like a wounded animal every time she rammed those twelve inches of rubber deeper inside him. She'd destroyed him, mind and body and soul.

Welcome to my world, Detective Esperanza.

Devona soaked in a steaming, soothing bubble bath, puffing on a cigar, surrounded by burning candles in crystal jars, which filled the bathroom with soft, dancing light and the intoxicating scent of violets. The bathroom was spacious and immaculate. Everything from the custom-designed marble sink to the tiled walls and floor was pure white. Her body became slack as the water's heat massaged her muscles. She rested the cigar in the octagonal glass ashtray, at the edge of the spacious white marble bathtub.

Devona's biggest surprise was how much she enjoyed it when Esperanza was inside *her*. She wasn't crazy about being penetrated—very few men ever earned that privilege—and she allowed it to happen only when *she* was in complete control. There was something about Esperanza, though, something enticingly passionate and robust that made her want him again and again. If she were in a relationship with him, from time to time she might actually allow him to control *her*. How strange would that be?

She sat up and sensuously soaped her body with a plush bath sponge, moving slowly, caressing her gleaming skin, making herself shudder. As tiny, rainbow-colored bubbles floated through the air, Devona wondered where Esperanza was, how he was doing. Was he thinking about her? Thinking about her ravishing his body and his senses? Humiliating him. Stealing his manhood. She watched the videotape, and boy, did she get off on it. Wait until Esperanza sees their lovemaking. *Not that vanilla sex you and your woman probably have a couple of times a week. No. It was forbidden art, what transpired between you and me. Sex on the edge, the*

*way sex should always be. Can't wait until you see the tape.
It's in the mail, darling.*

Though Jason had been monumentally pissed, Devona
was glad she'd cut Esperanza loose. She wanted to possess
him again. *Would* possess him again. Couldn't do that if he
was dead. The best part of this whole situation was how it
set her husband afire. She hadn't seen Rybak so tenaciously
motivated in, like, forever, and it was a major turn-on.

Life is good. She slunk deeper under the hot water, and
sucked on the cigar and admired the lovely white orchids in
the thin ivory vase on the dainty cast-iron stool in the far
corner of the bathroom. Rybak had such wonderful taste in
flowers, and gave them to her all the time.

The door opened and Rybak marched in, head held up,
back erect, all pride and confidence. Carried a crystal flute
filled with champagne. Naked. Devona loved his hard, muscular body. He was virtually hairless, except for a line of
soft hair on his chest. His body was decorated with a variety of scars. Many more than Esperanza. Some were from
gunshot and knife wounds, others courtesy of his adoring
wife. He made himself comfortable on the edge of the tub
and handed her the glass of bubbly. He picked up a brush
and then roughly raked it through her damp hair, brushing
out the tight tangles. As much as Rybak hated to admit it,
Devona knew he was putty in her hands.

"You shouldn't have let him go," he said. "It was unprofessional."

"Oh, lighten up." Devona gulped down the champagne,
annoyed by his bitching. She didn't want to hear it. He was
wrecking her jovial mood. She handed him back the empty
glass and gave him a dismissive wave of the hand, as if he was
her butler. "You've become so stuffy lately. No sense of fun."

He stopped brushing her hair, took the glass and placed
it on the floor. "Bishop is going to be pissed."

"Fuck Bishop."

"Bishop's not the issue."

Devona could see the veins in his temples throb like baby snakes trying to slither their way out from underneath his skin. "You compromised us. Don't forget, Esperanza can identify us. You've put us both at risk."

"I hate to sound corny," Devona said, holding up her sinewy leg and lathering it. Too much stubble. Time for a waxing. "But isn't life all about taking risks?"

"Not stupid ones," he shot back. "We have to finish what we started."

Her face brightened, and she gushed, ripe with excitement at hearing the good news. She sat up, all attentive and girlish, and asked, "When do we go after him?"

"Soon. First I want to contact our friends in the department and find out a little more about your boy toy."

Her mouth began to salivate, and there was a warm throbbing between her thighs. "I can't wait to get my hands on him again."

Before Devona was even able to blink, Rybak placed his hand on the top of her head, dug his fingers in and dunked her underneath the water, holding her down for several seconds. Caught off guard, Devona struggled violently, thrashing her arms and flailing her legs and splashing water. She was swallowing water, and could hear herself struggle to break free. Rybak finally released her, and she popped up, gasping for air, and spat out gobs of wretched-tasting, soapy water.

"That's to remind you that this is business and we're going to handle it *my way*," he said, then threw her a fluffy, terrycloth towel and stormed out of the bathroom. Slammed the door so hard, she thought it would fall off its hinges.

Devona used the towel to wipe soap from her stinging eyes, and found herself quite moved by her husband's violently jealous reaction. This little adventure was getting better by the minute. Devona delighted in the idea that there might be plenty more surprises in store for all of them.

She turned on the hot water, and steam spiraled into the air as she rested her head against the tiled wall and smiled jubilantly, then picked up the cigar, stuffed it back in her mouth, puffed on it and closed her eyes, dreaming awake.

Dreaming of Esperanza.

Blissful slumber. No nightmares. No pain. Joy. Sunshine. Floating freely. Everything was fine. The rape never happened. He never suffered any indignities. It was all a long-forgotten illusion.

Esperanza stirred, sleepily opened his eyes and was happy to find himself safe in his own bed, lost in the geniality of Legs's embrace as she placed fluttering *besitos* on his neck and ear. He turned to kiss her on the lips, but instead found Devona next to him. Face half-covered by lustrous, fiery red hair as she grinned maniacally, a single-edge razor clenched between sharp teeth. Before he could do anything, she swung her head and slashed his jugular vein. He jolted up, clutching his throat as blood spurted from between his fingers. Blood soaked the silk bed sheets, and the chill of death gradually imbued his body.

"Nick," Legs shouted. *"Despierta."*

Esperanza was yanked out of his nightmare by Legs's voice. He found himself sitting up in the hospital bed, clasping his throat. Except there was no wound. No blood.

Exhausted and shocked, he dropped back on the hospital bed and muttered, "Fuck." He tried to collect himself, but his heart wouldn't stop pounding and it seemed as if he couldn't breathe. Every time he did breathe, it was like he was getting stabbed between the ribs with a knife.

Legs said, "You okay?" and dabbed his sweat-drenched face with a washcloth.

He nodded and cleared his throat. She filled a plastic cup

with ice water and handed it to him, and he guzzled it in an instant. "Bad dream," he said, his voice barely a whisper. It was difficult to see Legs, because of the blinding sunlight burning through the window behind her. "What day is it?" he asked, and squinted, trying to get her silhouette in focus.

"Monday."

"I've been here twenty-four hours?" He sat up again. This was not good. It was time to move. "You gotta get me discharged."

She scrunched her nose and tilted her head to the side. "I don't know if the doctors are going to allow you to—"

He scowled, and his neck muscles bulged. "Either you get me discharged or I'm walking out."

Esperanza could tell Legs was troubled by his decision, but knew he wouldn't hesitate grabbing his clothes and splitting, and no one was going to stop him. "Fine. I'll page the doctor and get you discharged," she said with a despondent gaze. "Look, this is probably a bad time, but Abuela's outside. Wants to see you."

He thought about it for a moment. *I can't face the old lady. I treated her request as a joke. I don't have time for this. Gotta get it together so I can get the fuck outta here and hit the streets.*

"Send her in," he said.

Legs walked out, and *la vieja* shuffled in and stopped dead in her tracks as soon as she set eyes on Esperanza. She quickly made the sign of the cross, her wrinkled, ebony hand trembling from the cold. By the expression on her face, Esperanza imagined he must look like death warmed over. He touched the bandages wrapped around his midsection and flinched. Abuela finally ambled to the bed, hunched over and kissed him on the cheek with chapped, cold lips. It was like being kissed by a corpse.

"I'm sorry this happened to you," she said, tears in her milky eyes, which were developing signs of cataracts.

The harsh smell of Ben-Gay coming from her made Esperanza back away slightly. "Please have a seat, Abuela."

She made herself comfortable in the high-back, vinyl hospital chair with curved, wooden armrests and unbuttoned the top of her plaid coat. The coat was way too flimsy for winter in New York. She removed her wool hat, angled forward and conspiratorially whispered, "If you wish to stop looking for my Alina, I will understand."

"I won't stop looking," he replied. "I promise."

Her elderly facade remained somber, yet she already seemed to know what his answer would be. "Thank you. You're a man of courage." She dipped into her bright red, pleather purse and produced black rosary beads with a silver crucifix at the end. She held them up in a loop between her now-much-steadier hands. Esperanza realized she was inviting him to wear the rosary. He'd never been a very religious man, and though officially a Catholic, he hadn't been to church in years and never wore a crucifix. To appease *la vieja*, he let her slip the rosary beads over his head, and she stroked his damp hair. "This rosary has been blessed, and it will protect you."

He fingered the crucifix now dangling over his welt-covered chest and said, "I'll give it to Alina when I find her."

Chapter 13

Inside the narrow walk-in closet of his office in Sueño Latino, hidden behind rows of designer Italian suits, supple leather trench coats and wool sport jackets, Esperanza pulled open the heavy door of a safe. It was four feet by three feet, and built into the concrete wall. Every move he made delivered a shockwave of pain through his body. The secret safe had cost Esperanza a pretty penny. Besides holding stacks of hundred- and twenty-dollar bills, as well as such important documents as the club's liquor license, the fireproof safe also contained an oversized aluminum attaché case. Esperanza hauled it out and dropped it on the desk. If it weren't for the painkillers, he wouldn't even be able to walk straight. He spaced out for a second as he tried to remember the combination. On the third try, he got it right and clicked the case open.

The Vicodin was keeping him in a state of wooziness, so he was downing shots of espresso and an occasional amphetamine, to keep his faculties in balance. Esperanza felt a calming sense of relief as he stared at the inside of the attaché case, which was lined with gray foam that snugly held several semiautomatic handguns, including a 9-millimeter Glock and a .380 Beretta.

As if brand new, all the guns were shiny clean. Esperanza went to the firing range with Havelock once a month and was meticulous about the maintenance of his weapons. Esperanza grabbed his favorite, a Sig Sauer P226. It was a matte black, rugged and accurate, one of the world's premier combat autos. Esperanza loaded a fifteen-round clip containing 9-millimeter Parabellum ammunition. Parabellum was a German trade name for these exceptionally accurate armor-piercing bullets. Word came from the Latin: *Si Vis Pacem, Para Bellum.* "If you wish for peace, prepare for war."

When the doctor reluctantly discharged him from the hospital, he told Esperanza, "Get plenty of bed rest, Mr. Esperanza. More important, no physical exertion." The doc was concerned Esperanza might tear the various series of stitches all over his body.

Regardless of what the uppity doctor said, regardless of the stitches, the welts, the bite marks, the scratches, Esperanza was going after Star and didn't doubt the pimp would tell him everything he wanted to know. *After Star, it'll be Rybak and Devona's time of reckoning. Those two'll find out what it's like to really suffer. They'll give up Alina in a heartbeat. If she's still alive. No, she is. She is.*

Esperanza adjusted the leather shoulder holster he was wearing over his black turtleneck. The brown holster was a holdover from his days on the job. It was worn and pliable. He'd kept it as a memento. He usually wore a hip holster, but there was something reassuring about going old-school. Never expected to be breaking out the shoulder holster, slipping in his Sig, hitting the streets again, back on the job, for real.

Esperanza grabbed the much more compact Kel-Tec P32 "mouse gun"—which cozily fit in the palm of his hand—and also loaded it. He jammed his scuffed hiking boot against the edge of the desk, pulled up the cuff of his corduroys. The olive cords were cargo style, cut baggy, with lots of pockets to carry extra ammunition clips, a can of mace and a knife.

No fancy clothes today. The gear he wore was efficient and comfortable.

He stuffed the mouse gun into his ankle holster.

Since the blinds were drawn, the office was dark except for the light spilling from the chrome desk lamp and the closet. Legs, shrouded in shadows, leaned against the windowsill, scrutinizing Esperanza's every move. Legs didn't like guns.

"Why don't you," she said, "at least take Havelock with you?"

He knew the question was coming. Legs didn't want him to go alone, not in his weakened condition.

"When the time comes," he said, "if I need Havelock, I'll ask for his help." And Esperanza knew Havelock would be down to take care of even the nastiest business. "Right now, this is something I have to do on my own, *nena*."

"What're you trying to prove? If you walk away, nobody'll think any less of you."

"I'm not trying to prove a fuckin' thing." Esperanza slammed the attaché case shut. "I'm doing what you asked me to. Find your niece." He returned the case to the safe, then closed the door and twirled the knob of the combination lock. When he spun back around, Legs was standing right in front of him, her eyes melancholy but stern.

"Maybe I don't want you to anymore," she said. Her voice was faltering.

Esperanza couldn't believe she'd said that. *I know she doesn't really mean it. She's scared. Scared I'll end up dead.*

"You know she's in serious danger, now you want to change your mind?"

Legs dropped her head, roughly scratched her scalp. Her hair whipped and bounced, and then concealed her face like a veil. She thought about it for a long moment, then said, "No. Of course not. Alina's got to be brought home. We're gonna have to take care of her for a while," and looked back up him, her gaze steadier, more self-assured. "I just don't want anything to happen to you."

Esperanza slipped on a black, leather jacket. Certain events had been set in motion, and there was no turning back.

"You always say you have more faith in me than in anyone else in the world. I hope that hasn't changed."

"No. Never." Legs zipped up his jacket, and stood extremely close, her face an inch away from his. "What did those animals do to you?"

"I already told you, I don't want to talk about it." Esperanza pushed past her, stepped behind his desk, opened the drawer and produced a switchblade. He flicked it open to make sure it still worked. It did. Legs winced. He closed the switchblade and dropped it in a leg pocket of his pants.

Legs grabbed his big, soft hand and pressed the palm against her chest. He could feel the whispered beating of her heart.

"Don't shut me out, *papito*."

Esperanza snatched his hand away.

"Are you fucking deaf? I don't wanna discuss it." He glared at her, very certain as to why he'd so easily lost his temper.

I'm pissed because I don't want Legs to know that Devona humiliated me like I was a bitch. 'Cause I don't want Legs to know that I liked fucking Devona. And, I can't ever let Legs know that for a moment, I even liked Devona fucking me.

Legs's silence was like a scream. She stepped aside, though. And Esperanza tore from the office.

As Esperanza hurried past the Sueño Latino employees who were waxing the dance floor, polishing the bar and getting ready for opening later that night, he noticed some of them nervously glanced at him. He imagined what kind of talk was going on behind his back. *Why is el jefe acting like un hombre loco?*

He didn't care what anybody thought. He drove all thoughts of Legs out of his mind.

Time to go hunting. Time to go make Star regret the day he was born.

Rybak was playing his second game of "Metal Gear Solid" against a guy named Hightower. They were in the newfangled arcade in Times Square, playing the popular, futuristic race-and-destroy video game. Rybak always met Hightower and Mangineli at the arcade. Mangineli hated it, but Hightower and Rybak were video-game junkies. They were always ready to try out the latest, to see who'd emerge victorious. Their skills were about equal, and while they were extremely competitive, they never bet money. It was about pride. Something an idiot like Mangineli would never understand.

Hightower and Mangineli were Internal Affairs cops. They were on Bishop's payroll. *Corrupt I.A.B. investigators. How perfect.*

Rybak appreciated Hightower because the light-skinned black man was stylish, well mannered and intelligent. Always dressed to the nines, sporting meticulously tailored, double-breasted suits of the finest materials. Always had the silk handkerchief sprouting from his breast pocket like a blooming flower. On the other hand, the wop could be a cast member of *The Sopranos*. With the lacquered pompadour, the gaudy gold jewelry, the seventies-style sharkskin suits, Mangineli seemed more a "made guy" than a cop. They were some pair, these two. Neither one dressed this way when they were busy investigating their brethren. Then, they stuck to standard-issue detective suits: single-breasted, dull colors, blandly unstylish. That way, Hightower and Mangineli never drew attention to themselves. But when they were freelancing, it was a whole other kind of fashion show.

"The papers nicknamed him 'Lotto Cop,' Mangineli said, in his grating voice. He cultivated his tough-guy demeanor to perfection as he bobbed his head and gnawed on a toothpick. Rybak never stood too close to Mangineli. Man reeked like a vat of Aqua Velva.

"Thirty million, huh? Lucky bastard," Rybak said, his body weaving as his fingers adeptly worked the game's controls. His monster vehicle careened through a post-apocalyptic landscape, laying waste to anything that came within its path.

"Meanwhile, the rest of us have to work for a living," Mangineli added.

The brilliant lights and the assault of beeps and whoops and electronic bells and whistles that filled the arcade over-whelmed the senses of anyone under twenty-one. *It's why teenagers barely have attention spans anymore.* They were satisfied as long as there were loud digital explosions, rap or rock music, and quick-cut, vivid, F/X-enhanced imagery. The arcade was filled mostly with white teens, swarming from game room to game room or across the winding over-head balcony.

Rybak blew up another vehicle. "Well, if he's livin' *la vida* loaded, why's he playing P.I., risking his ass for some little whore?"

"It's personal," Hightower said as he scored another thousand points. "The girl's his old lady's niece."

"Yep," Mangineli chimed in while inspecting his sparkling manicure. "And you geniuses are buyin' yourselves a shit-load of trouble." Rybak put Mangineli around fifty, even with the jet-black hair. He could stand to gain a few pounds, and he needed to stay out of the tanning salons. "Esperanza was a hell of a good cop, and a Navy SEAL to top it all off."

"A cop who often bent the rules," Hightower said. "And sometimes broke them, depending on whom you ask."

"What do you mean?" Rybak glanced over at the big man, but still kept his eye on the game. Hightower had a broad, very likable face. Wore a thick mustache over his lips and dark aviator sunglasses over his brown eyes.

"He was working undercover narcotics," Hightower said, "and I.A.B. investigated him on a couple of occasions, mostly stemming from accusations of excessive force." Hightower's attention was momentarily drawn away as a nubile black girl in skin-tight jeans strutted past, swaying her impressive bubble butt. "He was cleared every time."

Mangineli yapped on as if he were Esperanza's proud publicist. "Then on the hush-hush, he was transferred to Homicide, where he got to use his brains. He and his partner, Anibal Santos, cleared plenty of high-profile cases. After a few years knee-deep in murder, he hit the jackpot."

"Hey, you never know," Rybak said. Esperanza sounded like someone Rybak would like to run with. Too bad he was going to put him in the ground instead. Besides, this fascination Devona had with the Latin-lover ex-cop was making Rybak too emotional. He'd never seen his wife get all weak in the knees over another man. He didn't like it one bit.

"You goin' after this guy?" Mangineli said.

"Yes," Rybak said.

"So, an unstoppable force meets an immovable object," Hightower said and then let out a chuckle. "Should be quite the show."

Esperanza hunched over the wheel of an unassuming blue Saturn coupe. He was staking out Star's Harlem apartment building, on 137th Street, off Lenox Avenue. It was a part of the neighborhood that hadn't been gentrified just yet and was still pretty tough. Esperanza's Jag or any of his other fancy wheels would draw too much attention, so he secured a rent-a-car.

Star lived in a four-story, pre–World War II tenement

building. A long time ago, the place was a beauty, but now it was in terrible shape: bricks missing, layers of soot, cracks snaking down the facade like varicose veins. There was graffiti all over the lower part of the building, and the stoop was fractured and lopsided. It was crumbling like many of the structures lining the block. Other buildings were starting to go through the process of renovation.

A few emaciated pipe heads ambled in and out of an abandoned building, and a crew of black kids played b-ball in the late afternoon gloom. Their makeshift basket was a plastic milk crate with the bottom cut out, wired to a light pole. The black kids screamed and cursed and pushed, and mocked each other's skills and carried on loudly as they played. They seemed to move in slow motion. Every time the ball bounced on the asphalt, it was like a deafening explosion inside Esperanza's head.

About a half hour earlier, Star had swaggered by, accompanied by two *morena* working girls in faux fur and miniskirts, their hands crawling all over him, as the hoopsters whooped and hollered. Esperanza wanted to give Star and his lady friends enough time to get comfortable and get their freak on. He popped three Vicodins and washed them down with lukewarm, black coffee.

Slipped on leather gloves. Checked his watch.

Showtime.

In silent frustration, Esperanza worked the lock of Star's apartment door. The hallway walls were peeling as if diseased, and the smell of urine made him feel as if he'd been pissed on. It had been years since he used a lock-picking set, and it wasn't as easy as he remembered.

He finally got it to click. Then, the bottom lock was quicker. He drew his Sig and stepped into Star's crib. He could hear thumping hip-hop music coming from the bedroom, combined with scintillating moans and groans. The gaudy living room was a bachelor pad straight out of *Pimp's Monthly*. Walls the color of maraschino cherries. Furry white sectional sofa. Cheesy coffee table in the shape of giant dice. Sixty-inch, high-def, projection TV. Thousand-watt, state-of-the-art stereo system with speakers taller than Esperanza. Maroon velvet curtains and matching shag carpet. Classy.

Stop admiring the fine decor and keep it moving.

Esperanza stealthily made his way down the hall. Stayed close to the wall, to keep the wooden floor from creaking. He reached the bedroom door, which was slightly ajar. Peered in. Star, not wearing a stitch of clothing except for the leather, backwards-turned Kangol cap, was kneeling on the queen-size bed. It was black wrought iron, with spiraling bedposts and gold satin sheets. Star was busy banging one of the hookers doggie style, while she enthusiastically lapped and licked the other *puta's* bushy *chocha*. *Quite the party.* The bittersweet scent of pussy and the acidic stench of crack laced the air. Hanging over the bed was a huge, framed movie poster from *The Mack*. Other blaxploitation posters—from *Super Fly* and *Dolemite*—adorned the lime green walls. On the bedroom windows, there were sapphire curtains, and the floor lamp had a blue shade on it.

Esperanza ogled for a few minutes, lost in the decadent pleasures of the threesome, imagining himself ravaged by those two horny, plus-sized, chocolate goddesses. Esperanza saw himself screwing the girls in a variety of nasty sexual positions. It was like he was living in a porn movie. The room began to seesaw. Esperanza blinked. His legs wobbled. *Focus.* He took several deep breaths, remembered his mission, then stepped back and kicked the door in. Star and the two *putas* crashed to the floor in a knot of limbs as one of the girls shrieked. Star disentangled himself from the panic-stricken girls and reached for the nightstand, where there was a crack pipe, a huge bag of weed, several vials of crack and a small, .22-caliber semiauto.

"Move, and I'll drop you," Esperanza said. His gun was trained on Star, and the pimp froze. "Ladies, get your clothes and get the fuck out." The hookers quickly gathered up their belongings and, still butt-naked and frightened, ran past Esperanza and out of the apartment. He glanced up at the poster of *The Mack*, then back at Star. "Who the fuck you supposed to be? Quentin Tarantino?"

"That asshole Rybak obviously fucked up," Star said, acting the tough guy. "But you're dead, yo. You gonna get popped when you least expect it."

"Come over here."

Star reached to the floor to grab his underwear, and Esperanza cocked the hammer of his Sig. At the sound of the metallic click, Star's hand froze in midair. He stood up straight, eyes full of fury, head held up high in defiance. Clothes or not, he was still the man. That's what he seemed to be trying to project. Esperanza wasn't impressed. Star could afford to miss a few meals, and should probably lay off the forty ounces, since he was developing quite a beer belly.

In all his naked glory, Star reluctantly bopped over, and when he was standing a foot away, Esperanza coldcocked him across the temple, and he crumbled to the floor among the piles of dirty clothes.

"Keep dreaming."

Star awakened to find his wrists and ankles tied to the sturdy bedposts with extension cords. He was bleeding from the gash on his temple, and struggled to break loose without success.

"Muthafucka," Star said, raising his head an inch. "You better fucking cut me loose."

"Oh, I'm going to do some cutting," Esperanza said, and nonchalantly swaggered over to the bed and clicked opened his switchblade. "So you better tell me where to find your two psycho friends."

"I ain't tellin' you jack."

"Have it your way."

Esperanza was perched on the edge of the bed and held the tip of the switchblade right under Star's nostril.

"What the fuck you gonna do?" Star's macho front was quickly falling to pieces.

Esperanza lowered the razor-sharp blade and placed it at the base of Star's penis. "Cut your dick off." Then he sliced a tiny piece of skin, and Star yelped. "Oops. Nicked ya, son."

"Awright, muthafucka, awright! Chill! Please." Star begged, fought back tears and sniffled. "Rybak and Devona . . . asked me to keep an eye out for the girl. She liked cruisin' Eighth Avenue, hangin' with that tranny, Desire."

This bit of information took Esperanza by surprise. *I thought Alina was just a random target. That she was in the wrong place at the wrong time. Had she been previously involved with Rybak and Devona? Why? What went on between them?*

"They were specifically looking for her?" Esperanza kept the tip of the blade to Star's manhood.

"Said they knew her. Offered me a coupla grand if I found her." Star was wild-eyed, desperate. "I hit the tranny parties, ran into her, kicked it to her and brought her to them."

"What did they want with Alina?" Esperanza pressed and twisted the knife.

Star yelped again and talked a lot faster. "Word on the street is they involved in some kiddie-porn shit."

Esperanza's mind reeled. This wasn't what he expected to hear.

Child porn? What the fuck is going on here? What have they gotten Alina into? Are there other kids?

He backhanded Star across the mouth, splitting his bottom lip. "Rybak and Devona," Esperanza said. "They work alone?"

"I dunno," Star said, gobs of snot running down his nose as he broke down and wept so hard, for a moment Esperanza almost felt bad for him. "They . . . they . . . they don't pay me to ask no questions."

"How do you get in touch with them?"

"They got some voice-mail number. When I gots certain . . . merchandise, I leave them a message. We usually meet at the Malibu Diner in Midtown. I swear."

Esperanza believed him. The pimp was terrified. He'd definitely get in contact with them, given the right motivation. Esperanza brought the knife up to Star's face, grabbed him by his neck and jammed his thumb into the pimp's Adam's apple, forcing him to throw his head back.

"You're gonna leave them a message right now. Tell them to meet you in an hour at your usual spot." Esperanza pulled out his cell phone. "What's the number?" Star shouted out the number, and Esperanza dialed it. There was no outgoing message, just a beep. He placed the phone to Star's mouth, and the pimp left a quick message. "See," he said, "how nice it is to be cooperative?"

"I did what you tol' me. Cut me loose."

"Ain't gonna happen." Esperanza picked up a pair of Star's soiled silk underwear from the floor and stuffed it in the pimp's mouth. "You set me up, you fuck. Just be glad I don't clip you right now."

Because of Star, I ended up in Devona's hands. Now he's gotta pay the price. Esperanza slashed Star's face from the temple to the chin, then backed away and watched the pimp thrash and jerk while spurting blood. *How do you like it, cabrón? How do you like the fact that you'll never be the same?* Esperanza watched him for a moment, not showing a hint of emotion. *He's never gonna forget me now.*

As he exited the pimp's building and headed to his rent-a-car, all Esperanza could think about was that very soon, Rybak and Devona would be in his sights.

Chapter 14

It was already ten PM. Esperanza had been waiting for over two hours. Across the street from the Malibu Diner, the joint where Star usually met with Rybak and Devona, Esperanza sat in his rental car. Sig in his hand, the safety off, a bullet in the chamber. Watching the gradually thinning crowds of pedestrians zip by. *Where are they? What're you gonna do? Walk up and put a gun to Rybak's head? Kidnap them? Well, why not? No. Gotta do this right. This can't turn into a gunfight on a crowded Midtown street. Patience.*

Another hour passed. No Devona and Rybak. *These scumbags ain't comin'. Star played me. He must've given them some kind of warning somehow.* Esperanza hammered his forehead against the wheel of the car a couple times, then sped back to Star's place.

He staked out Star's apartment building for about half an hour, then paid a grungy crackhead a fifty to give him information. The crackhead, with her matted hair and filthy overcoat, leaned into the window of Esperanza's rent-a-car, grinning at the fifty-dollar bill being waved in front of her face. She was so emaciated, it seemed as if her brown skin had been stretched over her skull.

"Yeah, and an ambulance came. Took Star away. Yo, white boy looked fucked-up as shit." The crackhead let out a wheezy laugh. The funk coming from her body was as nauseating as a Celine Dion ballad.

Handing over the crisp bill, Esperanza said, "Thanks." The crackhead's eyes lit up, and she scurried off to make a big score.

Esperanza was going to wait a while longer to see if Star came back.

This is bullshit. I screwed up. Let my temper get the best of me. Should've taken Star with me, kept him in my sights until I found Rybak and Devona. Now he's gone. I'm not as good at this as I used to be. I'm making too many mistakes. Now what am I gonna do? Frustrated to the point of rage, Esperanza started the car and peeled out, leaving behind a cloud of burning rubber. He needed to go talk to Mark and see if his brother would help him. Then he had to figure out what his next move would be.

Though he was headed home, he drove around aimlessly, but it gave him a chance to clear his mind. He needed to slow things down. Think more clearly. Use his brains instead of letting his feelings get the best of him.

The whole kiddie-porn thing threw him for a loop. Drug dealing. Breaking and entering. Prostitution. Rape. Murder. He was intimately familiar with the kind of criminal acts the police handled every day. But perps who preyed on children, to have sex with them and videotape them and take pictures? This was something he knew little about. So he called his brother, since Mark used to be part of the F.B.I.'s Innocent Images, a division that specialized in online child pornography. It made him feel uncomfortable reaching out to his little brother, since he'd always been the protector. *C'mon, Nick, keep your ego out of this. You need all the help you can get.*

"So what's this about?" Mark said. He was in the field and could talk only briefly.

"Get me any information you can that'll help me get a

better understanding of the criminal element involved in child porn."

"Why?"

"Just do what I ask," Esperanza said, losing his patience. He didn't like the fact that Mark was asking so many questions. "I'll meet you at your office first thing in the morning."

"I don't have to jump just because you say so," Mark said.

Esperanza took a deep breath. "This is your big brother asking you for an important favor. For a second, forget all the official crap, and remember we're blood."

"Okay." Mark sighed. "Fine. Be at my office at eight."

The Federal Bureau of Investigation was located at 26 Federal Plaza, an imposing black tower near the bottom of Broadway. Mark's modest office was sparse: unappealing, government-issue desk, two wooden chairs and several file cabinets. On the beige wall, there was a framed color photo of President Bush and the F.B.I. seal, as well as a poster of the bureau's ten most wanted. The only personal touches were a diminutive cactus plant sitting on the windowsill next to a Homer Simpson doll. A few framed photos were on his desk. The eight-by-ten was of Mark's wife, Anita, a willowy redhead from Bogota, Colombia, smiling blissfully. Another featured Mark's two strapping boys, Joaquin and Gabriel. Esperanza loved his nephews. Both were bright and affable and extremely inquisitive. They looked adorable in matching First Communion suits. Both had blue eyes and red, curly hair. Esperanza picked up the third framed photo. His sister, Gloria. Photograph was snapped a few years before she died of breast cancer. Gloria was posing in front of El Morro, the majestic stone fort in Old San Juan. Holding on to her straw hat and flashing a crooked grin as a gust of wind blew strands of her wavy hair across her face. She'd been a social worker who dealt with foster children.

I wonder what she'd think of what I'm doing? Gloria loved kids. She'd probably tell me to do whatever was necessary.

The one other photo was of Esperanza's parents. Mark's wedding. Esperanza's parents were dressed to the nines, flanking Mark and Anita in front of a Catholic church. They looked so happy and so proud that day. A few months later, his father suffered a massive coronary and passed away. Esperanza thought his mother would soon die from grief, she adored his father so much. But she hung in there. She promised Pop she'd keep the family together and it gave her a sense of purpose.

"The only Devona Love that came up was a fifty-three-year-old biker–bank robber chick from Alabama," Mark said as his fingers rapidly ran across his computer keyboard. "Didn't fit the profile you gave me. There's no Jason Rybak either. Sorry."

Outside, the amber light of dusk bounced off lower Manhattan's canyon of glass skyscrapers, infusing Mark's plain office with a welcoming glow.

Esperanza shifted in his chair. He was still uncomfortable sitting for extended periods of time. He wanted to go to the bathroom, pop another couple of painkillers, but changed his mind. The constant Vicodin fog was making it difficult to concentrate. At least pain kept him alert.

"Don't worry," he said. "I'll find them soon enough."

"Tu esta' bien?" Marked asked, as he swiveled away from the computer and eyed Esperanza suspiciously. "You look kind of out of it."

"I'm fine."

It was strange to be kind of working with his *hermanito*. They were very close as kids growing up in East Harlem. Esperanza, being the older, more physically imposing brother, always looked out for the baby of the family and made sure he was safe. Esperanza was a hero to Mark, who was a nerd back then, face always buried in books, and a major target for bullies. Meanwhile, Esperanza was a hard case. Rambunctious and short tempered, he constantly got into street brawls. The family expected Mark to become a doctor and worried that Esperanza might end up in jail, even though he often talked about becoming a detective for the N.Y.P.D. After an incident in which seventeen-year-old Esperanza threw a local gang leader a serious beat-down, there was a crew of thugs gunning for him, so his father forced him to sign up for the Navy. Following a couple of tedious years doing duty on a battleship cruising the Panama Canal, Esperanza decided to try out for the SEALs. Figured why not? He'd get to carry guns and shoot bad guys. While Esperanza was doing his SEAL training, he received a letter from his mother (who sounded terribly disappointed) saying that Mark changed his mind about going to med school. Instead, he decided to attend John Jay College of Criminal Justice with the intention of becoming a special agent for the F.B.I. Esperanza always believed that his parents blamed him for Mark's new choice in career because Mark looked up to him and wanted to follow in his big brother's footsteps. Maybe there was some truth to it back then. Not anymore. Mark was his own man.

Mark opened his desk drawer, pulled out two thick manila file folders. There were notepads, papers, pens, a phone and a digital clock on the desk, all neatly organized.

"I put together some information for you regarding the world of child pornography. Statistics, trends, profiles, things like that."

"I still want you to fill me in."

"Okay. Besides the F.B.I., C.P. is also under the jurisdiction of U.S. Customs and Justice, since most of it is bought, sold and traded over the Internet," Mark said. "Makes it an international problem. Often involves cooperation between Interpol and police agencies all over the world." Mark fastidiously rolled up the sleeves of his crisply starched white shirt. "The Internet's also the way a lot of pedos spend their time hunting the innocent."

"The miracles of modern technology."

"That's why the bureau's Crimes Against Children division created the Innocent Images Initiative. You know I worked for them, for . . . a little under a year. Agents go on the 'Net posing as kids, to bait the predators." He sounded very official, as if he were holding a press conference. *He's in full agent mode now. Confident. Determined.* Esperanza smiled to himself. *Regardless of the gun and the badge, he's still my baby brother.* "It was started after the bureau handled several cyber-predator cases that led to homicides. I was glad when they transferred me to counterterrorism."

"I guess tracking down tangos is way less intense." "Tango" was what Navy SEALs called terrorists.

"I know you were Mister Super-Elite Counterterrorist Unit and all that, but trust me, it is less intense. Agents in Innocent Images tend to burn out real fast, and some of them end up with serious psychological problems." Mark glanced at his family photographs. "I didn't want to deal with those kinds of sickening crimes day in, day out."

Esperanza wondered why Mark was getting agitated. It was subtle, and if you didn't know him well, you wouldn't even spot it. It was a slight tremble of his cheek and the tugging of his earlobe. These were signs that Mark was seriously disturbed by what he was talking about.

"You need to relax a little more, you know."

Mark said nothing. Instead, he pushed the file labeled EVIDENCE across the desk, toward his brother. Mark's stare was grim, his face taut.

Esperanza took the heavy file, which contained dozens of photographs, eased up slowly from his uncomfortable chair and leaned against the wall near the window.

The first image was of a girl, maybe eight years old, a spiked leather collar around her neck. Her forearm was folded across her eyes, her mouth was wide open, crying out in agony, as a grown man raped her. The next one featured a boy and a girl with bright blue eyes and blond hair, kindergarteners, who could be siblings. They stared up, wide-eyed, at the camera while kneeling between a man's open legs and clutching his erection as they licked it. Esperanza's stomach got queasy. Thick, bitter bile rose in his throat. He flipped through a dozen more pictures featuring nightmarish images of different children, performing a variety of sex acts with adults and each other. Esperanza noticed that the faces of the adults were always concealed from the camera's lens. Even considering all the brutality he'd witnessed during his career in homicide—headless torsos, a ten-year-old kid shot in the face, a homeless man doused with gasoline and burned alive, a family of ten tied to chairs and their throats slit during a home invasion—nothing compared to the perversity of these photographs. Esperanza thought he'd seen the worst of humanity. He was wrong. This was purity destroyed and defiled for pleasure and profit. Evil running rampant. God's light extinguished.

He heard Abuela's voice, a faint echo in the back of his mind. "These people do the work of the devil."

What the fuck am I dealing with here?

Esperanza closed the file, dropped it back on the desk. He sat down again and slouched as if all the energy had been sucked out of him.

"Jesus fucking Christ."

"It's way worse than what you just saw," Mark said. "You don't hear about it, because people don't want to believe child porn even really exists. It's hard enough dealing with priests molesting kids. Who wants to hear about rape videos? About thousands of photos of children being produced and distributed all around the world?"

"I still think of child porn as being about a couple of perverts selling grainy videotapes through the mail."

"It's a new era. And you, like most of the general public, stay blind to it. As the Internet's grown, so has C.P." Mark went over to the window and stared down at the tiny cars and people rushing though the streets below. Gloom shrouded his face. "These animals are getting smarter and more high tech and really difficult to catch. Quiet as it's kept, when there's some huge bust on the news, those perps are newbies. Inexperienced collectors who were sloppy and easy to bust." Mark turned and gazed at Esperanza. "The hardcore players, that's a whole other story."

"It's like nailing the street dealers, but never getting the major suppliers."

"Exactly."

"This helps. Thanks for not letting me down."

"Sorry I was a little testy last night."

"Ain't no big deal." Esperanza spaced-out for a moment, the images of those kids flashing in his mind, accompanied by horrific screams. "One other thing I want to know. Is child porn profitable?"

"Sometimes. Not too long ago, a nice, so-called normal, upper-class, married couple from Dallas were busted for operating a commercial C.P. Web site. They were netting close to one-point-five million a month. But most of these guys seem to be more into trading, sharing pictures and videos. The 'Net makes that a very easy thing to do."

"New technology, new ways to commit crimes." Esperanza noticed the strokes of silver on Mark's temples and the little crows feet at the corners of his eyes.

"And we haven't been at all successful at nailing the sickos who actually make the stuff."

"That's the side I might be dealing with."

"That's what it sounds like. They don't seem to be run-of-the-mill pedophiles, though. You may have stumbled onto a very dangerous and sophisticated underground network. So you better watch your ass." Mark sounded worried.

"Trust me, I am." *If only Mark knew the dark humor his comment held.*

"That other file you can take with you," Mark said. "I know you don't spend time online, but you can get a bunch of other information from Web sites like those run by the International Centre for Missing and Exploited Children and Interpol."

Mark was right. Esperanza never bothered with the Internet. Didn't even do e-mail. That was Legs's thing. *Life's too grand to waste sitting in front of a computer monitor, traveling through a virtual world.* He'd ask Legs to find information for him. She'd appreciate being able to lend a hand.

"*Gracias,*" Esperanza said.

Mark checked his Cartier watch, a gift Esperanza had given him for his birthday. "*De nada.* I gotta roll. Briefing to attend." Then he snatched his suit jacket from a hook on the back of the closed door and put it on. "I went by Pop's grave with Mom last week. You know it's been ten years since he passed."

"Yeah." Esperanza stood up. His legs wobbled for a second.

"How come you never go, Nick?"

"I guess 'cause I don't want to remember him like that," Esperanza said, and jutted his chin in the direction of their parents' photo. "That's how I like to remember him."

"Fair enough. But it's probably harder for Mom to understand."

"I know. Trust me, Mark. There's isn't a day that passes that I don't think of Pop."

"Yeah." Mark ran a comb though his thinning hair. "Listen, if these thugs you're dealing with are involved in producing child porn and kidnapping, you have to bring the bureau in on it, Nick. I know how you are. Don't turn this into some personal vendetta," Mark said as he buttoned his single-breasted jacket. Esperanza noticed Mark's tie was a little crooked, so he straightened it out for him.

"I'll contact you," Esperanza said. *After I'm finished with them.* "But I have to find them first."

"If you need any more help, you know I'm here for you, bro'."

"I appreciate that," Esperanza said, and got all choked up with emotion. He loved his *hermanito* and was extremely proud of the man he'd become. "I know."

They hugged tightly, patted each other on the back and gave each other a warmhearted kiss on the cheek. These two tough men, dedicated to taking down criminals and killers, never had a problem expressing their love for each other. It was something their extremely doting father taught them. Besides, they were Puerto Rican. Being affectionate was as common as rice and beans.

Devona and Rybak's silver BMW 7 series 750i sedan cruised in to the parking lot of the West Side Pier, the vehicle's high-intensity headlights severing the darkness. Devona was alone. She turned off the radio. The techno music she'd been blasting was replaced by the sound of gravel being crushed under the car's tires. Devona was there to meet Star. He'd left a message telling them to meet him at the Malibu. Rybak figured it was a setup because Star didn't use the usual code words. Later on, Rybak reached Pimp Daddy on the cell phone he'd given him a couple of months before (Rybak liked to call it the Bat phone). Star immediately began whining about how Esperanza was gunning for Rybak and Devona. How Esperanza cut up his face in the process. Poor boy.

The pimp was in his colossal, cherry-red Lincoln Navigator. Devona hated that every idiot now owned an S.U.V. They took up too much damn space, and all looked like pickup trucks with extra seats. Ugly things. She appreciated

THE DEVIL'S MAMBO / 153

the elegance of cars. The vehicle you drove was an accessory. Like Harry Winston diamonds or a Prada handbag.

She parked opposite the Navigator, and without shutting off the engine or cutting the headlights, climbed out of the Beemer. The S.U.V.'s door opened, and Star emerged from a cloud of blunt smoke. Squinted because of the glare from the headlights. The whole left side of his face was bandaged, his right eye was black-and-blue and his lip was split and swollen.

Nice work, Nick. I see you got no problem taking matters into your own hands.

Though Devona could see only a squiggly image of her reflection in the Navigator's freshly waxed exterior, she knew she looked quite fabulous in her new pistachio-colored rubber raincoat. It had a wide collar, and draped her body perfectly, falling all the way down to the top of her boots. Hair stylishly held up over her head in a swirl by two silver Chinese hairpins. Delicate strands cascaded down the side of her face and the back of her head. She brashly strutted over to the pimp. He looked ridiculous in a white mink coat and matching bowler hat. *Men should never wear fur.* But Star wasn't much of a man anyway, so it didn't matter.

"You see what that muthafucka did to me?" Star said, pointing to the thick bandages.

Devona imagined that it must've required a hell of a lot of stitches to close up such a lengthy gash. "At least he let you keep your good side."

"You got jokes? Well, it ain't funny, yo," Star said. "If y'all woulda done what youse supposeta, I wouldn't be all fucked up right now."

Devona was having a difficult time keeping herself from laughing. "We got sloppy. Happens, dude."

"I coulda bled to death. Lucky one of my bitches called nine-one-one."

"You did what Rybak said, kept your mouth shut,

right?" Star had wanted to press charges against Esperanza, but Rybak convinced him it would be a bad idea to get the police involved.

"Not a word. Why am I even talkin' to *you,* anyway?" Star said pugnaciously. "Where's Rybak?"

"Had more pressing business to attend to. Talk to *me,*" she said. "What did you tell Esperanza, Star?"

"I said, not a damn thing."

Devona slid closer and seductively tilted her head as a frosty breeze made the loose wisps of her hair flutter across her face. "You wouldn't lie to me, would you?"

No matter what situation he was in, Star immediately turned to mush when dealing with a beautiful woman. He was one of those kinds of fools. "Of course not, boo," he said flirtatiously. "You know I'm a man of my word."

"I believe you." Devona was certain he'd told Esperanza *everything* he knew. Fortunately, everything wasn't much. "Don't worry. We'll make Esperanza disappear."

Star's eyes marched up and down her body. "Damn, youse one fierce bitch, you know that?"

"My, you have a way with words." She giggled girlishly. "Are you coming on to *moi?*"

"I know you be checkin' *me* out. Been wantin' to tap that ass evah since I first saw you." He held his coat open as if making an invitation. She noticed the massive erection straining his silk pants. "This is juss the first time I got you to myself."

She unbuttoned the top of her raincoat, revealing a leather bustier, which showcased plenty of cleavage. "Think you can handle this?" she asked as she ran her fingers down her chest.

"Fuck yeah."

Devona stepped into the coat, and he wrapped her in the fur. She rubbed her body against his and went wild, sucking and nibbling his neck and pinching his nipples under his silk shirt, as Star moaned in delight. Without warning, she backed away and flashed Star a perversely sinister smile.

Time to play.

Star was perplexed by the strange, expectant expression on her face. But then Rybak was behind Star, wrapping a garrote around his neck and strangling him, and Star realized he was on a short journey to the grave as he flayed his arms and legs like an epileptic. All the struggling in the world didn't do the pimp any good, since Rybak was too powerful and the thin metal wire cutting into Star's throat was unbreakable.

Now it's my turn to party. Devona pulled one of her long hairpins from her hair, clutched it in her hand, then rushed forward and stabbed the pimp in his stomach. *Gotcha.* Star desperately kicked at her. Devona effortlessly dodged him. *Too slow, Super Fly.* She cackled, and stabbed him in the thigh. Rybak took his time strangling Star. *Oh, this is getting me so hot,* Devona thought.

Rybak and Devona were in perfect, murderous synch. She stuck Star in the arm. Then his eye. Blood spurt all over her raincoat. *Say good night, Gracie.*

One more stab to the heart, and the pimp was finished.

Rybak let go, and Star's body slumped to the ground. Devona leaped into her husband's arms and clamped her legs around his waist. They passionately tongue kissed while Rybak stood over the pimp's bloody corpse.

Lost in her husband's embrace, Devona recalled the first time she and Rybak met, when she was a commercial domme working at a private Upper East Side dungeon named Latex Kiss, which catered to affluent S & M players. She was the most popular domme at the dungeon, and it cost a thousand dollars an hour for her specialties, which included "electrical play," asphyxiation, "human ashtray" and heavy-duty corporal punishment. Rybak showed up for a session one day. To Devona, he was simply another client into extreme pain. Then she discovered that he wasn't weak like those C.E.O.s and movie stars. She did things to Rybak that none of her other slaves could've ever tolerated. He even refused to have a "safe word" that would alert her that the pain was too much for him. Rybak could take it as well as she could give it. He immediately became her favorite regular and hired her once a week, like clockwork, for several months.

Then one frigid winter evening, after indulging in a two-hour scene, Rybak confessed to Devona that he was in love with her and wanted to spend the rest of his life with her. She thought he'd lost his mind. Sure, she was extremely attracted to him, but she had no intention of running off with one of her clients.

The playroom they were in was lit solely by candlelight. The walls and floor were cinder block, and there were a Saint Andrews Cross, an old-fashioned barber's chair covered with red leather and a couple six-foot-tall wrought-iron cages that allowed very little movement. There were racks of masks, whips, chains, paddles. A full complement of torture tools. So romantic.

Out of nowhere, Jason quoted Devona's idol, the Marquis de Sade: "'Crime is the soul of lust,'" he said as he pulled an automatic from his leather gym bag and expertly loaded it. "What would pleasure be if it were not accompanied by crime? It is not the object of debauchery that excites us, but rather the idea of evil." He placed the barrel of the gun between her legs and tenderly rubbed her. Devona was both petrified and aroused like never before. She came in a matter of seconds. Rybak stuffed the gun into the waistband of his jeans, put on his corduroy suit jacket, kissed her hand and then added, "Come with me, Mistress Love, and I'll open a whole new world for you."

Devona did go with him that day, and her life had been, unequivocally, changed forever. She'd found her soul mate. Rybak helped her discover the darkest, wildest part of her soul, and it was a revelation. He also trained her to kill with every kind of weapon, including her bare hands.

On the pier, Rybak spun around, carried Devona to the BMW and dropped her on the hood. The heat from the car's engine warmed her back, and its rumble made her body tingle. Rybak yanked her skirt up, spread her legs in a wide V. He pulled her vinyl panties to the side and dove in face-first. His mouth only talked at first, then he sang to her. Jazz. Opera. Heavy metal. He passionately sang from deep inside and carried her off into blissful delirium. Cold air. Hot tongue. She hammered her fists against his brawny shoulders and let out tiny squeals of delight. Her high-pitched calls combined with the distant sounds of cars honking and the polluted water of the Hudson lapping at the edges of the pier made for a surreal aural concert.

Devona craned her head and stared at Star, a twisted, bloody corpse on the ground, illuminated by the jarring beams of the BMW.

Tears filled her eyes. She wanted this moment to last forever. Only Rybak was capable of granting her this kind of joy and pleasure. During special moments like these, Devona understood why nothing in the world was more precious to her than her wonderful husband.

Chapter 15

Las Palmas Restaurant was a hole-in-the-wall on upper Broadway. Joint was famous for melt-in-your-mouth *Cubano* sandwiches and ultra-caffeinated coffee. Esperanza wanted to see if Havelock knew anyone who worked in the sex industry.

Havelock was his best friend. A man with whom he'd jumped out of planes. With whom he'd endured BUD/S, the most grueling military training in the world. BUD/S "evolutions" included two-mile swims in frigid ocean waters. Fifty-yard underwater pool swims while holding your breath. (Most students had to be revived afterwards.) Fifteen-mile boat paddles after three nights of zero sleep. Gut-wrenching obstacle courses. Then there was Hell Week, which consisted of nearly twenty-four hours of training for five straight days. The SEAL instructors pushed students to the breaking point, and beyond. Way beyond. Instructors liked to say, "It's about mind over matter. If you don't mind the pain, it won't matter."

Once they became SEALs, Esperanza and Havelock fought side by side through covert counterterrorism missions in the Middle East and *always* watched each other's backs. Havelock was the man Esperanza trusted his life with. Yet he chose to tell Hav nothing about his sexual torture and humiliation at the hands of Devona. And his *amigo* asked no questions. All Havelock knew was that Esperanza had been abducted and badly beaten. That was enough. Havelock offered his services—lock, stock and smoking automatic.

Las Palmas had a lengthy Formica counter on one side and wobbly tables jammed together on the other. Merengue pumped from the jukebox while cute Dominican waitresses with white blouses, tight black jeans, sweet dispositions and thick Spanish accents zoomed back and forth. All the wide hips swaying and big boobs bouncing kept the male customers' eyes quite busy and the female customers *celosas*— jealous. Might explain why Las Palmas was usually packed with *hombres*.

Since Esperanza was somewhat of a celebrity at Las Palmas, he was given what could be called a semi-private table in the corner. This meant there was more than two feet of space between his table and the next. The two friends sipped *café* and munched on lightly toasted, heavily buttered bread. Plus *tostones*—fried, flattened green plantains smothered with a garlicky oil called *mojito*. The food, the coffee, the savory aromas of garlic and green peppers and cilantro were comforting to Esperanza. Even brought up his energy level—at least a little.

Havelock handed Esperanza a business card. It had a Chinese calligraphic symbol at the center and a phone number at the bottom.

"If anybody can give you an assist," Havelock said, "Lady Chen can." Then he dunked a piece of bread into the coffee and ate it.

"How do you know her?"

"Close friend from my Hong Kong days." Before returning to New York and working at Sueño Latino, Havelock was a personal bodyguard for a Hong Kong real estate tycoon. "We still hook up for drinks from time to time."

"You think she'll—"

"I set up a meet, for eighteen-hundred hours. Tomorrow. Address is on the back."

Esperanza flipped over the card. There was a handwritten, Upper East Side address and the cherry lipstick print of a woman's lips.

"The only way you can get in is with Chen's kiss of approval," Havelock said. He was trying to keep things light, but Esperanza didn't respond. Just continued staring vacuously at the card.

Havelock's face shrouded with concern. "Legs is really worried about you."

"I fucked up big time, bro'." Esperanza dropped the card into the pocket of his wrinkled flannel shirt. "Treated this whole thing as a joke." He drifted off again and gazed down at the place mat underneath the clear plastic tablecloth. It had a colorful map of the Dominican Republic. The hum of voices and merengue and silverware clanking became a dull buzz in his head. Esperanza couldn't get over the fact that he'd been taken down so easily. It was too humiliating for him to tell Havelock he'd been captured like a civilian. SEAL training had taught him to move as a team, but he'd tried to move alone. And alone he'd finish it. More importantly, he was taught that even if he was the last man standing, never ever surrender. The BUD/S motto was: "It pays to be a winner. Second place is first loser."

Havelock gently placed a massive hand on his friend's slumped shoulder. "I know you want to handle this business solo, but don't let your ego get you buried."

Esperanza looked back up at Havelock. "I won't," he said with unwavering determination.

"You don't look so hot, my man. When's the last time you got some sleep?"

Sleep was the least of his concerns. Havelock was right, though. Esperanza looked like shit. Eyes bloodshot, hair a mess, face pallid and in dire need of a shave. Esperanza was the kind of man who always made sure he looked his best. But since the "incident," he didn't care much about his appearance.

"Why don't we head downtown? Hit the gym, do a couple of laps in the pool, then get a shave, a steam and a massage?"

"Think I need a little cleaning up?" Esperanza flashed a smile.

"I think you need to relax. Clear your head. Be objective."

"Feel like takin' a ride with me? Doin' a little B & E?"

"I'm down."

Esperanza and Havelock. Moving as a team. The idea made Esperanza feel better already. Time to stop feeling sorry for himself and start making moves again.

They cruised around the Meatpacking District as Esperanza tried to carefully retrace his escape route. It took them nearly two hours, with plenty of dead ends, but they finally found the back entrance of the warehouse where he'd been held captive by Devona and Rybak. The alley was filled with dented aluminum garbage cans, a couple of bins overflowing with pieces of Sheetrock and rotted wood. Esperanza could smell decaying flesh. He glanced around and noticed a dead black cat a few feet away. Maggots were crawling from kitty's eye sockets. *That's not a good sign.*

"You sure this is the spot?" Havelock asked, as he tied his long dreadlocks in a ponytail and then pulled a black fleece beanie over his head.

"Pretty sure." Esperanza stared up at the fire escape.

"Lemme give you a boost, then."

Havelock interlocked his sausage fingers, Esperanza placed his boot in and Havelock hoisted him up with little effort. Esperanza grabbed the edge of the ladder and had to use his hands to climb up one rung at a time. It was painful, but he quickly made it to the first landing of the fire escape. There were slivers of peeling black paint on his hand. He dusted off his palms on the back seat of his blue jeans, then tried to unlatch the ladder, but it was still stuck. *This has gotta be the place. I remember I couldn't unlatch it when I climbed out the window. That's why I had to jump.*

"You okay up there?"

For a moment, Esperanza stared down at Havelock, waiting below. He smirked, said, "Never felt better," then stepped back and furiously kicked the latch several times until it came loose. He released the ladder, which dropped down like a guillotine. Havelock easily scaled his way up and joined Esperanza.

"That an expensive scarf you got on?" Esperanza said.

"Of course." Havelock snorted. "Cashmere, baby."

"Hand it over. I'll buy you a new one." Esperanza wrapped the rust-colored scarf around his hand and made a fist. "Let's hope there ain't an alarm." Esperanza turned his face away and rammed his fist through the window. No alarm went off.

"Not big on security, huh?" Havelock said.

Esperanza unlocked the window and pulled it up. Havelock reached under his leather trench coat and drew an ultra-compact 9-millimeter Luger. Stainless-steel finish. Three-and-a-half-inch barrel.

"Nice weapon," Esperanza said, whipping out his larger Sig.

"Bought it a coupla weeks ago. Let's see if it gets field-tested today."

They entered the warehouse and found themselves on a catwalk. They held their arms straight out, left hand supporting the gun hand, shoulders relaxed. Esperanza took the lead, Havelock brought up the rear. The warehouse was drenched in shadows, except for a single work light. With his hand, Esperanza signaled to go down the stairs. No talk between them. Not until the place was clear.

The warehouse seemed to be out of commission. There were only a few stacks of boxes and wooden crates. And a single, aging forklift.

It took them several minutes to look around the vacant warehouse.

Esperanza pointed to the wood-and-glass door with "Supervisor's Office" stenciled on it. They entered, gun barrels methodically swept left, then right, making sure the office was vacant. It was hard to see, since the office was illuminated by nothing more than the light from the street coming in through a dusty window. The office was tiny enough that Havelock and Esperanza would knock into each other if they turned too fast. There was a battered metal desk and two file cabinets. While Esperanza checked them, Havelock kept his gun aimed at the door, his index finger loose and limber on the trigger. Desk and file cabinets were empty. The office had a back door. Esperanza pulled it open, and Havelock went through, eyes glued to the sight of the Luger in front of him and the area beyond. There was a larger room filled with more crates. At the far end, there were two steel meat-locker doors. Esperanza headed for them, and Havelock followed. They heaved the enormous doors open, and Esperanza took a deep breath and cautiously stepped inside. It was pitch black. Esperanza's left hand crawled along the wall. He found a light switch and flicked the light on. The spacious meat locker was bare.

Esperanza looked around in disbelief. *This was where I was tortured. I'm sure of it.* Place had been completely cleaned out. Not a whip, a chain, a manacle, nothing. Only meat hooks dangling from the ceiling. There wasn't even a trace of blood by the floor drain. It reeked of pine cleaner and bleach.

"I don't believe this."

"Not what you expected?"

"No. It's like . . ." *The torture chamber never existed.*

"What?"

"Hold on." While Havelock kept his Luger aimed at the meat-locker entrance, Esperanza crouched near the drain. He clicked open the switchblade, stuck the tip into one of the holes and scraped along the edges. He held the knife up to the light.

"Blood," Esperanza said.

"It's a meat locker, ain't it?"

"Yeah. But I'm pretty sure these blond hairs don't belong to an animal."

For most homicide detectives, the morgue was a second home. So it was for Esperanza and Santos. They'd spent endless hours talking to the medical examiner about such postmortem details as time of death, angle of bullet entry, gunpowder residue, blood-spatter patterns, presence of defensive wounds and plenty of other gory murder details.

And here they were, like old times.

Santos, Havelock and Esperanza hovered over the covered corpse lying on the stainless-steel table. Santos lifted the corner of the sheet. It was Star. Quite dead, and obviously quite murdered.

"All the hookers in the city gotta be in mourning," Esperanza said. By the vicious nature of the pimp's injuries, Esperanza figured this was Devona and Rybak's handiwork.

"Found him this morning," Santos said, "floating near the West Side Pier." He turned on the bright, circular work lamp, which lit up the bloated body and most of the room. "I don't know, Nick. Seems like everybody you interview regarding your case ends up a stiff." Santos's voice dripped with sarcasm, but Esperanza knew he was very serious. After leaving the warehouse a few hours before, he called Santos to ask him to do a trace on who rented or owned the property he and Havelock had searched. Santos said he'd been looking for him. Needed him to come to the morgue.

Esperanza slipped on a pair of latex gloves, painstakingly inspected the lacerations on Star's neck. *This is like being back working homicide.* Esperanza shivered. *It's freezing in here. There's the sour smell of death and chemicals in the air. Damn, I forgot how much I miss being a detective.*

"No water in his lungs, right?" Esperanza said. Star's face was light blue. *Star wore the same freaked-out expression as Desire's corpse. Experienced a lot of pain before death.*

"Nope," Santos said. "Dead when he was dumped in the river."

"They used piano wire," Esperanza said and then glanced up at Santos. "So, at least you know it wasn't me. I would've just broken his neck."

Havelock said, "What was the actual cause of death, anyway?" He leaned against the steel counter and lackadaisically played with a microscope. He had little interest in forensics. Police work wasn't his thing. Since he became a Navy SEAL at the age of twenty, Havelock had always been a search-and-destroy man.

"M.E. hasn't done a full autopsy yet," Santos said. "But the preliminary report says he was simultaneously strangled and stabbed. Puncture to the heart most likely finished him off."

"Your kinky, fun-lovin' couple," Havelock said.

Esperanza examined the tiny stab wounds. "These punctures," he said. "Maybe an ice pick?"

"Something thinner," Santos said. "He also has those stitches on his face, only a couple of days old."

Esperanza gave the stitches a cursory once-over. They twisted their way down the side of Star's face Frankenstein-style. "Hmm. Wonder how he got those?"

Santos stared at Esperanza with leery eyes. "Right now,

there's no heat on this." He pulled the sheet over Star's face. "Nobody gives a shit about a deceased transsexual go-go dancer and a pimp. But if the body count keeps rising during this little investigation of yours? We're going to have a serious problem."

Esperanza pulled off the latex gloves and tossed them in the wastebasket. His cell rang. He checked the caller I.D. It was Legs. *She's gotta stop calling me so much. She's gotta have more patience.* He answered it. "What's up, babe?"

"Just wanted to see how it was going," she said, sounding worn-out. Esperanza was having a difficult time hearing her.

"Got some new leads. I'll be home in about an hour. I'll fill you in then."

"Okay. I'll be waiting up for you," she said. "I love you."

"Me too. 'Bye." Esperanza shut off the phone and slipped it back in his pant pocket. He turned his attention back to Santos. "Where were we?"

Santos pulled a folded piece of paper from his breast pocket. Unfolded it with a flourish.

"By the way, that warehouse you called about? The location where they held you, which you now *conveniently* remember?"

"Yeah. What is it, Santos?"

"It's owned by Miller Properties, Incorporated," Santos said. "Simon Miller. Real-estate and shipping bigwig. And, the building was leased to an L.A.-based company called New Visions. Import-export."

"And?" *Import-export. Shipping. Is there more to this than child porn? Maybe drugs and guns are also involved? Otherwise, what's the connection?*

"New Visions is owned and operated by one Nemec Wozak."

"What's special about him?" *I wish Santos would get to the point already. Always gotta be Mister Methodical.*

"He's a vic. Murdered under similar circumstances like your friends Star and Desire." Santos read to the bottom of the report, then looked up. "Two weeks ago, his body was found in some hooker motel out in Queens. Brutally tortured. Dick cut off. Wozak's so-called assistant, one Freddie DeNunzio, was in the other room. Single gunshot through the eye."

"Wozak have a sheet?"

"No," Santos replied and then smirked. "But DeNunzio did. Used to be a leg breaker for some Brooklyn loan sharks. Several arrests for assault. Charges usually dropped."

"Mob-connected?"

"Small-time."

Esperanza pursed his lips. *This might actually be going somewhere.* "So you figure Rybak and Devona whacked those two in Queens?"

"Similar M.O. The whole sexual-sadist approach."

More curious now, Havelock stopped fooling around with the medical equipment, folded his arms across his broad chest and attentively listened.

"Any good forensics?" Esperanza said.

"No prints. Or shell casings. Even the slug was removed from the wall." Santos said. "So nothing concrete. Those two sure know how to clean their tracks. Queens Homicide is stumped."

"Queens Homicide couldn't solve a children's puzzle."

"Don't be so elitist."

"I'm going to have to pay a visit to this Simon Miller," Esperanza said. *He owns that warehouse. He's involved somehow.*

"*We,*" Santos said. "Since I got the bad luck of catching Star's murder, you're gonna have to keep me in the loop, whether you like it or not."

The last thing Esperanza wanted was his by-the-book ex-partner tagging along. He'd go with Santos to interview

Miller only because it would make his visit an official one.
But that was it, as far as Santos's involvement was concerned. If he needed anyone by his side, it was Havelock.

*He'll cross whatever lines I need crossed. And until I get
Alina back safe and sound, the "book" is goin' out the window.*

"Gonna be like old times, *compadre*." Esperanza gave
Santos a big smile. "You do the talkin', I'll do the listening."

Santos rolled his eyes. "Meet me in the squad room tomorrow. Nine AM."

Chapter 16

Sprawled on the supple living room sofa, Esperanza gazed at the ceiling. Then he rolled back and forth, trying to get comfortable. The butterscotch sofa was made of full aniline leather. Most expensive leather available. He gave up and took another sip of Glenmorangie. Single Highland rare malt scotch whisky. Aged 18 years. Tulip shaped glass. Neat.

It was four in the AM. He was beat. Though badly in need of rest, he found that sleep refused to conquer. Most of the lights in the living room were turned off. The forty-inch, plasma television that hung on the wall was tuned to CNN. Sound was on mute.

Legs had lit a few candles. The floor-standing, iron candelabra spiraled and branched out like a dead tree. Beyond the sliding doors, beyond the wraparound balcony, the city nightscape sparkled. In New York City, skyscraper lights made up for the lack of stars in the sky.

He'd gotten to the bottom of his scotch. *I'm fried. Why don't I get my ass in bed and get some rest? Sleep seems impossible these days.*

Reflections of candlelight danced off Legs's collection of crystal bottles. She had every conceivable shape and color. Pink triangular. Mint green oval. Esperanza thought of pulling a book from one of the immense shelves lining the walls. *Maybe if I read for a while, I'll get sleepy.*

The far wall of the L-shaped living room was decorated with handmade *Vejigante* masks from Puerto Rican carnivals. Each mask represented a different town. A fusion of Spanish, African and Taino Indian culture. Esperanza brought a new one back every time he visited *la isla*. Some masks were papier-mâché, others were made from coconut shells. Most had hollow eyes, jagged horns and screaming mouths full of fangs. Kaleidoscopic paint strokes. Yellow polka dots.

With shadows falling across them, the *Vejigantes* seemed to stare at Esperanza in judgment. They usually gave him happy memories of his mother's hometown in Ponce, but on this night they were giving him the creeps.

On the tempered-glass-and-iron coffee table in front of him, Esperanza noticed a few packages next to the porcelain vase with droopy white tulips. He sat up. Swooped the half-empty bottle of Glenmorangie from the gleaming parquet floor, refilled his glass and took a sip. Then he leaned over and sifted through the six small packages. They were all addressed to Legs, except for one, which had his name on it. It was a padded envelope. In the return address line, written in spiraling, sophisticated handwriting, was M.D.L.

Mistress Devona Love.

He tore open the envelope. A D.V.D. In some part of his mind, he knew this was coming. The secret he'd been holding on to, a secret that was bound to come out because it had been recorded for posterity. On the D.V.D. was the evidence of his manhood's death. His heart punched his chest faster, and his hands got clammy. He limped over to the entertainment-system cabinet and opened the glass door. Digital surround receiver, D.V.D. player and C.D. changer. He placed the D.V.D. in the player's tray, grabbed the re-

mote, carefully sat in the overstuffed recliner and pressed
the PLAY button.

There he was, on his own ten-thousand-dollar television
screen, in full color, tied and gagged and getting sodomized
by Mistress Love. *Oh look, we have created enchantment.*

He found it both fascinating and horrifying seeing himself violated like that. Eyes rolled back. Drool dripping
from his chin. *That's not me. That man on the screen's being
used as a toy. Can't be me.* Devona eagerly thrust harder.
And harder. Pupils glimmering with gratification. She gazed
directly into the camera, wide grin spread across her lovely,
sweat-covered face. *You fucking cunt. You're relishing it so
much, making me your bitch.*

Rybak and Devona wanted to play a game of mental torture. Keep him off balance. Keep him glancing over his
shoulder. *They know where I live.* They knew much more
about him than he did about them. Gave them a clear advantage. *Now I have to make sure Legs is protected. The
only good thing about their game-playing is, it just might
keep Alina alive a while longer.*

Look at you, Nick. Jacked. I think I'm gonna throw up.
Esperanza's legs collapsed under him, and he fell back on
the sofa, spilling scotch all over himself. *I'm going to kill
the both of them. I swear it.*

"*Papito?*" Legs said with a yawn from behind him.

Esperanza instantly hit the STOP button. Turned around.
Tried not to look startled.

"What is it?" he snapped at her. Wasn't his intention.

She stood in the shadows and squinted, then rubbed her
eyes. Wore a silver, silk, Japanese kimono. It came down
mid-thigh. Hair was pulled back into a messy bun.

"It's four AM, honey." Legs yawned again. "Please, come
to bed."

"I'll be there in a minute, baby," he said warmly and managed a weak smile.

He waited. Listened to her footsteps disappear down the lengthy hallway lined with abstract sculptures. Then he rushed to the D.V.D. player and ejected the disc, and in quiet fury, snapped the disc into pieces.

Under a plush, forest-green quilt, Legs was curled up in the mahogany sleigh bed, fast asleep. The room was illuminated by the glow of a Japanese paper lantern, which sat primly on the antique vanity. Dead quiet but for the murmur of Legs's breathing.

The bedroom was their sanctuary. Fleecy, golden yellow carpet on the floor. Silk curtains on the windows. On the walls, tasteful, erotic, black-and-white prints of male and female nudes. On Legs's dresser, an endless assortment of body lotions and perfumes, but very little makeup. A padded, antique rocking chair in the corner, and beside it, a small octagonal table covered by stacks of Legs's dog-eared erotica paperbacks and her personal journals.

Esperanza, grim and still in his street clothes, sat on the suede padded windowseat, staring at Legs. Though he drank three glasses of scotch, smoked a joint *and* took a couple of Vicodin, he still wasn't sleepy.

What's Devona and Rybak's next move gonna be? They're coming after me soon. I gotta find them first. How? The video images of his assault kept playing in his mind over and over. *What if Legs had seen the D.V.D.? What if they sent it out over the Internet or some crazy shit like that?* While fingering Abuela's rosary, dangling from his stiff neck, Esperanza focused his attention on the outside world. *Don't let them get to you, Nick. That's what they want.* Perched on the eighth-floor ledge of the building across the street was a gargoyle, its mouth locked in an eternal snarl. The creature flashed sharp fangs, and its bat-like wings were stretched wide apart, as if it was about to take flight. Esperanza stared into the gargoyle's wrathful eyes, and swore that the gargoyle tilted its head slightly and stared back at him without blinking.

"God will *not* deliver you from evil," the gargoyle said, though its mouth didn't move. "You will burn for your sins."

Am I becoming delusional? What sins? What is it with the religious symbolism? This ain't like me. I have to regain control. Think like a cop. Act like a soldier. They'll come to me. Patience.

He studied the gargoyle for several seconds. Devona's giggles echoed inside his head.

You will burn for your sins.

Stop it. Go to sleep.

Esperanza's eyes swept over Legs from head to toe. While tossing and turning, she'd knocked the quilt from her body. She was on her stomach, the side of her face resting on her folded arm. Gloriously naked except for skimpy lavender panties of fine lace. Her body seemed to be calling to him. Esperanza cautiously peeled off his own shirt, and his fingers inspected the series of stitches covering his upper torso. *I'm always going to have these scars. To remind me of that terrible night. Every time I see them or touch them, I'll feel ashamed.*

He crept into bed with Legs and lovingly stroked her hair. He watched her sleep for a minute, then leaned down and planted gentle little kisses all over her face. *I need her. Her tenderness. Her love.* Though her eyes remained closed, Legs smiled and wrapped an arm around his neck. Kissed him deeply. Their kissing intensified as he rolled on top of her, their bodies squirming with longing.

Legs drowsily opened her eyes and said, "Are you sure you want to do this?"

Is she worried I won't be able to get it up? Or is she worried about my injuries?

"Yes," he said. "I need to be close to you."

To forget. At least for a moment.

She stripped off her panties, and Esperanza rolled on his back. Legs climbed on top, taking him inside her, a little at a time, savoring him, as his palms delicately caressed and kneaded her breasts.

"*Ooh, papi.* I've missed you," she said, enchanted hips gyrating faster. "You've been so far away."

"*Ay, mi amor, si,*" he crooned, lost in her pleasure. "I'm sorry. You know how much I love you, right?"

"*Seguro.*"

He threw his head back and moaned. *Falling, falling.* Into her gentleness. Her warmth. Feeling safe. Protected. Consumed by Legs's compassion, her love for him, always unwavering and unconditional. He felt alive. Blissful.

Then he closed his eyes. Saw distorted, grainy, colorless visions of Devona castigating him. *Get out of my mind, you fucking cunt.*

Esperanza's eyes popped open, and Devona was riding him, pelvis vaulting turbulently as she injected her nails into his chest, drawing blood.

"Don't you want to hurt me?" Devona said. "C'mon, lover. Take my breath away."

He reached up and tightly clamped his fingers around Devona's slender throat. She smiled expectantly and rode him fierce and fast as he squeezed tighter and her face turned deliriously flush.

Die, you bitch, die.

He blinked and was horrified to see Legs desperately struggling to break free of his lethal grip. It took him a moment to realize he was strangling her, not Devona. Legs's eyes pleaded for him to let go as her fists pounded his forearms.

He abruptly released her, as if the palms of his hands had been seared by fire. She jumped off of the bed, and gagged and coughed and stomped her feet, fighting for air, fighting to breathe.

Esperanza sat there for a moment. Frozen. Mouth agape, staggered by the violent act he'd committed. How could he hurt the woman he loved?

He dashed over to Legs, attempted to embrace her. She pushed him away.

"What the fuck is wrong with you?" She was hoarse.

Esperanza attempted to speak, but no words came. *I'm losing my mind. Devona's infected me, a deadly virus coursing through my veins. A virus that's pushing me toward madness.*

Legs sat, poured a glass of water from the carafe on the nightstand and gulped it down. She coughed a few more times and then somberly gazed up at Esperanza, who stood naked before her, head lowered, arms dangling at his sides, shoulders slumped.

What have I done? Am I gonna lose Legs forever?

"What did they do to you, Nick?" Legs said. Her body quivered. She hugged herself. "You gotta tell me."

They sat cross-legged on the bed, both still naked, facing each other. It was a position they took any time they needed to have a serious talk.

Esperanza was finding it incredibly difficult to open up to her.

She wasn't even sure if she wanted to hear the whole story. Legs was frightened of what the story, whatever it was, would reveal about her man.

He came clean, though, and details poured out in a torrent of pain, rage and embarrassment. Esperanza cried, and she hadn't seen him cry since his younger sister, Gloria, passed away.

But this pain was different. It came from a place deep inside, a forbidden place, where there was darkness, and hate. Esperanza seemed unable to bear facing the man he'd become. Uncertain. Weak. Haunted. His body heaved as he let out disturbing, animal-like sobs.

Legs listened, caressed his cheek. Stroked his hand. "It's okay, honey," she said. "It's okay to experience feelings of shame and guilt."

Meanwhile, I'm hiding my own emotions. Because I gotta be strong for him. But I don't want to be strong right now. I want to scream and cry. This is all my fault.

Legs was stunned into silence as he told her in graphic detail how Devona raped him, how he fucked her and how she beat him, and choked him, and debased him, and nearly killed him and then set him free.

"I managed to crawl to Fourteenth Street, where the cops picked me up."

"Jesus. Jesus." She wanted him to stop talking, wanted to run away, wanted to hide.

"I'm used to being in control," Esperanza said, wiping tears from his eyes with his forearm. "Lookit me. Can't seem to get it together. I'm jumpy. I'm losing it."

"You can fight this, Nick," Legs said. "You're a brave man. You've faced death most of your life and never even blinked."

"Yeah, right. Meanwhile, some psycho broad and her husband turned me into a walking disaster."

It made her queasy. It was also breaking her heart to see her man shattered like that. Who was this Devona Love, this viciously sadistic creature who left Esperanza troubled and volatile, left him shaken to the very core? Legs could see it in his eyes. The loss of confidence, the uncertainty. Something she'd never thought she'd see in Nicholas Esperanza.

She always knew there was something shadowy inside of Esperanza. A part of him that was dangerous, that served him as a cop. A part of him that both of them were smart enough to never explore. This Devona person seemed to have wholeheartedly tapped into that part of him. She unlocked a cage. Set something dark loose. Something Esperanza couldn't control. Something violent and twisted and utterly terrifying.

"Is there a part of you that wants to be with her again?"

"I want to kill her."

He said that statement with such conviction, it made her recoil. "That's not you, Nick."

"Don't be so sure." He stared up at the ceiling for a moment. Legs could see his Adam's apple palpitate. "Those fucking freaks . . . the joy they got from degrading me . . . they made me wish I was dead," he said, his words razor sharp with loathing. His troubled gaze locked with hers. "That crazy bitch, what I saw in her eyes . . . scared the shit outta me." His expression turned sinister. "I've looked into the eyes of more killers than I can remember, but I've never seen anything as cold and ruthless and purely wicked as what I saw in Devona's eyes."

Legs really had no idea what to say. *How do you find the right words for a situation like this one?* Her mind was reeling. She wanted a drink. A joint. Wanted to erase the past few days from their life like math problems on a blackboard. But that wasn't going to happen. Legs had to keep it together. *Just talk to him, girl.*

"I don't understand how you could've suffered through such a horrible experience and not shared your feelings with me," she said. Needed to bite down hard on her tongue to prevent herself from crying.

Esperanza gazed at her. There was such profound vulnerability in his eyes, it floored her.

"A part of me died that night," he said, choking on the words. "Now I look in the mirror and I see someone completely different. Someone vulnerable. Insecure. I don't know how to even start talking about how I feel. Can you understand that?"

"Yes," she replied solemnly, then embraced him, and he buried his face in the crook of her neck, his warm breath growing faster and deeper. "We'll get through this. . . ."

Legs wanted to plead with Esperanza to quit looking for Alina. She couldn't stand the thought of him being killed. Also couldn't stand the idea of turning her back on her niece, her *familia*. Besides, Legs also knew that no matter what she said, she wasn't going to be able to convince him of anything. He was obsessed. On a quest. And he'd be relentless in his pursuit of Alina. No matter what the cost.

He backed away. "I also keep seeing those pictures my brother, Mark, showed me. Visions from hell," he said, wagging his head as if to shake the terrible images from his consciousness. "Kids raped and tortured. Forced to commit unspeakable acts. I know Alina's suffering. And they'll kill her. That's why I can't stop. Won't stop until I find her and put these scumbags out of business. Permanently."

Legs buried her face in her hands. No matter how out of control her niece was, no matter the drugs and the sex, she was still a child. A child who was being sexually tormented. She loved Alina. Her sister's baby. Her blood. After hearing what these monsters had done to Esperanza, she couldn't bear to imagine the kind of agony Alina was going through. Legs clutched her stomach as the knot got tighter and tighter. She didn't want to hear any more. It was too much for her to handle.

Legs could no longer be strong for him. She began to cry. Cried for Esperanza. Cried for Alina. Cried for herself.

They held each other tightly, until the orangey sunlight of dawn bled through the windows. She was afraid to let go of him. Afraid of what they'd have to face next.

Chapter 17

Bishop was taking one of his late-night strolls through Soho, and since there were no hordes tonight overwhelming the formerly artsy, gritty, graffiti-covered neighborhood, he actually enjoyed himself. It's why he walked so late. When Bishop first moved to the area in the seventies, Soho was cutting-edge New York. The area teemed with painters, sculptors and photographers, and was packed with used-book stores and galleries that forever changed the New York City art scene. Now Soho was filled with fancy eateries and designer-clothing boutiques. Wealthy, pseudo-artsy yuppies owned the cavernous lofts once rented cheaply to struggling artists on-the-verge.

Bishop glanced over his shoulder. Felt uneasy, sensed someone shadowing him. He pulled up the collar of his charcoal-gray, wool overcoat.

Honk! Honk! Bishop recoiled, turned to see Rybak's BMW pulling alongside him. The tinted driver's-seat window smoothly rolled down. Rybak said, "Get in, please."

Bishop quickly scoped out the deserted block, then immediately climbed into the car and slammed the door. Rybak peeled out, since there was little traffic except for a smattering of taxicabs cruising for fares.

"Have you lost your mind, mate?" Bishop said, his Cockney accent even more guttural than usual. "We've got to avoid being seen together in public, yet you have the nerve to show up where I live."

"Don't have a cardiac," Rybak said, turning on West Broadway and heading south. "It's urgent. The problem is Esperanza's old-school. Hard-boiled."

Bishop retrieved rolling papers from a brown leather pouch, carefully dropped tobacco into a tiny sheet of paper and proceeded to roll a perfect cigarette. "Spare me the street poetics," he said, then gently ran his tongue along the edge of the paper, sealing it. This ex-cozzer who was searching for Alina was becoming more of a nuisance than anticipated.

"He's not going to stop looking for the girl," Rybak said. "So I suggest you get rid of her."

"I'm not finished with her yet," Bishop replied. Smiled to himself thinking about Alina. She was an unusual one. Tenaciously defiant. *I'm taking tremendous pleasure in training her. I have no intention of giving her up any time soon.* Bishop did as he pleased. No snooping ex-cozzer was going to change that. "How did Esperanza get away?"

Rybak kept his eyes on the road. "I got sloppy." His fingers drummed the steering wheel.

"Lying doesn't suit you, Jason," Bishop said. "You've never been 'sloppy' while doing a bit o' work. It probably has to do with that psychotic tart of a wife—"

Rybak exploded. Spasms of rage. He hammered his fist against the dashboard. Bishop didn't flinch. He wondered if Rybak was more insulted by hearing his wife called a tart or psychotic.

"Never, never, never," Rybak growled, "talk about Devona that way."

"There's no need for a show." Bishop couldn't believe how damn emotional the bloody Americans could be sometimes about what they thought was love. Rybak used to be dependable to a fault. Then Devona came along. "All this frothing won't get us anywhere."

Rybak chuckled. "I can kill you with my bare hands right now, and there's nothing you can do about it." He didn't say it as a threat. He said it as a matter of fact.

"I'm aware of that," Bishop said. "Yet you didn't manage to kill Esperanza. Do you appreciate my concern?"

"Don't worry." Rybak seemed to be coming back to his senses. "It'll be handled."

"Good. Now what is the real reason you came to see me?"

"Two reasons. One, Simon called in a panic. Wants to see you right away. Esperanza showed up at his office, asking questions about Nemec."

"Bloody 'ell," Bishop said. "This just keeps getting better." Bishop felt a slight regret at having ordered Nemec's death. Nemec had been a loyal partner for nearly twenty years. *Why'd he have to go and steal from me? The boy didn't matter, but Nemec knew how much I fancied Alina. So Nemec paid with his life. Now I have to deal with Simon.* "What else?"

"I'm resigning," Rybak said flatly.

"You're resigning."

"Yes." A smile of satisfaction filled Rybak's rigid face. "Devona and I are going to do some traveling."

"Why am I not surprised? After Devona came into the picture, I knew it was only a matter of time." Bishop stubbed out the cigarette in the car's ashtray. He was disappointed by Rybak's decision, but gave no indication. He wouldn't argue with Rybak about it. Devona had spun her web. She had a hold on Jason that no other human being could break. Love was all about control, as far as Bishop was concerned. He lived for control, but had no use for love. "You've been a grand chap in my firm. So I won't stop you," he said. "But before you go off on whatever . . . adventure you and the . . . missus got planned, do your job to its completion. Make Esperanza dead."

Esperanza was escorted into the vast living room of Lady Chen's establishment by a height-challenged, middle-aged, white man. Conroy. He looked spiffy in a black tux, and as soon as Esperanza saw him, he was tempted to call him Jeeves.

But I'm sure Conroy won't appreciate the joke.

Unfortunately, the morning visit Esperanza and Santos made to Miller's office had been a bust. Miller, with his salt-and-pepper hair, two-hundred-dollar haircut and thousand-dollar suit, was typically arrogant and impatient. The way rich people tend to be when being questioned by cops. Or questioned by anyone. Miller was very busy, could spare them only ten minutes of his precious time. Didn't know Nemec personally. As far as his underlings told him, New Visions was a good tenant, always paid on time. Told Esperanza and Santos to check with the managers who run his day-to-day operations. But why bother, since two homicide detectives from Queens had already interviewed his staff regarding Nemec's murder, and as far as anyone knew, Nemec ran a legitimate business. Miller excused himself, had important business to attend to. If they needed anything else, call his assistant. That was that.

Esperanza took Havelock's advice and went for a steam, a massage, a shave and a haircut. Even did several laps in the pool. Made him feel much better, more confident, and helped clear his mind. He kept thinking about what happened with Legs the night before. Hated himself for hurting her. Hated burdening her with his rage, his guilt, his shame, but the purging of emotions lifted some of the weight from his shoulders. He was blessed and honored to have Legs in his life. Any other woman would've run as far away from him as possible after hearing his confession. Not Legs. He knew she'd be there for him no matter how tough it got.

All right, Nick. Stop thinking about last night. Focus on the task at hand. Find Rybak and Devona. Find Alina.

Lady Chen conducted her business from a stately, three-story townhouse on the Upper East Side. On the aristocratic, tree-lined block, there were brownstones and townhouses in which C.E.O.'s, movie stars and a few New York blue bloods lived—and played. Lady Chen had to be exceedingly well connected—since she was essentially operating a whorehouse. It made sense, though. The madam catered to the rich and powerful. An hour at Lady Chen's cost a grand. Two grand, if it was an out-call.

"Wait here," Conroy said with an air of arrogance. *You work in a ho house, homeboy. Lighten up.* Esperanza unbuttoned his dark-navy wool-crepe blazer and marveled at the dozen drop-dead-gorgeous, Asian working girls lounging on a luxurious teal leather sectional and a couple of matching love seats. The lighting was romantically low-key. Walls were painted a subtle peach, decorated with framed prints of impressionist art. Vivaldi's joyfully melodic "The Four Seasons" played softly from hidden speakers.

The *chinitas* perked up. Smiled and giggled sweetly. Mostly, they were in elegant evening gowns, though some wore thigh-and-cleavage-baring silk-and-satin lingerie.

"Good evening, ladies," Esperanza said. "But I'm here to see Miss Chen."

"That's Lady Chen, darling." The voice came from behind him.

Esperanza turned to see Lady Chen gliding down a spiral staircase. Her entrance was befitting of a glamorous dame in a forties film noir. Lady Chen was exquisite. Pigtails. Latex bra. Plaid miniskirt and white, thigh-high stockings. Converse sneakers with five-inch, rubber platforms. Willowy figure. Plump lips. Pearly flesh. Honey-soaked voice with a slight Chinese accent.

She reached the bottom of the stairs. "You must be Nicholas." Chen held out her hand. Esperanza, not missing a beat, pretty much tangoed across the gleaming marble floor, drew her hand to his lips, lost himself in her confident, coal-black eyes. He kissed the top of her fingers, held his lips to the smooth, lilac-scented skin.

"Pleasure to meet you," he said. "Wow. Havelock told me you were ravishing. He's a master of the understatement."

To his surprise, it felt really good to flirt, to feel manly. For a moment, he forgot his injuries, his humiliation, and savored feminine grace and sensuality.

Lady Chen fanned herself playfully. "I was warned that you're a charmer." She hooked her arm through his. "What do you think of my girls?"

"Heaven," he replied and grinned gallantly.

"Let's go somewhere and talk," she said, and easily led him away from the ebony-haired beauties, guiding him through a door Conroy obediently held open for them.

The Très Vieux was an exceptional, unblended champagne cognac. Esperanza savored the drink. It was dark and rich, and went down smoothly. Might be a nice addition to the bar at Sueño Latino. Went perfectly with the San Cristobal Cuban cigars he and Lady Chen were smoking while they chilled on the silk, overstuffed sofa, which was dark plum and featured a richly detailed white-orchid print.

"My girls aren't kidnapped, beaten, drugged and forced into working at my house," Lady Chen said, "as many girls are, in plenty of the Asian spas around the city." She brushed cute bangs away from her eyes. "My girls are educated.

Sophisticated. I train them in the art of seduction and love-making."

"I'm sure you're . . . an exceptional teacher."

"I might even be able to teach you a thing or two."

They were lounging in Lady Chen's private parlor, her quiet retreat. Carroty, silk scarves were draped over the shades of antique brass lamps, which drenched the room in a sensuous glow. There was an assortment of glossy, well-tended plants. African violets with scallop-shaped, furry leaves blossomed with deep purple flowers. Towering parlor palms added a tropical touch. Vine-like plants with heart-shaped leaves crawled along redwood bookshelves, as delicate, ivory-lace curtains fluttered in a breeze coming in through the impressive French windows.

"How do you know Havelock?" Esperanza said as he squirmed, just a little. He still had some aches and pains. "He was kind of . . . vague."

"Havelock lent me a hand back in Hong Kong. Some Japanese *Yakuza*—gangsters—tried to take over my business." She blew out rings of smoke from those fabulous *labios*. "I've always been independent. Never rely on men to run my business. But because I make enormous profit, the criminal element often try to extort me. How do you say? Get piece of the action."

"They tried to hurt you?"

"Threatened to burn down my establishment and anyone in it. Beat up customers. Scared them away." She shook her head, then smiled slyly. "Fortunately, I have friends like Havelock. He made my *Yakuza* problem go away.

"He's good at that sort of thing."

"I will always be in his debt. So I'm willing to help you." Lady Chen placed her crystal snifter on the lacquered mahogany coffee table. Under the glass top was an elaborate Chinese landscape carved into the wood. "The people Havelock told me about—they're *very* underground. But if this dominatrix ever worked the legitimate S & M scene, I will find out about her."

Lady Chen smelled as if she'd just stepped out of a honey-milk bath. There wasn't a single blemish or wrinkle on her skin. Esperanza guessed she was in her late thirties, though she didn't appear to be a year over twenty.

"Be careful, though, who you ask," Esperanza said, awestruck by her seductive eyes. There was a certain mystery that Asian women possessed. An exotic sensuality that made most American men—white, black or Latino—fantasize about making love to one. "These people don't want to be found, and I've seen the corpses to prove it."

"Don't worry about me, lover." She reached out and played with his hair, her long fingers crawling down the back of his neck. He squirmed again. *Goose bumps. Girl's got magic hands, I'm sure.* "Discretion is what has made me so successful."

"You personally involved in the S & M scene?"

"When the mood strikes. Why?"

"What can you tell me about sadists?"

I need to be in Devona's head. She's been in mine.

"Sadists mix cruelty and love," she said. "I've worked as a domme in the past. But I am not a genuine sadist. If Mistress Love is, she's extremely dangerous. And most likely predictable."

"Why?"

"She craves attention."

And doesn't believe any rules apply to her. A true sociopath. Esperanza knew they were extremely rare. Specially a female one.

"I want to know about the psychology," Esperanza said. "I'm talking about when the so-called slave hasn't consented.

"Ah. The real thing. Aggression eroticized." She scrutinized Esperanza for a second. He could tell she wondered what compelled him to ask such unusual questions. Fortunately, she was classy enough not to say anything. "A true sadist relishes in the victim's suffering. Takes pleasure in the victim's torment. Sometimes breaks the person, makes him or her their psychological slave. Whether the person truly wants it or not."

"Sounds like Mistress Love."

"There are submissives who yearn for dommes like that. Subs who want to go *too* far. To the edge of . . . death even." She tugged on one of her pigtails. "There were times when clients requested I do things that were so vile, I refused. Even when offered a ten-thousand-dollar payment. Or more. I have limits."

"These people don't. So again, I warn you, be very careful."

"I appreciate your concern."

"And I appreciate your help."

Lady Chen smiled brightly and rested her long legs across Esperanza's lap. He glanced down at the bits of lean thigh exposed between the tops of the stockings and the bottom of the skirt. Milky white and smooth. She so enticed him, he wanted to stroke the exposed patch of flesh, to kiss it and to work his way up to her secret place. Swallow her whole.

"I'm always willing to assist a friend in need," Lady Chen said.

Lady Chen must've sensed that Esperanza was fantasizing about the kind of dirty things he'd like to do to her, because her cheeks flushed and her eyes narrowed. She provocatively licked the tip of her cigar. Though he didn't accept the silent invitation, Esperanza was quite flattered. And for the moment, felt like his old, roguish, *papi chulo* self again.

Chapter 18

Holding a lighted a match to one of his hand-rolled cigarettes, Bishop had a clear view of Rybak and Devona on the aging leather couch across from him. *Those two are always so frisky. Can't keep their hands off each other.*

Bishop lounged behind the desk, in the dimness of the office of one of Simon Miller's warehouses. Bishop enjoyed the darkness. And the silence. Long Island City was an industrial area of Queens. Manhattan seemed very far away, when it really was just over the Queensboro Bridge.

Bishop was ambivalent when it came to Devona. He admired her ruthlessness, yet despised her sometimes unprofessional tactics. *Crazy bitch always wants to play by her own rules.* He didn't like the fact that Rybak brought her along in the first place.

Miller, all prim and snooty, waltzed in and turned on the light. He glanced at Rybak and Devona, nice and cozy on the maroon sofa. Rybak wore a three-piece suit. Blue pinstripe. Wire-rimmed glasses. Leather briefcase on his lap. He'd fit in at any Wall Street investment firm. Devona, on the other hand, was sleek in a dark green, velvet bodysuit. Plus a hooded sable coat.

"Greetings, Simon," Bishop said. "Been waiting for you."

"You've made quite a mess of our arrangement."

Bishop wore a burgundy cardigan. Cream, silk shirt with an open collar. A gold cross dangled from his wiry neck. He tapped a silver letter opener against an empty coffee mug.

"I'm here to have a civilized chat with you, mate," Bishop said. He tossed the letter opener on the desk, then rose and indicated for Miller to sit behind it.

Miller hesitated. He nervously glanced at Rybak, who stared at him with emotionless eyes. Devona paid little attention. She was nibbling on her husband's neck. Miller fell into the chair, loosened his paisley tie and unbuttoned the top button of his yellow shirt. Simon, with his aristocratic features, keen walnut eyes and neatly trimmed, salt-and-pepper hair, reveled in his class superiority by talking to everyone as if they were a servant. Bishop mocked him by sometimes calling him Mister Howell.

"I want out," he said

Bishop was stone-faced. *What is this with everyone suddenly rebelling?* "Like you have a choice."

Bishop first made contact with Miller in a secret Internet newsgroup. It was for collectors and admirers of child pornography. Miller typed on and on about the dream he had of making love to a ten-year-old boy. Bishop told Miller he ran a very special club, but that it would cost him five grand to join. First, Miller had to send an encrypted e-mail with at least a hundred images of kiddie porn so that Bishop would know he wasn't law enforcement. (F.B.I., Justice and the locals weren't allowed to send out child porn even as part of an undercover sting.) After the images were e-mailed, Miller wired five-thousand dollars to Bishop's anonymous bank account, which was a part of his shell corporation in Panama. Once Simon became a member of the Candyland Club, he was able to download thousands of pornographic still images and videos of children. New stuff. Not boring, over-traded collections from the seventies.

But for Miller, the constant flow of fresh faces and bodies wasn't even the best part, wasn't really what he was paying the big bucks for.

Twice a month, the club featured live, online molestations, for which members from around the world were able to type in what sexual acts they wanted the adults to perform with the children. Eventually, Miller offered Bishop twenty large to arrange for him to have his way with a blond-haired boy—without the threat of legal repercussion. Bishop, true to his word, made it happen. Miller was hooked. Miller also became a valuable asset to Bishop, since Miller's shipping business allowed him to easily transport children and teens (some were paid for, some were abandoned and some were snatched) from Eastern Europe, Russia and Asia to the States, Canada and other parts of Europe. Bishop's "firm" had branches in Montreal, England, Sweden, Germany and Spain. They were like terrorist cells: they never met in person. All transactions were conducted via computer. Monies were moved electronically. The trafficking of children for the purposes of prostitution, pornography, sexual slavery, factory work and even organ harvesting had become quite lucrative. Bishop needed Miller and his shipping business. Since their partnership began, Bishop's ability to move merchandise worldwide had greatly improved. There was no way he was letting Miller "out."

"Look," Miller said, his voice calm, though Bishop could detect a slight tremor, "we helped each other out over the years, right? But now homicide detectives are snooping around. The last thing I can afford is to be connected to you in any form or fashion. So, we're finished."

"We're not finished 'til I bloody say so." Bishop held up his manicured hand. Rybak opened the briefcase and produced a manila envelope. He tossed the envelope, and Bishop effortlessly caught it, his eyes never leaving Miller's. "This contains your potential future. Shame. Jail. The end of your career. Your marriage. Your whole fucking life." Bishop leaned against the edge of the desk, close to Miller, then reached into the envelope, pulled out a tiny, digital video-tape and dangled it. "Imagine how the press would pounce on a story of a prominent real-estate and shipping magnate, caught on tape, engaging in lewd sexual acts with boys."

Miller remained impressively insolent. "I knew you'd pull this. I know who you really are. Don't forget, if I go down, you go down. Rupert Alladice. Mister Great Protector of Children. Founder of The Sanctuary. Pimp and porno-grapher. That would make some story, too."

Miller was one of the few people who knew Bishop's real identity. Miller had discovered the truth purely by accident two years ago, when his wife, Ellen, dragged him to a fund-raiser for The Sanctuary. Miller had kept his cool and do-nated five-thousand dollars.

The Sanctuary was the perfect playground for Bishop, as his personal preference was for teens. The place gave him unending access to confused, vulnerable and unwanted twelve-to-seventeen-year olds. He chose the runaways he knew no one was looking for. He did his research. Took his time. That's why Bishop was taken by surprise when Esper-anza came searching for Alina. With her history of sexual promiscuity and drugs, on top of the fact that she was from the housing projects on the Lower East Side and was being raised by an ailing great grandmother, Bishop expected no one to come asking questions. Certainly not a former N.Y.P.D. homicide detective.

Simon really thinks he can talk to me like that and get away with it?

Without warning, Bishop moved closer, grabbed Miller by his shoulders, jerked him forward and smashed his knee into Miller's solar plexus. "Mister Howell" doubled over.

Bishop grabbed Miller by his hair, flipped him over, threw him on the desk and choked him. Bishop leaned down, his face just a couple of inches from Miller's.

"You're fucking with the wrong guy. Stupid cunt." Bishop grabbed the letter opener and jammed the sharp tip right below Miller's left eye, piercing the skin. Now that he had Miller's undivided attention, Bishop softened his voice to a purr. It was like he was whispering a romantic declaration to a lover. "Let me make myself clear. Break our arrangement? I'll torture you for days before I finally disembowel you. I'll have your wife giving five-dollar blowjobs in back alleys in Tijuana. Your little girl, Aimee? She'll be starring in videos . . . getting buggered by farm animals." Bishop pulled away the letter opener and released Miller. Gagging and hacking, Miller crumbled to the floor, covered his face with his hands and wept. "I hope I've made myself quite clear." Miller, all the arrogance gone, looked up and nodded. Devona giggled as she and Rybak disentangled and stood up. Bishop casually dropped the videotape on Miller's lap. "Do me a favor," Bishop said before leaving. "Take a vacation. A long one. Give us some time to clean up this bloody mess."

At Sueño Latino, Esperanza was hunched over in his booth staring at Alina's Polaroid snapshot. His back stiff. Arms sluggish. Eyes distant. He sipped coffee and nibbled on a croissant. He was waiting to hear something from Lady Chen. Waiting to hear something from Devona and Rybak. Waiting for something, *anything* to happen. With every passing hour, he was becoming more frustrated. His gut told him Alina was running out of time.

"What are the chances?" Legs said as she slipped into the booth.

"Huh?" Esperanza put the snapshot in his pocket.

"Of finding Alina alive?" He just blankly stared at her. Didn't have an answer for that. "How are you feeling?"

"Like I could crawl under a blanket and sleep forever."

"That's the last thing you'd do."

"Which is why I have to leave my feelings about 'chances' out of this situation."

Legs patted his shoulder. Esperanza supposed the gesture was one of encouragement. "I need another cup of coffee," she said and made her way to the bar.

Right then, Esperanza's cell phone rang. It was Mark, wanting to know if he'd found any leads. Esperanza watched Legs as she slipped behind the bar and poured herself a mug of freshly brewed coffee, then started checking inventory while quietly chatting with Maria. The two of them laughed. Legs stroked Maria's still-flat belly. *Baby on the way.*

"No, Mark. I haven't found out anything concrete—yet. Yeah. I promise, I'll call you."

Esperanza sipped his *cafecito*. Spaced out. Wasn't sure if it was because of the painkillers or his erratic frame of mind. The club's staff busily swept, mopped, polished and carried in supplies, getting the place ready for another night of festivities. Esperanza was always amazed by how different Sueño Latino looked during the day, when the work lights were blazing. They sucked all the color and sensuality out of the place.

His eyes were drawn to the mirrored wall on his left. He noticed two men. They were wearing black trench coats, sunglasses and baseball caps. Maria hurried over, pleasantly smiled and asked them what they wanted.

Wait a minute. It's a dim, cloudy day. Why would they be wearing sunglasses?

Esperanza reached for his gun. The men opened their coats and whipped out Uzi submachine pistols. The first thug shot Maria. It was point-blank to the chest. There was no time for her to scream. The force of the gunshots sent her flying backward, her arms reaching out to grab onto something, but her hands grasping only air. She crashed against the bar and bounced to the floor, landing on her back.

The other shooter let out a salvo of slugs. The sound was ear-shattering. Each boom like a kick to the head. Legs ducked behind the bar as Esperanza leaned over the booth, quickly aimed his Sig and fired. The perp who shot Maria took the first 9-millimeter to the stomach. Instantly followed by one to the chest. Finally, clean through the forehead. Collapsed to the floor. Dead.

The other shooter fired at Esperanza and nailed a busboy in the process. The club's staff was screaming and scattering for cover. Esperanza ducked as bullets ricocheted inches from his head. He swiftly crawled along the floor, searching for better cover behind one of the wide pillars.

They sent hitters. You didn't anticipate that. You expected them to go for a more intimate approach.

Esperanza made it to a pillar and slid upward, his back pressed against the cement. Cries and moans flooded his head, but he muted them, stayed focused. He peered out, spotted the shooter kneeling behind an overturned table. They simultaneously aimed and fired at each other. Esperanza missed this time and jerked back as puffs of dust and chunks of cement spewed from the volley of bullets striking the pillar.

Esperanza instinctively spun to the other side of the pillar, returned fire and managed to graze the hitter, who clutched his shoulder but let out another swarm of steel projectiles. Esperanza checked his gun. *Empty.* He searched his pockets for another clip, though he knew there wasn't one. *Think of something. Fast.* He heard the shooter slap another magazine into his Uzi. The shooter fired several short bursts at Esperanza, keeping him cornered. The shooter waited a moment, then crouched and kept his gun aimed as he zigzagged across the dance floor, making his way toward Esperanza. *He knows I'm outta ammunition. Otherwise, he wouldn't be so confident.*

"Give it up, Esperanza," the hitter shouted in a British accent, "and nobody else gets hurt."

Though he knew it was a bad idea, he didn't have a choice. He wasn't going to let any more people die because of him, so Esperanza reluctantly stepped from behind the pillar, his hands in the air. Shooter probably didn't intend to leave any witnesses, but Esperanza was praying that Rybak and Devona's errand boy might get cocky. Come close enough so he could disarm him.

The perp was bleeding from his shoulder, and he was smarter than that. He stopped a few feet away and leveled the barrel of his Uzi at Esperanza. Legs suddenly appeared behind the shooter, clutching a pot of steaming coffee in her hand. She shouted, "Police!"

The shooter whirled around, and Legs splashed the scalding liquid in his face. He let out an animalistic shriek. Gun went off. Esperanza lunged and tackled the thug to the ground, and they rolled along the slippery dance floor, struggling for the weapon. With ruthless precision, Esperanza nailed his forearm into the man's broad face, shattering the bridge of his nose, and then snatched the Uzi away from him. He kicked his would-be assassin in the chest, sending him rolling backward. He didn't want to kill him. The man could lead him to Devona and Rybak.

Screaming and half-blinded, the skin on his face blistering, the perp still didn't intend to give up. He reached for a firearm tucked inside his coat.

Esperanza squeezed the trigger, and the man was virtually cut in half by a barrage of his own 9-millimeter bullets. Blood was splattered on the bar, the floor, the tables. The smell of cordite laced the air. Someone yelled, "Call nine-one-one." Though it seemed like minutes had passed, the violent turn of events had taken less than ninety seconds. Esperanza scrambled to his feet, dashed over to Legs and grabbed her by her shoulders and shook her.

"You okay? Have you been hit?" He couldn't believe she'd taken such a stupid chance. She could've been killed.

Then again, she would've been killed anyway. She didn't just save my life. If she hadn't stepped up to the plate, everyone in the club would probably also be dead.

"I'm fine," she replied, a little too calmly. Then she turned and saw Maria splayed out on the floor, not a twitch of movement. *"Ay, Dios mío."* Legs ran to her friend. Maria was drenched in crimson, eyes glazed over as she struggled to breathe. Esperanza heard Maria wheezing and recognized the sound of death. Legs dropped to her knees, and carefully, lovingly placed Maria's head on her lap and held her hand. "Hold on, *Mami*. Please, hold on."

Though he knew it was hopeless, Esperanza squatted and applied pressure to Maria's gunshot wounds. Legs did the same. He glanced up at Carlito, one of the maintenance men. He appeared to be in shock. "Get some towels!" Carlito snapped out of it, darted behind the bar and came back with a bunch of towels. Esperanza placed the folded towels between the wounds and the palms of his and Legs's hands. Staff members, though weeping and frightened, came to the aid of the fallen busboy.

Rybak played me. E'tupido. This was his doing, not Devona's. Rybak sent two hitmen in broad daylight to his club to whack him, and it was the last thing Esperanza expected. He'd been counting on Devona's personal attachment to him. She let him go, so Esperanza figured she didn't want him dead. Havelock should've been at Sueño Latino, locked and loaded, protecting the club during the day, and there should've been additional armed security at night. The only reason Esperanza was still breathing was because his girlfriend had heart *and* guts. Now she was holding one of her closest friends in her arms. Watching her and her unborn child slowly die.

Chapter 19

"One dead and two wounded," Captain Killian said from behind his spanking-new desk, which was cluttered with reports, memos and Nicorette gum wrappers. "You want to tell me what the hell's going on?"

"Two hitters tried to clip me," Esperanza replied. He was standing opposite Killian, coat folded over his arm. Killian didn't keep a chair. He didn't want anyone sitting, wasting more of his time. Killian had been Esperanza's supervising officer during his days in homicide. They'd always gotten along well, but at the moment, Killian stared at him with grim, accusatory eyes.

"Why?"

"Because of Legs's niece, Alina. I'm sure you've already been briefed." Killian wasn't about to cut him any slack, but Esperanza was still going to be as straightforward as possible. Esperanza glanced at the wall behind Killian. It was covered with plaques and framed photos of Killian with the commissioner, the mayor and other New York City politicos. There was even the *New York Post* headline about Esperanza winning the thirty million. "She disappeared two weeks ago. I've been looking for her."

The office had a window that looked out to the squad room, but the dusty venetian blinds were drawn for privacy. Killian rolled up the sleeves of his white shirt, as if getting ready to rumble. He had colossal hands and burly, freckle-peppered forearms. "Detective Santos has been assisting you—with this private investigation of yours?"

He knew this question was coming. Killian went by the book. If he found out Santos was lending a hand, the captain wouldn't hesitate to place Esperanza's ex-partner on desk duty. Or worse.

"No," Esperanza said firmly. "I've been giving him information, which, in turn, he's been passing on to Missing Persons."

The captain's oversized head angled forward, bulbous eyes remaining leery. His turgid face was acne-scarred and clean-shaven. The only light in the office was coming from the banker's lamp on the desk. Lit from below, Killian seemed more menacing than usual. Along with a Bugs Bunny mug filled with sharpened pencils, there were dozens of toy soldiers lined up along the front edge of the desk, making Killian look like some kind of giant. "Commissioner's in an uproar," he bellowed, "because an ex-homicide detective, formerly under my command, turns his nightclub into a bloodbath."

"They came after *me*," Esperanza said. "What was I supposed to do? Let them whack me?"

"If you weren't poking your nose around in the first place, impersonating a police officer—"

"I wasn't impersonating an officer."

"—No one would be gunning for you." Killian ran his fingers through his wavy, chestnut hair. He was always fussy about his hair, happy that at sixty, it was neither receding nor thinning, and there wasn't a fleck of gray. "And a pregnant girl wouldn't be dead." Ashamed of himself, Esperanza looked away. In the corner of the office was a fold-out bed, for those extra-long nights when going home wasn't an option. "You keep up this investigation," Killian continued, "I'll throw you in jail. End of story."

Esperanza returned Killian's caustic stare.

"Thanks for the support."

Killian clasped his hands together and cracked his knuckles. Esperanza noticed he was no longer wearing his wedding band. Only his high school graduation ring. "You were a great cop. You got lucky, got rich. But you're not getting any special treatment from me, Esperanza. Stick to having fun. Leave the police work to us." Killian pulled tortoise-shell glasses from his shirt pocket. Put them on. They made his eyes appear twice as big. "Speak to the detectives handling this case. Then Internal Affairs wants to chat with you."

"So I'm just supposed to drop everything and forget about Alina, even if I believe she's been kidnapped and is being tortured?"

"You suddenly think the N.Y.P.D. is inept because you no longer work for us?" Killian said. "We're going to vigorously pursue this case. That's why I assigned some of our best people. We'll do everything in our power to find the girl."

Killian picked up one of the many reports piled on his desk and began to read it. He paid no more attention to Esperanza.

I can't believe this, cabrón. He owes me some respect for all the cases I cleared. For the years I gave to the job. Life on the line—day in, day out. Now he just wants to blow me off.

"Is there anything else?" Killian said without looking up.

Esperanza walked out. Didn't bother to close the door behind him.

Detectives Batiato and Creiger spent three hours grilling Esperanza. They were investigating the shooting at Sueño Latino as well as the apparent abduction of Alina Perez. Batiato was stout, bursting out of his shirt. He looked like he pumped iron five times a week. Creiger was gangly. Had a bad comb-over. Batiato and Creiger didn't know Esperanza personally, but over the years, they'd heard great things about him. They both treated him like a brother in blue, patiently drawing from him as much information as they could.

"We want the same thing you want," Batiato said. "We're not tryin' to jam you up. The more you help us, the quicker we can figure this thing out."

Esperanza told them everything he knew regarding the case (leaving out only the small detail about the sexual assault). Possible child-porn ring. The kidnapping of Alina and the murders of Desire, Star, DeNunzio and Nemec were all most likely committed by Devona Love and Jason Rybak. Why he thought Nemec might possibly be connected to Simon Miller.

Batiato and Creiger were on his side. They wanted to help him. Esperanza appreciated that, especially after the way Killian dissed him.

After the camaraderie of the Creiger-Batiato session was finished, in came the I.A.B. guys, Mangineli and Hightower. The two of them belligerently interrogated Esperanza as if they had a personal investment in the situation. Went for the hardball approach, doing their best to intimidate him. It was a pointless exercise, though, and a total waste of energy. Esperanza wasn't impressed by their antics.

Mangineli paced back and forth in the claustrophobic interrogation room. The single, steel-barred window was covered with soot. Esperanza glanced at his reflection in the one-way mirror and wondered if Killian was behind it, listening and watching. Esperanza ran his fingers along the tabletop, badly scarred with cigarette burns. The heat was turned way-up high to keep suspects as uncomfortable as possible. Esperanza didn't break a sweat.

"We'll send you to the Tombs if we have to," Mangineli said, like he actually had the authority to put Esperanza in a cell. Mangineli had an unlit Tiparillo cigar clenched between his teeth. He was a straight-up greaseball. Kind of man who chose to become a cop instead of a mobster only because he could probably get away with more crimes by carrying a badge. *Who's watching the cops who watch the cops?* "I'm sure you'd run into a lot of old buddies there."

Hightower sat at the head of the table, reading through the police report neatly laid out before him. He'd remained cool the whole time, saying very little. These two were accustomed to putting the fear of God into cops who desperately wanted to keep their pensions, their careers and their freedom.

Esperanza leaned back in the chair, foot propped on the edge of the table like he owned the interrogation room. In many ways, he did. He'd spent countless hours in this very same room, interviewing witnesses and interrogating suspects. This was *his* house. "By the way, Mangineli," Esperanza said, "where are your floppy shoes?"

"What?" Mangineli turned to Esperanza, hitched up his too-big beige, polyester slacks.

While picking lint from his cashmere sweater, Esperanza asked, "Don't clowns usually wear big, floppy shoes?"

Mangineli pulled the skinny cigar from his mouth and grinned. His teeth were so straight and so white, Esperanza ventured to guess that they were false.

"You think this is a joke?"

"No," Esperanza said. "I think *you two* are a joke. You come in here leanin' on me like I'm some two-bit perp, just to impress me." Esperanza gazed at Mangineli with contempt. "What's that all about?"

Hightower dramatically pounded his fist on the table, then leapt out of his chair and got in Esperanza's face. At least his breath was minty fresh, and he had about him the hint of balmy cologne.

"You think you're God's gift," Hightower said, "don't you?"

"I just know your type," Esperanza said, rocking back and forth in his chair, on the verge of exploding. "Guys like you never did a day of honest police work in your life. Too busy taking payoffs from bad cops and nickel-and-dime dealers."

"Fuck you," Hightower said.

"Yeah, yeah, yeah."

Esperanza propelled the heel of his hand into Hightower's chest, tired of having his personal space invaded. Hightower stumbled backward, quickly regained his equilibrium, then charged at Esperanza, who was already on his feet, ready to take down the lofty brother. Fortunately for Hightower, Magineli was quick. He got in between them, kept his enraged partner at bay.

"Calm down, Hightower," Magineli said, holding his spindly arms out. Hightower huffed and puffed for a moment, then reluctantly stepped back. Mangineli turned his attention to Esperanza. Sat on the edge of the table. Esperanza noticed that Mangineli's shoes—shiny, brown wingtips—weren't cheap, like his suit. "Let's be civilized. You don't carry a badge anymore, Esperanza," he said. His tone was matter of fact. "I'm warning you: Immediately cease this investigation into the kidnapping of Alina Perez."

"Or what?" Esperanza said, jutting his chin out in defiance.

"We'll arrest you for obstruction and hindering a police investigation to start with," Hightower replied, fingering the American flag pinned to the lapel of his black suit jacket. "Now, I want you to tell us everything you know about Devona Love and Jason Rybak."

Why are they so interested? Why are they interviewing me in the first place? These rat-squad bastards are up to something.

"I already talked to Creiger and Batiato," Esperanza said and stood up. "I ain't got shit to say to you."

"I read your I.A.B. file," Hightower said. "If any of those charges had stuck, you'd be in the pen right this minute. You fuck with us? You're goin' down."

"My accountant's scarier than you two assholes." Esperanza snatched his coat, which was folded and hanging on the seat back of an empty chair. "And since you got no jurisdiction over me . . . fuck off."

Irritated, Esperanza hustled from the station house, then stopped at the top of the steps to collect his thoughts. He was exhausted, and his body swayed back and forth for a moment. It was already dark. Snowflakes fluttered through the crisp air, leaving a dusting of glittery white on the streets. Uniform cops relaxed in their cruisers, sipping coffee and eating snacks, before heading out on patrol. Esperanza hated his two years in uniform. After six years as a Navy SEAL, being a beat cop—writing parking tickets, settling domestic disputes, chasing turnstile jumpers—was a bit of a joke, but he had to pay his patrolman dues to become a detective.

But they were much simpler days, weren't they?

A bus roared by. Left behind a nasty cloud of black smoke. Esperanza coughed, and headed toward his car.

"Nick. Hold up." Santos came rushing after him. "*Que paso?*"

"Got chewed out by the captain, got questioned by two detectives. That I expected," Esperanza said. "What I want to know is, why did two rat-squad scumbags interrogate me?"

Santos wasn't wearing a coat or a jacket, so he stamped his feet to stay warm. Man couldn't stand bitter winters in Nueva Jork. In a couple of years, he intended to retire to a two-bedroom house in Arecibo, Puerto Rico. Finally finish that novel of his.

"Supposedly because you're an ex-cop."

"I don't buy that. There's something suspicious about those two pricks," Esperanza said. "Why don't you see what you can find out—"

"No," Santos replied. "*Con lo que paso en* Sueño Latino, you're done. Killian's putting out a memo. Any detectives who assist you are gonna be busted down to writing traffic tickets." Santos was turning red from the frosty air. He hunched his shoulders and stuffed his hands deep into the pockets of his wrinkled wool slacks. Licked snowflakes from his ashy lips. "Look, Bats is a fine detective. Give him as much information as you got, and walk away."

"You know I can't do that. I'm still gonna search for Alina."

"Why? You have Homicide and Missing Persons working this case now."

"I don't care if the whole department is working this case." Esperanza thought of Abuela for a moment. Then Legs. "I made a promise. And I'm gonna keep it."

"It's out of your hands, Nick," he said. "Let it go. It could've been Legs that was killed today."

Without warning, he grabbed Santos by his shirt collar and rammed him against a police car. His face trembled with indignation as he glared at his friend, ready to rip his head off. He'd run out of patience, tired of everyone telling him what to do. Santos raised an eyebrow, showing more disappointment than fear. "You're outta control, *compai*." A couple of uniform officers, hands on their nightsticks, were headed toward them, but Santos waved them off. "It's over," he whispered.

Esperanza released Santos, then straightened Santos's polka-dot tie. Gave his ex-partner a tender pat on the face.

"It's not over until Alina's found."

"I can't believe you sent Goodis and Sinclair after Esperanza," Devona said, fiddling with the van's radio until she found a smooth-jazz station. "*We* were supposed to take care of him."

Devona removed a perfume bottle from her purse and sprayed some in the air, hoping to mask the funky odors of urine and sweat wafting from the back.

"I thought it should be handled in a less . . . personal manner."

Rybak, with a knit cap on his head, was behind the wheel of the battered van. They were parked on a desolate street near the waterfront in South Brooklyn. Mostly abandoned or run-down factories. Two-story, depressingly gray, brick-and-cement structures. Not a single car on the narrow street, which was barely visible, as the falling snow became heavier by the minute. Every few seconds, the windshield wipers squeaked as they swooped across the windshield and wiped away snow.

"Yeah, right. Real professionals, those two," Devona said. "In the middle of the day, guns blazing, everybody hit except their actual target?" The radio kept fading in and out, and Devona kicked it. It went dead. The van's engine rumbled loudly. "It'll be all over the front page of the *Post* and the *News* tomorrow. Full-color photos. Bishop will appreciate the publicity."

Rybak drummed his fingers on the wheel, eyes staring straight ahead. Devona found the habit annoying.

"Enough already, Devona. I screwed up. Okay."

"It's not okay, Jason." With all the strength she could muster, she punched her husband in the shoulder. Barely phased him. "You said *we* were going to handle this. You and I." Devona angled forward and hissed in his ear. "You lied to me. You should never lie to me."

"I'm sorry. I don't know what I was thinking." Rybak hung his head. "I wanted to finish Esperanza quick, get out of town and start over with you." She grabbed him by the chin and pulled his head up so that she could see his face. His boyish remorse made her heart melt for a second.

She squeezed his face. "Promise me we'll finish Esperanza together."

"I promise," he mumbled.

The inside of the van was suddenly flooded with light as a second van pulled up behind them. "Time to work," Devona said. This would be the last job they'd do for Bishop. Otherwise she'd die of boredom.

Devona and Rybak climbed from their vehicle, and she pulled the hood of her fur coat over her head. A rampageous wind—the kind that sucked the energy out of you and made your muscles cramp—blew in from the Gowanus Canal. It made snowflakes swirl like swarms of white locusts.

From the other van emerged Mato Dragoslav. The lardaceous Serbian sported a puffy, red parka and leather baseball cap. He limped over and made crunching sounds in the snow with his hiking boots.

Dragoslav smiled from beneath a heavy, unkempt beard.

"Greetings, my friends," he said and then grinned. He held out his hand, and Rybak shook it. Looked at Devona and nodded respectfully.

"Cargo arrive okay?" Rybak asked.

"Yes."

Devona was always amazed at how flat Dragoslav's face was. If he turned sideways, it was as if he didn't have a profile.

They followed Dragoslav to the back of his white van. He unlocked the doors and pulled them open. Inside were eight teenaged girls in cheap vinyl coats huddled together and trembling. All blond and blue-eyed. Pretty faces misshapen with fear. All bound together by a single rope. *A girly chain gang.*

"Oleksei will be happy," Rybak said. Oleksei was a former Soviet K.G.B. operative–turned–mobster who was a big shot in Little Odessa in Brighton Beach. The Brooklyn community was an enclave of hardworking Russian immigrants, as well as a ruthless criminal element, which included many gangsters, but none as feared as Oleksei. Aside from gambling and drugs, Oleksei ran a couple of popular whorehouses for the past fifteen years. He specialized in fresh-faced girls. "They all check out?"

"No diseases," Dragoslav said. "All very, very pure."

"A parade of sweet virgins," Devona said as she surveyed the girls. Very Slavic. Slanted eyes. Round faces with high cheekbones. They'd been transported from the Balkans on one of Miller's freighters. Poor little angels thought they were coming to work legit jobs in the States. Instead, they'd end up hooked on heroin, spreading their legs for an endless flow of decrepit Russian men in the outskirts of Brooklyn. *Pity.* "Come on, ladies," Devona said. The girls didn't move.

Dragoslav screamed something in Serbian, and they all hurried out, heads lowered as Devona herded them to the other van.

Devona watched Rybak hand the Serb a thick envelope filled with cash.

"Take good care of my girls," Dragoslav said.

Rybak smirked. "I'm sure they're all gonna get the best education."

Dragoslav howled with laughter as if it was the funniest joke he'd ever heard.

A symphony of automatic gunfire and screams echoed in Esperanza's ears. *Maria. She and her baby are dead. How many people are going to die because of my incompetence?* The heaviness of his heart left him paralyzed for a moment. Again, he was stretched on the sofa in his living room, his hands tucked behind his head, fingers interlocked, contemplatively staring at the ceiling. He was supposed to be a man of action, a man able to get things done. *I'm a fucking joke. Alina's probably dead by now. And I'm not getting any closer. All I'm gonna end up bringing home to Legs is another corpse.*

Esperanza figured he must look ridiculous dressed in black leather pants, leather vest and motorcycle boots. He donned the outfit at the suggestion of Lady Chen, whom he was meeting at Club Purgatory. It was an exclusive, members-only S & M club down in the Meatpacking District. Lady Chen told him he wouldn't be able to get into the club un-less he dressed the part. She'd made contact with someone who could give him information about Devona and Rybak.

Maybe I'll finally catch a break and nail those two psy-chos. Then maybe I can find my way back from my own madness.

But the image of Maria on the floor of Sueño Latino, her body riddled with bullet holes oozing rivers of blood, kept flickering in his mind. Then he heard Lucho, wailing at the news of his wife's and unborn child's deaths. Esperanza covered his ears, but Lucho's cries only grew louder. He turned and stared at the bottle of Vicodin on the coffee table next to his cell and his spanking new Beretta 92FS pis-tol. The Beretta replaced his Sig Sauer, which the police had confiscated. Esperanza reached for the bottle of Vicodin, but his hand froze in midair. *No. Your mind has to be sharp from now on. Pain is your friend.*

Instead of picking up the pills, he sat up and grabbed his cell.

Legs, in a T-shirt and sweatpants, emerged from the bathroom after taking a long bath to calm her nerves. Her damp hair was tied in a ponytail, and she was dabbing her nose with a tissue. Sniffling. Face ashen, eyes puffy from crying, she dropped into the overstuffed leather chair as if the sadness was too much to bear. The shooting had hap-pened several hours ago. But by how shell-shocked Legs looked, it seemed like only a few minutes had passed.

"I can't believe Maria's dead."

Esperanza wasn't sure if she was talking to him or to herself.

"I'm sorry." That was the best he could come up with. What could he possibly say to her to make the hurt go away? *Nothing. Nothing.*

She squinted, dark pupils burning with acrimony. "Find my niece, Nick," she said, her voice gravelly, her tone indomitable. "Hunt those motherfuckers down like the animals they are and make them pay for what they've done."

Esperanza dropped the cell, and it bounced off the Persian rug and onto the hardwood floor. Deep in her eyes, he saw an unwavering thirst for revenge, for justice. It unnerved him. Because he saw himself. He remained frozen, staring at her. *Does she really want that? Or is she just caught up in her emotions?*

Havelock came in from the kitchen carrying two mugs of tea, interrupting the uncomfortable moment between them. His red crewneck sweater and straight-leg black jeans didn't seem to go with the brown shoulder holster and nickel-plated, .45 automatic. Hefty gun like that had serious stopping power. Havelock placed the mugs of tea on the coffee table and sat on the sofa. Legs picked up the mug with the Puerto Rican flag on it, blew into it and absentmindedly sipped the tea.

"You two okay?" Havelock was hesitant about getting in their business. Legs didn't speak. "What do you need me to do?"

"Stick with Legs," Esperanza said. "At all times."

"Done."

"I'm going to meet Lady Chen. She says she's got a solid lead about Rybak and Devona." Esperanza grabbed the Beretta from the table, stuffed the gun in his waistband. "Don't let your guard down, Havelock. I did, and look what went down."

"I'll protect her. With my life."

That's what Esperanza needed to hear: Legs was going to be fine, no matter what. He was entrusting her safety to Havelock, and she couldn't be in better hands. *Not even mine.* He slipped into his leather coat and headed for the door. Legs suddenly leaped from the chair, bolted after him, grabbed him by the arm and forcefully spun him around. She searched his eyes for a moment and then embraced him, her arms tight around his neck, as if holding on for dear life.

She whispered in his ear, "You're my heart," and kissed his earlobe.

He shuddered. "And you're mine," he replied, and gently held her face in his sturdy hands and kissed the warm, salty tears streaming down her cheeks.

Chapter 20

Esperanza descended concrete stairs. Club Purgatory. He entered through a graffiti-covered door, and it was as if he'd been transported to another dimension.

The room was as cavernous as the Holland Tunnel. All the walls, floors and ceiling were painted shiny black. From overhead, spotlights fired harsh red and blue beams, creating pools of light. Hypnotic and sparse Euro-techno dance music pumped through the place. Purgatory's clientele—leather-bound people in hellish heaven—congregated around the bar. In between drinking and chatting, they fondled and spanked each other.

Esperanza stopped by the bar. Didn't see any folks of color hanging around the joint. Except for him. The long bar was plated, unpolished steel and shaped to look like a lightning bolt. The stools were smooth, bent pieces of iron. Everyone was dressed or stuffed into leather, chains, rubber, vinyl or latex. Combined with the music was a kinky fantasia of screams, moans, curses and demands. It all came from deep in the bowels of the club.

The hairs on the back of Esperanza's neck stood up. Considering his last experience with sexual-power types, this was the last place he wanted to be. Someone bumped into him. He turned to see an obese woman in a rubber bodysuit wav-

ing over the bartender. Huge breasts jutted from the two holes
cut into the chest area, and her nipples were pierced with
silver rings the size of quarters. She was way past forty and
had a ton of white makeup plastered on what had once been
a cherubic face. *If I ran into her in a dark alley, she'd scare
even me.* The corpulent woman took a drag from a cigarette
and tugged the dog chain she was holding. His eyes followed
the chain until he saw a scrawny man in a leather jockstrap.
He was blindfolded, but crawled toward the woman like a
dog. Then he sat up, opened his mouth and stuck out his
tongue. His mistress stubbed the cigarette out on his *lengua.*

Esperanza closed his eyes for a moment. His nostrils
filled with the nauseating stench of cooked skin. *I gotta find
Lady Chen in a hurry. If I stay in this place for too long,
bad things are bound to happen.*

"Excuse me," Esperanza said to the hairy bartender. He
had on rubber overalls and green-tinted goggles. "Where's
the lounge?"

The bartender pointed, his bony fingers encased in silver
rings.

On the other side of the room were two enormous, scarlet doors. Esperanza pushed through the mass of bodies,
pulled the doors open. The screams and moans were clearer.
Listen to that. Jesus. How twisted is this place gonna get?
Esperanza hated to admit it, but he was uneasy. At any
other time, he probably would've found it fun exploring the
world of dominatrixes and slaves, masochists and sadists.
But not on this night.

He reluctantly made his way down a lengthy, tunnel-like
hall. The floor was made of rusted sewer grates, lit from underneath by intense white light.

He passed a row of rubber mummies. They lined one side
of the hall. Men were inside inflatable rubber suits, covered
from head to toe in bulging black, only two thin tubes jut-

ting out from hidden nostrils. Kind of looked like the Michelin Man spray-painted black. Esperanza felt like he'd stumbled onto the set of some bizarre sci-fi movie. A bald dominatrix, wearing strips of black electrical tape over her nipples, a metallic codpiece and knee-high combat boots, pranced up and down the line of rubber mummies, momentarily squeezing the tubes, cutting off their air supply. Esperanza tried to look away, but couldn't. He was too fascinated by the ritual he was witnessing.

Other slaves were dangling upside down, enclosed in leather body bags that reminded Esperanza of cocoons. Except he didn't expect something as lovely as a butterfly to emerge. *I thought I'd seen it all. Boy, was I wrong.*

He made a sharp left and suddenly found himself before an altar. *Lookit this. Candles, stained-glass windows and a six-foot statue of Jesus. The whole nine yards.*

Kneeling at the altar were five men, naked but for transparent vinyl thongs. Their hands were manacled behind their backs, and ball-gags were stuffed in their mouths. Two curvaceous women in latex nun costumes, faces covered by World War II–style gas masks, pranced around, roughly spanking the kneeling masochists' asses with wooden paddles, while several couples who were hidden by shadows eagerly watched the proceedings.

Past the nuns, Esperanza saw another doorway. He went through it and down another tunnel-like hallway. *Does this fucking maze ever end? No wonder they charge a hundred and fifty bucks to get in.*

Then a petite woman in a ruby hobble skirt appeared from nowhere. The latex fit snugly, from waist to ankles. She could take only tiny steps, like a geisha. Her matching leather corset, decorated with metal studs, gave her an exaggerated, hourglass figure. She quickly cut in front of Esperanza and grabbed him by the arm, feeling up his muscles.

"Powerful," she said lustfully. She licked her wrinkly lips and added, "Slap me."

"Get the fuck away from me," Esperanza said. He tried to push her away, but she had quite a strong grip and refused to let go.

"Slap me hard." He slapped her. And liked it. "More," she said. He slapped her again. Felt even better. She laughed. "That's all you got?" This time, Esperanza backhanded the woman across the mouth so hard, he sent her to the floor. She looked up at him and gave him a bloody smile of appreciation.

What am I doing? I'm enjoying this . . . What the fuck is wrong with me? What has Devona turned me into?

Shaken, Esperanza trotted down the corridor. *Gotta get outta here.* He made a right, stepped through yet another doorway. *Here we go again. Stay in control, Nick. Please.* This time, he found himself inside a medieval dungeon. Rough, gray cinderblock walls and a wooden torture rack in the shape of an X. Esperanza stopped, mesmerized. A slim, baby-faced woman dangled upside down, blindfolded and gagged with a scarf, her soft, naked body tightly tied in an elaborate, complicated web of knotted white cords. *She looks like a teenager.* Made him think of Alina. Plastic clothespins were clamped to the girl's labia and nipples. Esperanza shuddered as a dominatrix in a black, rubber bodysuit and thigh-high stiletto boots and a chainmail veil swung a bullwhip with relentless precision. There was a loud whack every time it connected with the girl's alabaster flesh. The thin strip of leather left scores of pink bruises. The girl let out deep groans. *Those aren't groans. They're screams. Just like I screamed. Except she's enjoying her pain.* Images of him being whipped by Devona flashed in his mind like some demented S & M music video.

Then he saw Devona hanging upside down while he ferociously whipped her. Except she laughed hysterically and said, "That's the best you can do? You're not man enough."

Esperanza's face twitched. He fought back the images from his mind. *Get out of this place, Nick. Get out before you lose it.*

Racing from the dungeon, down another long corridor, he finally found himself in a lounge. Several horseshoe-shaped booths were almost concealed by darkness. Only a few tiny candles provided a weak glow. He caught his breath as a river of sweat poured down his body. *I'm glad to finally get away from all that craziness. Just gotta relax. Take care of business.* Esperanza wiped his face with a hand-kerchief and surveyed the lounge. Cherry, padded vinyl walls and a circular bar at the center. Overhead monitors featured a video of a woman tied to a bed while several men urinated on her. Another clip was of a woman sticking her entire fist in and out of a man's rectum. All this while tranquil concer-tos softly spilled from tiny speakers. *What if my video suddenly pops up on those screens? Mistress Love fucking me in the ass. This crowd would think I fit right in. Maybe I do. . . .*

He spotted Lady Chen at one of the booths. She saw him and enthusiastically waved him over. Esperanza was amazed at her metamorphosis. Lady Chen had donned a latex nurse's outfit, her face was covered in Kabuki style makeup and she wore a fiery, waist-length wig. Next to her was an androgy-nous guy with a Mohawk of metal spikes protruding from the top of his head. He sported enough piercings and elabo-rate tattoos to make Marilyn Manson envious.

Esperanza gave Lady Chen a peck on the mouth. "Good to see you, doll," he said. "Nice place. Fun for the whole family." He sat down beside her.

"This was the only place Rudeboy was willing to meet."

Rudeboy raised his gleaming eyebrows. The hairs had

been plucked and "replaced" with miniature, red-eyed-skull piercings. A three-inch spike impaled his septum, and a bunch of rings hooked into his bottom lip. "I hear you have a problem," he said. "With Rybak and Mistress Love." Rudeboy's body movements were edgy. His voice was supple and soft. He sported a rubber vest with heavy buckles.

"That's one way of putting it," Esperanza said.

"Rudeboy says Rybak and Devona aren't the one's you should be worried about." Lady Chen placed her hand on Esperanza's knee, and as she spoke, she seductively stroked his thigh. He didn't stop her.

"Who then?"

"His name is Bishop." Rudeboy showed a hint of repulsion. He took a sip of his beer, then stared at Esperanza with haunted, pale blue eyes. "Have you ever wondered, Mister Esperanza, about the nature of evil?"

The dank attic of Bishop's Bridgehampton, Long Island, house was lit by a single, bare, overhead light bulb. On a blood-stained, dirty mattress, among cardboard boxes filled with old clothes, was Alina. She was hog-tied. Gagged with a balled sock. Alina was naked and shivering. Looking up, through spirals of reddish brown hair, her eyes were hot with raw hatred.

Bishop stepped out from the darkness. He carried a large plastic bucket filled with water and ice. Shirtless, his whitish skin seemed to glow. On his sagging chest, underneath silver clumps of hair, there was a tattoo that read. GOD SAVE THE QUEEN.

"Hello, my little one," he said, and tapped the light bulb so it swayed back and forth, throwing shadows on the walls. Bishop smiled. He enjoyed the cheap, dramatic effect.

He placed the bucket on the floor, crouched and reached out to caress Alina's face. She tried to squirm away, but her bindings tightened every time she moved. Bishop pulled the saliva-soaked sock from her mouth. She gasped for air.

"Better, luv?" he asked.

"Go to hell, muthafucka. *Lo juro. Te voy matar.*"

"Is that a bloody fact? You think you'll get the chance to kill me? Idealistic, aren't we?" Bishop admired Alina. *She's a tough little tart.* Tough as he'd ever encountered. She didn't understand, though, that the harder she fought, the more it exacerbated her agony. She was giving Bishop endless amounts of pleasure. Her unflagging rebelliousness was the only thing keeping her alive.

Bishop reached into his pocket and produced a chocolate candy bar. Alina suddenly looked less resilient. She licked her parched lips, anxious for sustenance. Bishop fed her pieces of chocolate, and Alina hungrily consumed them, barely bothering to chew.

"By the way," Bishop said, lighting a cigarette, "do you have an aunt named Magaly Rivera?"

There was a glint of recognition in Alina's eyes. "Her name's Legs."

"Her boyfriend . . . his name is Nicholas Esperanza. He's searching for you."

"Now it's on, you fuckin' bastid. Nick ain't no joke. He's gonna fuck you up." Alina was filled with bravado again.

"That may be," he said. "But I'm going to make sure he never finds you." Alina smelled rank. She hadn't been bathed in days. Bishop was aroused by the musky odors, though. Blood. Urine. Sweat. Dirty little whore.

With the back of his hand, Bishop stroked her cheek, and Alina ferociously sunk her teeth into the skin between his thumb and forefinger. Bishop smirked, withstanding the pain for a long moment. With his other hand, he pinched Alina's nostrils shut. Unable to breathe with her mouth clamped shut, she finally let go. He pulled his hand away and held it up to the light, rotating it back and forth, curiously inspecting the damage. Blood droplets oozed from Alina's teeth marks. *Vicious cunt.* She was getting him very excited.

"You're like a stray dog," he said, then sucked the blood from his hand. It was salty and sweet. "Biting the hand that feeds you."

"Fuck you."

"Don't worry. That's on the menu. Your arse is mine," he said, "as always." Bishop stood, removed his wide, leather belt from his trousers and folded it in a loop. "But first, you must be disciplined." Bishop wasn't one for whips, or torture racks, or any of the other elaborate S & M accoutrements Devona and Rybak were so fond of. He preferred to keep things simple. Whatever was at hand would suffice.

Burning cigarette drooping from the corner of his mouth, Bishop beat Alina, and she screamed and cursed, but refused to shed a tear. Bishop didn't show even the remotest hint of emotion as he struck Alina until she was covered with swelling welts. Then he lay down next to her and whispered in her ear. "Tell me you love me," he said while pawing her wounded, lissome body.

"Fuck you."

"Have it your way." Bishop quickly got on his feet, grabbed the bucket and dumped the freezing water on her. She gasped for air between screams, her body going into spasms. Bishop was hard now. He unzipped his pants and touched himself, eager and ready to pleasure Alina while she was still in a state of shock. She was crying, finally.

Now she was ready for him.

Esperanza asked Lady Chen if she didn't mind excusing herself while he spoke with Rudeboy. He believed that the less she knew about what was going on, the better for her. Lady Chen said she'd cruise the scene for a while. Maybe she and Esperanza could hook up later and play? *On any other night* . . .

"I encountered Bishop sixteen years ago," Rudeboy said. "I was a fifteen-year-old rent boy, working the Deuce." Under all the S & M posturing, there seemed to be a well of vulnerability waiting to spill over. "He picked me up, offered me a lot of cash and smack to go back to his house. Wanted to do a stag film."

"You remember where the house was?"

"Maybe Long Island. Or Connecticut. Some ritzy suburb. Don't know for sure."

Esperanza sipped his seltzer, for a moment lost in the sound of fizzing water and clinking ice. "What happened?"

"After I was pumped fulla heroin, we went to the bedroom." Rudeboy leaned forward. His voice faltered. "There were a boy and a girl there, much younger than me, maybe eight or nine, all doped up. Bishop wanted me to have sex with them and with some older guy."

Esperanza suddenly thought about the kids in those photos at Mark's office, the emotional scars that they must've ended up carrying for the rest of their lives. *If there was a rest of their lives.*

"Do you know the other man's name?"

"No. Just one of Bishop's sicko friends." Rudeboy tapped his fingers on the tabletop. His black nails were like talons that could rip your throat open. There were winding tattoos of barbed wire and inked-in droplets of blood running up his strapping arms. "Anyway, the cameraman, Ernie, and his assistant show up and flip out when they find out they're going to be shooting kiddie porn. Ernie says, 'I ain't doin' it.' Bishop puts a gun to Ernie's head, so Ernie filmed it, of course. Later on, Bishop took me to his room and . . . did horrible things."

"Did Rybak work for Bishop back then?"

"Not that I'm aware of."

"Is Rybak into kids?"

He shrugged and leaned back. "Can't tell you for sure, but I don't believe so."

"He just enjoys torturing people," Esperanza said, pushing back rising anger. *Get a grip. Stay focused.*

Rudeboy smirked, and for a moment reminded Esperanza of that sneering gargoyle on the ledge of the building across the street from his. "His wife, Mistress Love, got him into that. He was a natural."

"How do you know all of this?"

"I've been into the S & M scene for years. Mistress Love was a very popular domme—for those into extreme pain. But after she hooked up with Rybak, she became something more . . . something scary. Suddenly she lost all sense of control. Forgot about boundaries. She and Rybak still make the rounds from time to time, even though there are many places they're no longer welcome. There have been rumors. Whispers in the night." Rudeboy held up his beer bottle. "Bishop's supposedly a trafficker. His commodity is innocence." Rudeboy guzzled the rest of his beer and belched, then wiped his mouth with the back of his hand. Esperanza noticed there were several jagged scars on his wrist and inner forearm. *I wonder how many times Rudeboy has tried to commit suicide.* "I want to make something very clear, Mister Esperanza." Rudeboy glanced around at the other pain aficionados. "Those of us who are into dispensing and receiving pain? We do it by choice. We do it because it gives us great pleasure. We have nothing in common with monsters like Bishop."

"Is Bishop his real name?"

"I doubt it," Rudeboy said. "The only thing I can tell you is that he's a Limey. A low-class, Cockney gangster."

"Any idea how I might be able to locate him?"

"No," Rudeboy said. "It's like trying to find a ghost."

"Anything concrete you can give me?"

"I can tell you where to find Ernie the cameraman. He knew Bishop back then. Maybe he still does."

"How come you remember Ernie so well?"

"He's a big time porn director named Jake Hardon," Rudeboy said. "And his camera assistant is now Giorgio Amore, the world's most famous male porn star."

Chapter 21

At the edge of an elaborate bedroom set, in the vast film and video production studio in midtown Manhattan, Esperanza relaxed in a canvas director's chair. He was amazed to be watching Giorgio, the legendary porn star, in all his naked glory. Giorgio was doing what he did best: kneeling on a king-size circular bed, banging the hell out of his voluptuous Brazilian co-star, Nina. A tiny video crew observed the salacious performance with professional detachment.

Giorgio was a blond beefcake and spectacularly endowed. He'd become internationally famous because he was one of the few male porn actors who was genuinely passionate about his work. He took tremendous joy in pleasuring his co-stars, and was actually exciting to watch. He was popular among women, straight men and gay men. Esperanza remembered being in a video store once where two black women were singing Giorgio's praises. They talked about how he was the only white man they didn't mind watching sex up a sista. They thought he was a straight-up hottie.

Esperanza was also a fan. Giorgio was the only male porn star whose D.V.D.'s Esperanza purchased. He was turned on by Giorgio's passionate ways. While most male porn stars were simply a large penis attached to a body, Giorgio was in a league of his own. He took his time, constantly talked to the women, touched and licked them like they were the most precious things on earth. Legs got her lust on every time she watched Giorgio do his thing, and it was worth the price of his D.V.D.'s.

The director, Jake Hardon, was busy directing, as well as shooting first camera. This was to be the latest opus in his long-running *Bootie Sex* series. Hardon was a whirlwind of energy. Middle-aged. A bit chunky. Khakis, plaid shirt and tinted, tortoise-shell glasses. He was considered the Spielberg of the adult-film industry.

"Stick in it slowly, Giorgio," Jake ordered.

Giorgio decelerated his rhythm as he thrust his cock in and out of Nina's gaping rectum. Busty Nina, who had caramel skin and short, ruby hair, giggled and groaned in delight, urging Giorgio on. The blond star, awash in soft, amber light, tenderly ran his fingers down her arched back, then slapped her fleshy ass several times.

"That's it, Nina," Jake said with whimsical enthusiasm. "Spread those cheeks some more. Just like that. Beautiful."

Watching Nina gyrate those hips, hearing her talk dirty in her Portuguese-accented English, smelling her sex scent and rose perfume, all made Esperanza's head swoon. *Damn, she's hot. Built for sex. Giorgio's workin' Nina like there's no tomorrow. Where do they find these girls?*

Esperanza watched them shoot for about twenty minutes, until the crew broke for lunch. He kept his coat on his lap because he had an erection. *Some things you just can't control.*

Jake and Giorgio invited Esperanza to join them for lunch. He could tell by their puzzled expressions, that they were wondering what an ex-N.Y.P.D. homicide detective wanted to talk to them about.

Behind his antique desk, Jake hungrily munched on a crisp Caesar salad. Giorgio, wearing a silk robe, sat on a blue, velvet love seat next to Esperanza. Watching the way Giorgio wolfed down his steak sandwich dripping with sautéed onions and barbecue sauce, Esperanza figured that making porn was hard work indeed.

Esperanza looked around. The office walls were covered with cork from floor to ceiling, and there were Polaroid snapshots of hot, young and very naked women of every size and color. All potential starlets for Jake Hardon Video Productions. By the endless number of photos, you'd think one of every kind of babe in America wanted to become a porn star. *Women like them must be making the feminists really happy.*

Lady Chen hadn't been exaggerating when she said she knew everybody in the sex business. She'd easily set up this meeting with Jake and Giorgio, the two men who Bishop had forced at gunpoint to film that kiddie-porn reel nearly twenty years ago.

Esperanza told Jake and Giorgio the reason he was there was to talk to them about Bishop. The blood drained from their faces, and their chipper moods turned dismal. They stopped eating. They were obviously reluctant.

"Look, gentlemen," he said. He hoped they sensed his urgency. *If not, I'm gonna make them.* "My niece's life depends on whatever information you can provide me."

"Rumors." Jake dabbed the corners of his thin lips with a paper napkin.

"Beats a blank," Esperanza said with a shrug of his shoulders. *C'mon, spit it out already.*

Jake hesitated and then dramatically dropped his fork in the nearly empty aluminum food container. "I hear he's connected to some very influential, very twisted individuals."

"And?"

Bishop might be more connected than I thought. That would explain those I.A.B. assholes tryin' to shake me down.

"Judges. Politicians," Giorgio said with a slight Italian

accent. "The richer they are, the more deviant they are." Giorgio had stunning aqua eyes and was square-jawed. Plenty of physical presence and a sunny disposition.

"Over the years," Jake said, "I've heard rumors. Bishop kidnaps children, buys them from pimps, whatever, you name it." He unwrapped a piece of gum. Shoved it in his mouth and chewed it for a moment. He vacillated again, seemingly disgusted by the words coming out of his mouth. "He shoots videos. Rents kids out."

Giorgio stared at Esperanza. "Bishop would've had us killed if we said anything to the cops. We hightailed it to L.A. right after that. Took almost ten years before we got the nerve to come back here."

"Giorgio and me—we make mainstream porn." Jake opened a bottle of sparkling water and took a sip. "That night, when Bishop made us film that . . . encounter? I still have nightmares every once in a while. What he put those kids through. I still wish I coulda said no, coulda done something to stop it. But when I looked into Bishop's eyes, I knew he'd pull the trigger."

"You were right about that," Esperanza said.

"Look, I'm gonna tell you something," Jake said. "But you didn't hear it from me." His voice cracked with nervousness. Then he did something that Esperanza would have thought impossible: He turned paler than he already was. "There's a company called Blue Orchid Productions. It's run by this lowlife, Ray Streiber. He makes 'craptacular' soft-core porn, for cable." Jake spit his gob of gum into the dented wastebasket beside him. "Word is, it's a front. Streiber supposedly shoots videos and handles all of Bishop's secret Web sites."

"What do you mean, 'secret Web sites'?"

"You can't find actual child-porn sites just by using a search engine and typing in a U.R.L.," Jake said. "It's a very tricky, complicated world out there in pedophile cyberspace. You gotta make contacts through chat rooms and newsgroups." Jake took a bent cigarette from the crumbled Marlboro box on the desk, started to light it, then changed his mind.

Esperanza produced his small notebook and started taking notes.

"These guys who trade and sell kiddie porn," Jake continued. "They use all kinds of sophisticated encryptions. Proxies. Web sites that are in existence for only a few hours at a time."

"Streiber works out of New York?" Esperanza wanted to keep things in the real world, not cyberspace.

"Yeah," Giorgio said. He removed the plastic lid from a cup of steaming cappuccino, then took in the aroma like it was an expensive glass of wine. "You can find his production company in the phone book."

This puts me a step closer. I hope there's a straight line between Streiber and Bishop. I can't afford to waste any more time.

"That night at Bishop's," Esperanza said. "The other man there—do you remember his name?"

Jake thought about it for a moment. "It was odd-sounding."

"Nemec," Giorgio said. "I think his name was Nemec."

Miller had some further explaining to do. *It's not a coincidence that Nemec worked for Bishop.* Miller was rich and connected. Esperanza couldn't just show up at his office and start slapping him around. *I'll end up in jail.* So Esperanza needed to do *mucho* bluffing to break Miller. Esperanza thought about calling Batiato and Creiger, but then they'd take over and leave him out of the loop. He needed to talk to Miller first. Alone.

Esperanza stepped off the elevator into Miller Properties' Midtown offices. The waiting area was done up in shiny aluminum and smoked glass. The receptionist sat behind a desk that looked something like a flying saucer. She was Hispanic milk chocolate, hair bleached blinding platinum. Blue contacts. Like she was going to actually pass or something.

"Buenas," he said, resting one elbow on the desk, and gave her his best smile.

"How can I help you?"

"Tu nombre es Rosalita, verdad?" La recepcionista lit up like Esperanza was going to ask her out on a date. "I'm here to see Simon Miller. I'm the police. Remember me from the other day?"

"Sure." Rosalita beamed. She had a nasal Brooklyn accent. "You're a hard one to forget. Your name again?"

"Detective Esperanza."

Hell, Killian's already accused me of impersonating an officer. Why not take it to the full extent?

Two minutes later, Jenna, Miller's personal assistant, appeared. The scrawny redhead didn't look too happy about Esperanza's unannounced visit. She thought the police were done with speaking to Miller. Esperanza explained that some new leads had come up and he needed additional information from her boss regarding the murder of Nemec Wozak.

"Mister Miller is," Jenna said, "on an extended vacation."

What a surprise. "I have to speak with him immediately," Esperanza said, sounding as official as he used to. "This is an urgent police matter."

"We can't reach him. Not at this time." She had a smarmy attitude, and Esperanza could tell she wasn't going to budge. "If you leave your number, when he checks in, I'll make sure he gets the message."

"He's the C.E.O. of the company and you have no way of reaching him?"

She pushed her short hair behind her ear. Didn't answer.

Esperanza decided to take a chance. He took a step forward so he towered over Jenna. "We can do this the easy way or the hard way. I'd hate to have to drag you to the precinct."

Jenna wasn't buying it. Probably remembered that when Esperanza and Santos had come to see Miller a couple of days ago, Santos was the actual detective.

"Do you have some kind of warrant?"

Silence from Esperanza.

"May I see your badge, please?"

More silence.

"Please leave, sir," Jenna said, "or I'll call security and have you escorted out."

What a bust with Miller's assistant. Esperanza weaved between cabs and delivery trucks as they honked their horns, like noon gridlock was going to move any faster. *Uppity bitch.* On vacation. All that bit of info did was confirm that Miller was somehow involved in Bishop's child-porn ring. *What if Miller is Bishop?* He'd fax a picture to Jake and Giorgio, and see. Esperanza pulled out his cell and called Mark. *Don't bust my balls this time, hermanito.*

Esperanza stopped by a hotdog stand. Hadn't eaten all day.

"I need you to do me a solid," he said to Mark. "Get me some financial records for Simon Miller of Miller Properties." He took in the images before him. It was a funny thing about Manhattan. All these modern, grandiose towers reaching up to the clouds, surrounded on the ground by sprawling plazas and elaborate fountains. Yet there were always old-fashioned, aluminum hotdog stands with big yellow umbrellas on almost every corner. "Also, I need you to check the sex-offenders database for a Raymond Streiber. And I need the information fast."

"Are you crazy?" Mark said. "I can't do that."

"You're F.B.I. You can do whatever you want these days."

"Only when it involves possible terrorist activities. How come you can't get this info through Santos?"

"Let me get a dog with mustard and sauerkraut," Esperanza said to the old dude wearing a parka and a Mets cap. Then he continued speaking to Mark. "After the shooting at Sueño Latino, Captain Killian cut me outta the loop."

Esperanza paid for his steaming hotdog and took a huge bite. Bun was nice and soft. Onions flavorful. The dog juicy. Solid, healthy cop's lunch. *Just what I need.*

"I'll see what I can do," Mark said, sounding exasperated.

"*Gracia', hermanito,*" Esperanza said, chewing. "I owe you big-time."

Chapter 22

Long Island City refused to be gentrified. Even with a couple of new, vainglorious condos at the waterfront, the neighborhood was still dominated by working-class Russians, Puerto Ricans, Greeks, Chinese and Dominicans. It remained largely an area filled with factories and warehouses. Not for long. New York was quickly becoming a city for the upper middle class and the rich.

Esperanza sat behind the wheel of the Saturn across from a two-story storefront. It was night. Not a single pedestrian. Barely a car drove by. The storefront Esperanza was watching had a sign done in simple black letters: BLUE ORCHID PRODUCTIONS.

At around two, Raymond Streiber emerged from his company's production office. He pulled down a metal gate. It made noise like it hadn't been oiled in years. Carrying a leather shoulder bag, Streiber got into a dented Toyota, which, clearly, had seen better days.

A few hours earlier, Esperanza broke into Streiber's one-bedroom apartment. Thoroughly searched it. Found nothing incriminating. The only thing he could be arrested for was for being a slob. There was no computer. No photos, D.V.D.'s or videotapes. *That makes me even more suspicious.* Any single male was going to have at least a couple of porn

D.V.D.'s or stroke mags at his crib. Yet Streiber, who *produced* soft-core porn, didn't own a V.C.R. or D.V.D. player.

Esperanza wanted to break into Streiber's office. *But that ain't possible. No way I'm getting through that roll-down gate.* Besides, the joint was wired with an alarm system. He'd have to get his information the old-fashioned way.

Streiber's car choked and whined. The engine finally came to life as the car's muffler spewed a toxic cloud of smoke. The Toyota sputtered, then pulled out of the parking spot. Esperanza followed.

"I want you," Rybak said, "to bring his girlfriend to us."

He was watching Hightower in the rearview mirror.

They were in Rybak's BMW. Devona was in the front passenger seat, next to her husband. Mangineli was in the back, with Hightower. Devona didn't like the I.A.B. cops. Didn't trust them. Felt they were a couple of losers who'd sell each other out in a second if they ever got caught in their shady dealings. The car was parked on Tenth Avenue, in Midtown, in front of one of those storage warehouses. The building was painted bright yellow and blue.

"Why don't *you guys* snatch her?" Hightower said.

Devona shifted around so she could look into their eyes.

"Are you paid to ask questions?" She already argued with Rybak about it, but he insisted that Mangineli and Hightower do the job. Said he trusted Hightower to get it done right. They'd handle Esperanza.

Hightower loosened his tie. Unbuttoned the top of his shirt. He never looked directly at Devona.

Maybe he thinks he'll turn to stone.

"No, but—" Hightower said.

"Just do what you're told," Devona said. "We're going to have a little fun with this Legs chick, before we have Esperanza join us."

"This is a whole different thing you're asking," Mangineli

said. He was the opposite of his partner. Couldn't stop staring into Mistress Love's eyes. "Kidnapping don't come cheap, doll."

Without turning around, Rybak tossed a fat envelope over his shoulder.

"How's that for an incentive?" Devona tilted her head, tapped her chin with her index finger. Had just gotten her nails done. They were painted shiny silver and were sharp as claws.

Hightower whistled as he ran his fingers along the crisp stack of C-notes.

"You guys are serious."

"Dead," Rybak said.

"Why the hoopla?" Hightower said, passing the envelope to Mangineli, who quickly began to count the cash. "Why not just ice Esperanza and be done with it?"

That's what Rybak wanted to do. But since he'd pulled a fast one on Devona by sending the two hitters to Sueño Latino, she wasn't having it. There was going to be a party with Esperanza before they killed him. Big party. Besides, they also planned to get some ransom money from the wealthy ex-detective. He knew what they'd do to his woman, so he'd pay a lot for her safe return.

Devona rolled her eyes. "You guys lack imagination," she said, taking off her fur cap and shaking out her rain of fiery hair. "Rybak and I like to have a little fun while we work."

Hightower took the envelope back from Mangineli, stuffed it in the pocket of his coat. "We'll handle it."

"Good for you. And don't hurt a hair on her." Devona's eyes narrowed, and her tone got sexier. "That'll be my pleasure."

On the playground at Union Square Park, groups of well-bundled children frolicked on swings and slides. They ran, chased, dodged and jumped, while mothers huddled together on wooden benches chatting and drinking hot tea and lattes, keeping one eye on the little ones enjoying the bright winter sun.

Esperanza sat on a bench pretending to read a newspaper. *Old school stake-out.*

Streiber lounged on another bench inside the playground, but away from the mothers, enjoying a hefty pastrami hero dripping with yellow mustard as he watched the kids play. Streiber was a rangy man with a crew cut and a slight limp. Looked ridiculous in a spiffy, maroon jogging suit and shiny cowboy boots and cheap overcoat. There was a constant smile on his craggy face. It gave Esperanza the creeps. A boy, around seven years old, with curly tangerine hair and freckles, kicked a soccer ball and then chased after it. The ball rolled by Streiber, and he stuck out his pointy boot and stopped it. Streiber reached down and picked up the ball, and the boy ran over. Streiber said something to him, handed him the ball and mussed the boy's hair. The boy smiled, and Streiber grinned happily and waved good-bye. Then he went back to his sandwich.

Esperanza cringed at the thought of what Streiber was fantasizing about doing to that kid. He wondered what drove men like him to commit such vile acts. There was a lot of kinky shit that people were into, a variety of sexual fetishes that included everything from "golden showers" to "fisting" to role-playing to spanking to tickling to swinging. Though Esperanza wasn't into any of that heavy-duty stuff, he simply shrugged it off as people's weird erotic fixations. *Who am I fuckin' kidding? I'm into more weird shit than I could've ever realized. I thought I'd explored all my fantasies, then I discover I have a bunch of new ones. Some I'd never want to admit to.* Whatever consenting adults did in the privacy of their bedrooms was cool. Lord knows, he and Legs could get their freak on every once in a while. Had experimented with a little bondage. Often used toys. Attended a couple of swing parties. Even indulged in a few three-somes, in which Legs explored her bi curiosity.

But what Bishop and Streiber and their crew were into was vile.

Don't try and figure out the hearts of darkness. Never could when I was cop, certainly can't now. Maybe there are no reasons. Maybe it's simply a matter of living, breathing evil.

Mark appeared out of nowhere, plopped down next to Esperanza, who instinctively raised his hands, as if to block a blow.

"Easy," Mark said.

"Don't sneak up on me like that," Esperanza said. "You could get hurt."

"Little jumpy, aren't we?"

Mark looked a hundred percent Fed in his gray overcoat, blue suit, white shirt and striped-red-and-blue tie. Mark followed his brother's gaze and noticed Streiber, the lone adult male in the playground.

"Streiber."

"Yep. Been tailing the little prick all day. He bought some computer equipment this morning, and that was it. Didn't meet with anyone." The afternoon sun glared off the windows of the building across the street, making it hard to see. Esperanza put on a pair of aviator sunglasses. "I checked his apartment. Nothing."

Mark raised an eyebrow and then shook his head. "Must be nice not having to deal with minor inconveniences like search warrants."

Esperanza's attention was on Streiber, but he quickly filled his brother in on the details involving Miller, Nemec and now Streiber. *I'm close to ending this. I'm getting to Bishop through Streiber. No matter what it takes.*

"The link between these guys," Mark said. "It's starting to make sense."

"You got something for me?"

"Yeah. But this is the last time, bro'." Mark pulled a folded manila envelope from his coat pocket. A skateboarder zipped by, did a gravity-defying spin, then disappeared.

"Fair enough." Esperanza took the envelope, pulled out stapled sheets of paper.

"Streiber's rap sheet. And Miller's financials," Mark said. "Miller's clean as a whistle."

"There might be something in the report you missed. I assume Streiber ain't so clean."

"Did time in eighty-six for soliciting sex from a minor while volunteering as a camp counselor. Arrested again in ninety for sale and possession of child pornography. Did a three-year stint at Sing Sing."

Streiber finished his lunch. He ripped open a moist towelette, wiped his hands and mouth. Then leaned back and relaxed, hands interlocked behind his head. The king surveying his kingdom. A kingdom of potential victims.

"What else?"

"No relatives." Mark stuffed his hands in his coat pockets and stared at the impressive buildings surrounding the block-long park. "Makes a living doing soft-core. A loner."

"Anything on Bishop?"

"Nothing," Mark said. "Obviously you're onto something as far as a kiddie-porn ring is concerned, so I'm going to have to pass this information on to Innocent Images." Mark looked back at Esperanza. "Sorry."

"Do whatever you gotta do," Esperanza said, putting the reports back in the envelope. "By the time the Feds start moving, Bishop and his crew will be buried."

"You became a cop to *uphold* the law."

"I ain't a cop no more."

Mark stayed silent for a moment, furrowed his eyebrows. "You fuckin' kill me, Nick. Sometimes I wonder—"

"Imagine your sons at your neighborhood playground and someone like Streiber watching. And waiting."

Nostrils flaring, Mark's eyes bore into Esperanza. "I'm quite aware of what men like Streiber are capable of." Mark's cheeks turned red. "But I'm not going to become a criminal just like them."

Streiber got up and shuffled out of the playground. "Gotta go." Esperanza slapped Mark on the back and went in pursuit of his own prey.

Chapter 23

Esperanza was seeing through the darkness. With his Rigel Tactical Night Vision Binoculars, he studied Streiber, who was in his car, parked in front of a warehouse. They were near the waterfront in Long Island City. *I'm glad I've kept up on the latest gadgets.* The image was bright green and sharp. Esperanza was impressed with how much night-vision optics had improved since he was a SEAL. It was one AM on a shadowy street, and Esperanza could see as if it were noon.

Streiber had been parked there for twenty minutes. Making calls on his cell. *This prick is up to something. My patience is about to pay off.*

Esperanza glanced in the rearview mirror of his Saturn. Headlights creeping up. He immediately ducked, and waited for the vehicle to pass. Then looked through the binoculars again and saw a black cargo van pull up behind Streiber's car.

Streiber got out, opened the trunk and hauled out three large duffel bags. Behind the wheel of the van was a thug in a leather coat. He turned off the engine, hopped out and shook Streiber's hand.

The thug pulled open the side door of the van. A second man stepped out. He was heavyset and had a buzz cut and stooped shoulders. Bulbous, frog-like eyes. Had on a goose-down parka. He held the hand of a boy, who appeared to be around ten years old. The boy wore a bubble jacket over pajamas. Bunny slippers. Though he was an older kid, he clutched a teddy bear and sucked his thumb. His hair was a mess of curls, and his eyes were half closed. The boy dragged behind the man as if in a daze.

Streiber and his two friends talked for a moment, then took the bags and the boy, and disappeared into the warehouse.

Esperanza lowered the binoculars. *I know what's about to go down. I got no choice but to intervene.*

His cell vibrated, startling him.

"Yeah?"

"It's me," Legs said.

"Not a good time."

"I was looking through Miller's financial records. Found something."

"Tell me. Quickly."

"Miller's not much of a philanthropist."

Esperanza hated it when Legs didn't get immediately to the point. "So?"

"In all of his financial records, there was only a single charitable donation," Legs said, sounding more excited. "Five grand to the Dream Foundation."

"Spit it out, *mami.*"

"I did some checking," she said. There was the sound of running water in the background. "The Dream Foundation is a non-profit organization. One of its affiliates is . . . The Sanctuary."

"He's a Limey . . ." Rudeboy's voice echoed in Esperanza's mind.

All this time, he was right under his nose. It couldn't be a coincidence. "Alladice," he muttered.

He heard Legs catch her breath. "The one who runs The Sanctuary, right?"

"Yeah." Esperanza's face got hot, and his jaw tightened. "I think he's Bishop."

"Holy shit."

"Hang tight, *negra*," Esperanza said. "I have to take care of something." Clicked off his cell.

Esperanza firmly clutched the steering wheel. Wanted to rip it out of the dashboard. He'd sat with Alladice, chatted and made jokes, listened to his speeches about disenfranchised youth. *Alina could've been in the next room, for all I know.* Had watched Alladice interact with those runaways, who looked up to him like a father figure. A savior. The wonderful and selfless program director. Esperanza had been played big-time. *I should've had Alladice thoroughly checked out. There might've been a clue in his background. I could've avoided all the shit that went down. Desire wouldn't be dead. I would've never been abducted by Devona and Rybak ... and gotten my mind and body fucked. Legs wouldn't be in mourning over Maria. Maybe if I would've taken this shit seriously since day one, I could've avoided a lot of pain and heartache. Maybe I ain't the man I used to be.* Esperanza pushed the rage back. No more games. No more mistakes. The enemy has a face now. He drew his gun from his holster, pulled the slide back and made sure it was ready to fire.

Stay cool. Save the boy first. Then have a chat with Streiber. I'm getting Alina back. Then I'm gonna burn Bishop's organization to the fucking ground.

The lock of the warehouse's back door was relatively easy to pick. Esperanza slipped inside the building. He left the binoculars in the car. Only thing he wanted to carry was his gun. It was tough maneuvering in the darkness. He finally saw a doorway. Harsh light oozed from underneath. He crouched and quietly opened the door. In an immense room, surrounded by large crates and stacked boxes, there was a makeshift "set" of a boy's room, brightly lit by floods. They had a couple of wooden wall flats painted sky blue, and on them hung posters of cartoon characters. The blond boy was on the single bed, in a fetal position, his head resting on the chubby man's lap. The chubby man was shirtless and stroked the boy's hair. On a tripod was a digital video camera, which was connected to a laptop computer sitting on a card table. Streiber was at the laptop, plugging in wires. Then he began working the keyboard.

"Start getting ready, Greg," Streiber said to the chubby man. "Live Webcast kicks off in ten minutes." Like it was a fun-filled sports event.

A thug leaned against a stack of crates, absentmindedly playing with an unlit cigarette. With his pockmarked face, bushy eyebrows and slicked-back hair, he might as well have been wearing a sign that said: TOUGH GUY. The man stroked the butt of his snub-nose revolver. It was in a holster clipped to the belt of his jeans. He tugged on the collar of his sweater. "Ray," he said, "I'm gonna go get coffee."

"Not now, Mario," Streiber said. "Bishop pays you for security."

Esperanza was crouched behind a stack of crates, watching. When he heard the name Bishop, his stomach churned. *I can't believe they're not only gonna videotape a molestation, they're gonna broadcast it live over the Internet.*

"Like anybody knows we're here." Mario lit his cigarette. Blew sloppy smoke rings into the air.

Streiber folded his arms across his puny chest. "You wanna put out that fuckin' cigarette? Give me a hand?"

Mario rolled his eyes. Dropped the cigarette to the floor and ground it out with the sole of his brown wingtip. *Probably the same thing he wants to do to Streiber.* Mario was about to go help Streiber when Esperanza noiselessly leaned over a crate and aimed his 9-millimeter at the bodyguard.

Esperanza cocked the hammer of the automatic.

Mario spun around. He must've been channeling Doc Holiday because he foolishly attempted to quick-draw his .38. His fingers had barely touched the gun when Esperanza blasted him. Mario's throat burst in a splash of scarlet as a hollow-point bullet tore into him. He clutched at his missing throat and crumbled to the floor.

Streiber and Greg froze, eyes wide, mouths agape. Esperanza quickly moved toward the set, his weapon steadily pointed at the chubby, frog-eyed man.

"Step away from the boy," Esperanza said.

Greg leaped to his feet and backed away, his gelatinous flesh bouncing and shaking. He held up trembling hands, fingers spread wide open. "Wait, man, please don't hurt me." His voice was high-pitched and annoying. "They're forcing me to do this . . ."

Esperanza wasn't in the mood for tall tales. *How many kids has he raped? How many kids has he emotionally crippled? Let's see how he likes being physically crippled.* Without taking his eyes off Greg's terrified face, Esperanza lowered the gun and shot him in the kneecaps. Steel shattered cartilage and bone, ripped through muscle and tendon. The pedophile was on the concrete floor, screeching and rolling around. There were two gaping holes where his knees used to be. *Now he can spend the rest of his days in a wheelchair.* The boy didn't even react to the violence. He just sat there, sucking his thumb, ghosts in his eyes. If he was that catatonic, Esperanza didn't even want to imagine how much he'd already been abused.

Streiber took advantage of Esperanza's momentary lapse of attention and tore out of there. For a guy with a bum leg, the man moved faster than Esperanza would've expected.

"Freeze," Esperanza yelled, and fired a warning shot into the air. He didn't want to kill Streiber. *Yet.* He needed information. Streiber vanished through a door. Esperanza raced after him.

Streiber dashed upstairs two steps at a time, Esperanza snapping at his heels. Esperanza heard him go through another door.

He stopped when he reached the fourth-floor landing. End of the line. It was the exit to the roof. Esperanza kicked the door open and stepped out into the night. The next thing he knew, Streiber slammed a three-foot metal pipe against his wrist, knocking the gun from his hand. Streiber swung at Esperanza's head with all his might, but Esperanza swiftly ducked, then came back up and rammed his left fist into the weasel's ribs. There was the sound of bone cracking, and Streiber cried out, dropped to one knee, and then toppled over. Esperanza picked up his gun, grabbed Streiber by his hair, heaved him up and jammed the barrel of his automatic under the child pornographer's chin.

"You ain't no cop," Streiber said. His shifty eyes were wild with pain and fear. "Who the fuck are you?"

"Your worst nightmare."

"What the fuck do you want from me?"

"Bishop."

In the darkness of the bedroom, Legs was curled up in bed, feigning sleep. She was tense. Heard the squeaking sound of the bedroom door opening. Two men entered the room. One of them was lofty and black, the other shorter and white. She could see their reflections in the vanity's mirror as they tiptoed toward her bed. They wore black trench coats and suits and ties and leather gloves. Looked an awful lot like detectives. Had to be Mangineli and Hightower, the two Internal Affairs cops Esperanza described in detail. They'd followed Legs around all day. They weren't very good at it. Legs had spotted them right way. Now they'd finally come for her.

Oh, my God. They're here to kill me. Calmate. Do as Havelock told you to.

She didn't move. Held her breath. The two men went to opposite sides of the bed. Mangineli clamped his hand around Legs's mouth. She struggled to break free, but they held her down. Then he shoved the barrel of a gun into her ribs, and she froze.

"Easy, sweetheart," Hightower said, and then whipped out a syringe from his jacket pocket. "We're going for a little ride."

Mangineli smelled of cheap cologne. Legs could make out his features a little better. He was smirking. "Your boyfriend should learn to mind his fucking business," he said. "Now you're both gonna end up floaters." Hightower was about to inject Legs when his hand froze in midair and his mouth dropped open in stunned silence. Mangineli's face turned into a knot as he wondered why his partner looked so shocked. "What is it?"

On Mangineli's forehead, there was the red dot of a laser sight.

"Don't move a fucking muscle," Hightower told his partner.

Havelock emerged from the walk-in closet, brandishing a compact submachine gun with a laser sight and a sound suppressor.

"My sentiments exactly," Havelock said. He was wearing a black crewneck sweater, black army pants and black combat boots. In the darkness, it was hard to see him. But you sure couldn't miss the glow of the laser.

Hightower and Mangineli were amateurs. While they were ineptly tailing Legs, Havelock was right behind them every step of the way.

"I got a gun in her ribs," Mangineli said.

"Then I suggest you drop it if you want to walk out of here alive."

Legs couldn't believe how completely calm Havelock sounded.

Mangineli cocked the hammer of his gun. Legs thought she was going to die right then and there. She couldn't breathe. Her heart raced out of control.

"No," Hightower shouted.

In the blink of an eye, one bullet pierced Mangineli's forehead and another hit Hightower square in the heart. Legs was splashed with droplets of blood, and the two rogue cops simultaneously fell dead on top of her.

In shock, Legs remained frozen with the two corpses on her lap.

Havelock stepped closer, his weapon still aimed.

"Move out of the way, Legs. Now!"

She pushed the heavy bodies away, scrambled out of the bed and rushed over to Havelock. There was blood all over her nightgown.

"Oh shit, oh shit." Legs trembled, as if wanting to shake off the specter of death.

"Chill," Havelock ordered. She got control of herself, took several deep breaths. "You okay?"

"Yeah." She wasn't, really. She thought she was going to puke, but she kept it in check. *Be strong. Be calm. You're okay. Havelock's here to protect you.*

She'd never look at Havelock the same way. Though she was aware of his past, his training, his work, she'd always known him as an affable, big-hearted brother. What she saw on this night was a soldier. How perfectly cool and collected he remained as he gunned down those two dirty cops. He didn't even seem to break a sweat. *Is this what Nick is really like, too?* The thought sent a chill crawling up her spine. She clutched her stomach and gagged.

With the machine pistol still aimed, Havelock carefully approached Mangineli and Hightower, then placed two fingers to each of their necks to check for a pulse. He turned, and looked at Legs and wagged his head.

"Too bad," Havelock said. "We're not gonna find out anything from these two. I sure hope Nick's having better luck."

Chapter 24

Dangling over the edge of the roof, Streiber wailed like a baby. Esperanza held him by his legs, ankles pinned underneath Esperanza's armpits. He'd kicked and punched and stomped Streiber, trying to get him to talk, but the rangy man was resilient. Seemed to be more afraid of Bishop. Esperanza decided to change his mind about that.

He caustically stared at Streiber. They were four flights up. There were no cars in the street, no people. Only the reaper, eagerly waiting.

"What's Bishop's real name?"

Streiber's face was streaked with blood. There was a gash on his cheek and an even bigger one on his forehead. Esperanza could see the white of his skull. "I don't know."

He jostled Streiber a couple of times, and Streiber let out an ear-piercing squeal. "Can you fly, motherfucker?"

"Please, I don't wanna die," Streiber said. Seemed like he was having an asthma attack. "Bishop's name is Rupert Alladice."

He jostled him again. Harder. "What does he do with the kids after he's finished with them?"

"Sells them off. Sometimes he . . . makes them disappear."

"There's a Puerto Rican girl named Alina. Used to be at The Sanctuary. Is she still alive?"

"Yes."

"Where's Alladice keeping her?"

"I don't know . . ."

Esperanza released Streiber's legs and caught him by his ankles before he could fall to his death. Streiber screamed. Called out for God and Jesus. Then he peed on himself. Urine ran down his stomach to his neck. By the wretched smell, Esperanza could tell he'd also defecated. *Who are you scared of now?*

"She's at Bishop's safe house." Between sobs, he spit out an address. It was a house in Bridgehampton, Long Island. Very upscale neighborhood. Whole other world from Long Island City, Queens. Sounded like the same house Rudeboy had been taken to.

Should I call the police, hand Streiber over to them, have them issue search warrants for Bishop's home? No. It'll take too long. Once Bishop knows Streiber is missing, he's gonna move quickly to clean his tracks. And eliminate Alina in the process.

He glared down at Streiber as his rage came to a full boil. The child pornographer was still begging for his life.

Does a sick creep like Streiber deserve to live? Do any of them? These pedophiles who rape and murder children for profit—shouldn't they pay the highest price?

Esperanza let go of Streiber's ankles.

Streiber shrieked as he plunged four stories. There was a loud thud as Streiber's head split open on impact with the concrete. He stared at Streiber's broken, twisted body, arms and legs askew, puddle of grim fluid forming around him.

Esperanza couldn't believe what he'd done. Yet at the moment, he felt no regret. No guilt. He was playing by Bishop's rules now. That meant only one thing: no mercy.

The Saturn flew across the Queensboro Bridge. Esperanza was on his way to a Manhattan hospital to drop off the kid. The boy was in the passenger seat, finishing a cup of hot chocolate, staring out the window like the outside world was totally foreign to him. Esperanza cautiously reached out and stroked his hair. Kid tensed up.

"It's gonna be okay, son," he said. "You're safe. Nobody's gonna hurt you anymore."

The boy turned and gazed at Esperanza with woeful eyes. "Can I go home to Mommy?"

"Yeah. You'll be home real soon."

The boy studied Esperanza for a moment. He seemed unsure whether or not he should continue talking. "Are you my guardian angel?"

"What?"

"Mommy always says that I got a guardian angel. To protect me from bad things."

Guardian angels don't murder people. Esperanza was shaken by the question. *How the hell do I answer?* "I'm no angel," he said, and affectionately squeezed the little boy's shoulder. "I'm a friend." Esperanza smiled brightly. "My name's Nick."

To his surprise, the boy also smiled, and his face transformed for a second. As if he'd suddenly rediscovered hope.

"My name's Bobby." Then he turned serious again, sighed, rested his head against Esperanza's arm and sucked his thumb.

The sight of shattered innocence was so heartbreaking, it brought tears to Esperanza's eyes.

Esperanza's cell phone vibrated. It was Havelock, who quickly filled him in on what went down with Hightower and Mangineli.

"Then I broke out," Havelock said. "Figured you'd need a hand. The cops could wait to talk to me later."

"I'm sure there's an A.P.B. out for the both of us now."

"I hated leavin' Legs in such a pinch."

"She can handle herself."

"Well, my brother, what's the plan?"

"I'm dropping off the kid, Bobby, at the emergency room. Get your hands on all the firepower you can and meet me down the block from Bishop's house."

Legs was wearing black sweatpants and an oversized T-shirt that read: PROUD TO BE PUERTO RICAN. In the breakfast nook, she sipped a steaming mug of green tea. She was rattled.

Death. Blood splattering from two bodies. She couldn't shake it off. She thought about Maria. Revenge wasn't what she expected. There was no gratification in it for her. Just emptiness. All Legs wanted—all she ever wanted—was for Esperanza to bring Alina home alive. Poor Abuela was consumed with anxiety. So was she.

Santos leaned against the counter, while Detective Batiato continued to interrogate Legs. Her and Esperanza's bedroom had been turned into a crime scene. Homicide detectives and Crime Scene Unit technicians moved around Mangineli's and Hightower's corpses. They took photographs, dusted for prints, collected other kinds of evidence Legs knew little about.

"I'm going to ask you once more," Batiato said. He stood over her. His breath smelled of acrid coffee and cigarettes. He was trying to intimidate her, but Legs wasn't even fazed. After what she'd experienced over the past few days, some overzealous cop wasn't going to scare her. "Do you know the whereabouts of Nicholas Esperanza and Havelock Walker?"

Legs folded her arms across her chest. "I told you a dozen times already. After Havelock called you, he split. He didn't give me his itinerary." Legs tried not to be irritated by the incessant squawking of police radios.

"Look, Miss Rivera, if you withhold information in a police investigation—"

"You're going to arrest me?" Legs stood up. Taller than

the detective even in her bare feet, she glared down at him. Legs was usually the image of sophistication and grace, but when pushed, the streets of El Barrio came out. She wasn't willing to take any shit from anybody. She had a hand on a hip and waved her index finger in Batiato's face. "Fuck you," she said. "Those men—those *police officers*—came into my house and tried to kill me, and you *dare* to threaten me? *Vete pal carajo.*"

Santos put his coffee cup down, came over and patted Batiato on the back. "Can you give us moment alone, detective?"

Batiato nodded and exited. Santos indicated toward the high-back chair at the sizeable oak table, and Legs sat down again. He sat opposite her, then slid his chair close, so no one could hear him. "This is difficult, *nena*. But it might be best if you told them what you know."

"I did, Anibal. I have no other information." Legs shook her head, her face twisted with resentment. "Grilling me like I'm a criminal." Over Santos's shoulder, through the open doorway, she saw E.M.S. personnel wheel out two body bags.

"They're only doing their job." Santos took her hand, gave it a squeeze. He spoke gently, almost tenderly. Legs was glad he was there. "Nicholas and Havelock are in a lot of trouble . . ."

"You're his friend," she said. "You're supposed to help him."

"That's what I'm trying to do."

Legs's eyes drilled into him. What he was saying wasn't good enough. Santos looked away. She could tell he was trying to figure out how to get her to talk. He should know that Esperanza and Havelock told her nothing. It was best that they kept her in the dark, so she wouldn't have to lie to the police. All she knew was, they most likely found out where Alina was being held and were on their way to rescue her. In the midst of her guilt, her bloody apartment, her fears, she felt a tiny bit glad. Glad that Esperanza was the man in her life. *No matter what, he's going to save Alina. I know it's going to be a tough road ahead for us. But we'll work it out. We'll get through this. Maybe we'll go away to Puerto Rico for a while, so we can put this madness behind us. I know it's going to be okay.*

"Are they gonna be arrested?" Legs said.

"There's a good chance of it," Santos said. "Take my advice. Get on the phone and call a lawyer."

An immense, two-story Victorian sat at the top of a hill on a sprawling piece of land. It was almost completely hidden by towering sycamore trees. The leafless branches reached to the sky like the hands of skeletons. There was thick, well-manicured shrubbery. The entire estate was surrounded by an imposing brick-and-wrought-iron fence.

Esperanza waited in his car, which was parked down the block. He kept his eyes glued to the gated entrance. No one had come in or out. He looked at his watch. *Where the hell's Havelock? He's taking too damn long. We have to get in there now.*

Headlights headed in Esperanza's direction.

They clicked off and on and then off again, remaining off. Esperanza clicked his headlights and off.

A black Range Rover pulled up and parked across the street. Esperanza hurried out and hustled over to Havelock, who climbed out of the big S.U.V.

Havelock sauntered to the back of his vehicle, and Esperanza followed. Havelock opened the rear door, pulled the zipper on a huge army duffel bag. Inside, there was a sawed-off shotgun. A Heckler & Koch MP5 submachine gun. A M1911 Colt handgun. Half a dozen 9-millimeter automatics. Flash grenades. Plenty of ammunition.

"You can still walk away, bro'," Esperanza said.

Havelock grabbed the sawed-off shotgun and began loading shot shells. "And let you have all the fun?" he said while pumping the shotgun. "No way."

Esperanza didn't smile, but he gave Havelock a hard slap on the shoulder. He grabbed the .45-caliber Colt. It was a cannon. Only seven bullets in the clip, but one was all you needed to take down even the most determined attacker. "Haven't used one of these in a long-ass time."

"How do you want to handle this?"

"Straight-up extraction," Esperanza said, slapping a clip into the .45. "Alina. And any other kids that might be in there. Every one else . . . take 'em out."

Havelock nodded. Esperanza was glad he'd be going into battle with his old friend by his side. He had no idea how many guns they might be facing, but between the two of them, and the firepower they had, they could take down a small army.

Esperanza put all his emotions in check. Emotion had no place in a firefight. Only instinct, experience and skill mattered.

He was no longer thinking like a cop. This wasn't about making a collar, about bringing in a suspect to be tried by a jury of his peers. This was a SEAL operation. They'd be fast, efficient and deadly.

Bishop, Rybak, Devona and anyone else inside that house wouldn't stand a chance.

Chapter 25

One of Bishop's guards patrolled the back of the huge Victorian. A strapping young man in a long leather coat. The guy was smoking a joint. Taking his duties casually. *Come a little closer.* He passed under a sycamore, stood there for a moment, taking long tokes. Smelled like primo weed. Sweet and pungent.

From behind the bodyguard, Esperanza dangled upside down, his legs hooked at the knee around a thick branch.

Esperanza reached out, grabbed the man by his hair, yanked his head back and, before the bodyguard could utter a sound, slit his throat with a switchblade.

With mounting impatience, Devona stared at the regal grandfather clock. It loomed from the far end of the dinning room. Devona hated Bishop's house. Too ostentatious. But she wasn't thinking about that at the moment. She wanted Esperanza. Wanted him *now.* The craving to destroy him again was unbearable. *Be careful, Devona. He could end up destroying you.*

Nah.

She was at the head of the stately cherrywood table, sipping Amaretto-laced coffee from an oversized mug. She tried to ignore the sound of her husband munching on pork rinds.

"It's getting late," she said.

"I'll try their cell again," he said and stuffed a handful of crunchy grease in his mouth. He chewed leisurely, eyes seething with jealousy.

Bishop entered, chest heaving. Face red and beaded with sweat. "You've heard from Mangineli and Hightower?"

"No," Rybak said. "Why?"

"Something's wrong," Bishop said. Had on his signature cardigan and tweed slacks. Even upset, not a silver hair was out of place. "I'm getting dozens of e-mails from members. The Webcast didn't take place." He planted the palms of his gracile hands firmly on the table. Devona swore she saw steam coming from his ears. Almost made her laugh. "I've tried Streiber's cell. He doesn't answer. Neither does Mario."

"Esperanza," Rybak muttered under his breath.

At the sound of his name, Devona felt a throbbing between her thighs.

"Brilliant bloke, aren'tcha?" Bishop closed his eyes for a moment. Inhaled. Deeply. Again. His eyes opened. "Clean up this bloody mess."

He's a cranky little monkey, Devona thought as Bishop headed back to his study.

"What do we do now?" she said.

"For the moment," Rybak said, wiping his palms together, crumbs raining on the table, "we wait."

"Boring," Devona said and hopped to her feet. "Gonna get some air. I'm tired of being cooped up."

She grabbed her steaming mug and stepped into the brisk winter night.

Esperanza studied Devona from his spot behind the sphere-shaped hedges. *Beautiful creature. Dangerous creature. The Devil in latex.*

Devona was in the lotus position on a bench in an intricately designed gazebo. The structure was painted ivory, except for the pagoda-style roof, which was varnished, natural pine. Looked like a tiny, open-air country church. Devona was holding a cup and staring at the full moon, seemingly unbothered by the cold. The wind sang, a melancholic trumpet solo. Esperanza could barely hear it, though. The sound of his heart doing a *mambo* was too overwhelming. His mouth went dry. Couldn't take his eyes off Devona. He ached for her. Parts of his newly healed body came alive with a vague, delicious pain. Bruises that had faded pulsed again. Places Devona had touched. Places that shamed him now invigorated him. Confused him, but somehow made him stronger. He knew who he was. A man who liked power, and serious, wild power games. He just wished this bitch hadn't been the one to show him the way. Esperanza wanted to destroy her, the same way she'd destroyed him. *There she is. What are you going to do now? Just can't stand here admiring her, fantasizing about her. Time to face your nightmare.* She closed her eyes. Face painted with pale moonlight.

Esperanza materialized from behind the hedges, gun steady in his hand. He moved like a shadow. Soundless. Invisible.

As he reached the steps of the gazebo, Devona opened her eyes. She registered no surprise. Instead, relief.

"Hello, lover," Devona said. "I've been waiting for you."

Esperanza hesitated for a moment. *Did she sense my presence? My fear?* He took guarded steps toward the gazebo, through a Victorian archway. Kept his Colt pointed at Devona's forehead.

"Miss me?" she said, then flashed a frisky grin.

"Lots," Esperanza said. He was having a difficult time swallowing. And breathing, for that matter. *Stay in control, Nick. Stay cool.*

Devona rose to her feet, slithered toward him, her movements languid and sensual. She had on velvet pants and a thin leather bolero jacket. Yet the cold still didn't seem to bother her. *Because it's the same temperature as her blood.*

"One more step, and you're dead," Esperanza said.

She stopped, moistened her inviting lips as her eyes gleamed with expectation. Devona coquettishly tilted her head to the side.

"After I spared your life, this is how you're gonna repay me?" she said. "You're gonna deny the unique bond we share?"

Esperanza cocked the hammer of his heavy automatic. "Don't move."

Devona took a confident step forward.

"You've been obsessing over me, haven't you?" she said. "I've been a constant guest in your dreams."

I should shoot the bitch right where she stands. Except his index finger refused to squeeze the trigger.

"Shut the fuck up."

"It's okay. You've been on my mind, too."

"You're fuckin' crazy."

"I'm the dark desire that's always burned deep inside you. You can't deny your own reflection. I've set you free." Devona leisurely pulled down the zipper of her onyx jacket, revealing a skin-tight bustier. Copper sequins and beading. Light sparkled from it. Seemed to make Devona glow. "I gave you what you've always fantasized about. You and I are one and the same. No need for rules." She let the jacket fall, and started caressing herself, fingers tracing the line of her neck, of her cleavage, up and down. *Up and down.* Her eyes seemed to grow darker. "All that matters to us is pleasure. Sheer, perfect pleasure."

In some ways, Devona was right. She'd opened him up, had erased the line between right and wrong. Taught him he was capable of *anything.* "I want you to make love to me," she demanded. "Right here. Right now."

She stepped closer, pressed her chest against the barrel of his gun. *Finish her, or you'll regret it, Nick.* He was paralyzed by the shadowy pools of her eyes. Her hand reached out, and her fingers crawled down his chest, his arm, to his wrist. Devona pulled his gun hand down. Esperanza lowered the gun to his side, uncocked the hammer and dropped the gun. The Colt bounced off the wooden floor, down the steps.

"I burn for you, Mistress," he said. His voice sounded like someone else was speaking.

"Yes, my slave." Devona kissed him delicately, drawing him into her sultriness.

I've been waiting for this. To be with her again. He encircled her with his powerful arms, and the kiss came alive with passion. Her mouth and tongue so spicy, he went into a feverish spiral. *This is so good.* His hands fondled her body with unabashed reverence as he crushed her against him and forgot about Alina, about Havelock. Even about Legs.

He was still Mistress Love's slave. She owned him. There was nothing he could do about it. *But this.*

Havelock pried the window open with a combat knife. From halfway down the lengthy hallway, he could hear a television and men laughing. He adjusted his tactical body armor. It was lighter than the vests the cops used. Gave you more freedom of movement. Havelock quietly slipped in. The sawed-off shotgun was in a holster attached to his broad back. The Heckler & Koch MP5 submachine gun felt good in his hands. *Like holding a beautiful babe.* Compact. Lightweight. Thirty-round magazine.

Havelock didn't like the idea of him and Esperanza splitting up. Their training had been all about teamwork, about watching your partner's back, taking an injury before letting a member of your team do so. But Esperanza insisted they separate, so they could cover more ground, more quickly.

Havelock crept down the hallway. Life-size oil paintings of knights, kings and queens hanging on daisy-yellow walls. *Bishop must think he's royalty.* Havelock could feel the adrenaline pumping. His senses were sharp. He sniffed the air. Buttered popcorn. Fresh-brewed coffee. *They're havin' a snack. Kickin' back. Not at all ready for an assault.*

Havelock was about five feet away from a double doorway. On the opposite wall, there was a colossal mirror. Baroque, wooden frame. Gave Havelock a clear view of the living room.

There were two men, relaxing and laughing, watching a sitcom on the big-screen TV. Both had shoulder holsters with automatics. The first cat was on a merlot-colored, velvet sofa, feet propped up on the antique coffee table, microwave bag on his lap, hand shoveling popcorn into his mouth. Crew-neck sweater and khakis and polished cowboy boots. The other one was sitting in an Eames chair, sipping coffee from a porcelain cup. He was bulkier. Fleece turtleneck sweater, matching olive cords. Shaved head. Havelock hated white boys with shaved heads. *They're just tryin' to take after the brothas.*

These guys were clowns, as far as Havelock was concerned. *They do have guns, though, and I don't know how many of 'em are in the house. Don't get too confident, mutha-fucka. Stay cool.*

Another man entered, from what looked like the dining room. Homeboy appeared to be a lot more serious. Havelock got the feeling it might be Rybak.

I'd be glad to waste him.

"You assholes havin' a good time?" The serious man spoke, and his boys sat at attention. "We have a situation."

"What is it, Rybak?" said the bald dude.

Havelock smiled to himself as he reached into his vest pocket for a flash grenade. *Time to get busy.*

"Chaz," Rybak said to the baldy, "I want you at the front gate. And I want Vince at the back of the house."

Vince put down the popcorn bag. "What's goin' on?"

"We might be getting some visitors."

At that very moment, Havelock pulled the pin on the flash grenade and tossed it into the living room.

Devona spun around, her back to Esperanza, taut ass grinding against his hard-on. Esperanza kissed and sucked and bit her neck and squeezed her breasts, and she went wild, her body rising and falling, as if possessed. Possessed by sex demons.

"I wanna ravage you," Esperanza whispered in her ear. He dry-humped her, losing himself in her decadence. *She smells of ripe mangos. Tastes like amaretto.*

Then it started. Maybe it was her scent that took him back. Visions suddenly began to flash in his mind. Devona whipping him. Biting him. *Raping me.* Laughing. An endless loop played his defiling over and over. *Wait. I can't do this.* Arousal turned to ire. Then to loathing. *I ain't gonna let her play me a second time.* He jerked his forearm around her neck and began to choke her. *Who's in control now?* He expected her to fight back, but she didn't even struggle. Instead, Devona seemed to be turned on by the cruel act. By the possibility of death. *Or does she think I won't really kill her?* She grabbed Esperanza's free hand and placed it between her legs. He unzipped her velvet pants, fingers digging in. Devona was soaking. *She's ready for me.* Esperanza played with her sweet spot. She reached behind her and stroked him. They undulated, both of them engulfed in a twisted, erotic dance.

Esperanza fingered her faster, and Devona's body became tense—a rubber band stretched to the point of breaking. *Yes, you puta. I'm going to take you as far as you wanna go.* She squeezed his *bicho* tight, until it hurt, then jerked her hand faster and faster. A flash of bright light came from inside the house. *Havelock.* Gunfire erupted. Didn't matter. Esperanza was lost in their profane coupling. *This is madness.* Devona shook, shuddered and trembled, as if hit with a thousand volts of electricity. The same sensation swept through Esperanza, and his knees buckled, but he still managed to stay on his feet.

Yes, yes, yes.

They climaxed together, and the rush was as exhilarating, as feverish as the first time. But this would be the last time. *I know who I am. I don't need a guide. Or a mistress who knows the alleys of my mind.*

Devona relaxed. *You won't haunt me anymore, Mistress Love.* Esperanza spun her around. She giggled. Crazy eyes half-closed. Strands of hair stuck to her damp face.

"I'll come visit you in jail," Esperanza said, then ruthlessly punched her across the jaw, sending her reeling to the ground. Devona moaned. Esperanza kneeled, punched her again. She lost consciousness.

He removed his leather belt, tied a loop around her ankles and then flipped her over on her stomach.

I should've killed her. But I owe her one. Too bad for Devona. I ain't setting her free.

He quickly pulled a bandanna from his pocket and tied her wrists behind her back. *Let's see how she likes being tied up.* Esperanza dragged Devona to the gazebo's rail, pulled her feet up and tied the end of the belt to the rail. He checked all the knots to make sure they were secure. *She ain't goin' anywhere. But prison.*

Esperanza picked up his weapon and headed for the house.

Chapter 26

Rybak and Chaz spotted the flash grenade rolling across the hardwood floor and dove for cover behind the ample redwood bar. Vince wasn't so lucky. Or so fast. A burst of intense white light, and he was blinded. Struggled for his weapon. Havelock let out a short burst of gunfire. Vince was hit three times in the chest. The impact of the bullets back-flipped him over the sofa. *Finally got himself some cover. Too bad he's already dead.*

Rybak sprung from behind the bar and tumbled like a gymnast. Havelock's bullets ricocheted off the floor, barely missing him. Rybak managed to make it through the dining room doorway, and returned fire.

Havelock no longer had the advantage of his view into the living room because the mirror on the wall exploded, with shards of glass flying through the air. He waited for a moment, then grabbed a piece of broken mirror and held it up, angling it so he could see without sticking his head out. Chaz leaned over the bar, weapon aimed. His gun hand was shaking, just a little.

He's afraid to die.

Havelock set his MP5 to full auto. He checked the gleaming parquet floor. Recently waxed. Nice and slippery. Havelock took several steps back, then ran and dove to the floor. As if lying sideways on a sled, he zoomed by, past the doorway, pulled the trigger and let out a torrent of gunfire, emptying the rest of the magazine in less than two seconds. Chaz didn't stand a chance. Though Havelock saw for only a moment, the top of Chaz's head was definitely blown off.

Havelock stood up, back pressed against the wall. His shoulder burned. There was a jagged piece of glass sticking out. *That's what I get for bein' fancy. Ain't no thang.* He gritted his teeth and pulled out the shard.

Through the window, Esperanza spotted Rybak, who was crouched by the doorway of the dining room, adjacent to whatever room the action was in. Havelock had detonated a flash grenade and fired a shitload of rounds, so there were plumes of smoke floating in from the other room. *Now it's your turn, Rybak.*

His gun aimed at Rybak, Esperanza quietly opened the French doors at the back of the house. *Let's see how he likes head games.* Rybak dropped the clip from his piece and was about to load another when Esperanza cocked the hammer of his Colt. Rybak spun around, automatic in one hand, clip in the other. He froze.

"Your wife's dead," Esperanza said, stepping toward him. "She came and went at the same time." Rybak was a statue. Face a blank canvas. "Drop it and kick it away."

Rybak dropped his weapon and the clip, and kicked them across the room.

Esperanza heard a footstep to his right. He swung his gun hand. Barely made out the figure of a hulking guard sneaking in from the kitchen. Esperanza fired once. Thug went into a swan dive. Ate glass as he crashed headfirst into a cherrywood china cabinet. Esperanza swung his gun hand back around, about to blow away Rybak. Too late. Rybak was already on the move.

"Devonaaa!" Rybak screamed so loudly, every single one of his dead victims must've heard him.

Rybak tackled Esperanza to the floor, grabbed his gun hand and slammed it against the floor until Esperanza let go of the Colt. Esperanza pulled out the Beretta tucked in the small of his back, but Rybak kicked it out of his hand. Rybak didn't bother trying to go after any of the weapons. His eyes were insane with grief as he began to strangle Esperanza with his bare hands.

Heart broken? You low-life scumbag. Good. Next it's gonna be your neck.

Esperanza twisted his hip and smashed his knee into Rybak's ribs. Knocked him over. They scrambled to their feet and circled each other. *Okay, let's do this hand to hand. See what Rybak's really made of.*

Sweeping his submachine gun's barrel from side to side, Havelock entered the living room. He'd heard Rybak scream like a crazy man, and it was followed by the sounds of a scuffle. As Havelock dashed to the dining room, looking to pop Rybak, Esperanza yelled, "Hav! Find Alina."

Havelock wondered for a moment what the hell was going on, but he quickly turned around and trotted from the living room and down the hall. *I hope Nick ain't doin' something too crazy. But he sounds like he's got a handle on the situation. This is an extraction. Time to extract.* There was a door. He pulled it open. Wooden stairs led to a basement. He slung the MP5 over his shoulder. Drew a small Maglite flashlight with one hand and the sawed-off with the other, then cautiously went down into the blackness.

They carefully circled each other. Warriors looking for an opening so they could go in for the kill. Esperanza could've let Havelock finish Rybak off, but he wanted the pleasure of doing it himself. His hands were up, one fist slightly higher than the other, arms loose and limber. Rybak had his arms wide open, as if he was ready to play catch.

"You killed my wife," Rybak said. "I'm gonna rip your fucking heart out."

Rushing forward with impressive speed and power, Rybak tackled Esperanza again, and they tripped over the china-cabinet corpse and stumbled into the spacious kitchen. The refrigerator, the sink and every appliance was shiny stainless steel. Esperanza bounced off the oak cabinet with the marble countertop and used the momentum to elbow Rybak in the jaw. Rybak threw several wild hooks, but Esperanza easily blocked and parried.

This motherfucker's had some serious hand-to-hand combat training, but he's got no discipline.

Rybak moved like a bull with swords in his back, and Esperanza, the matador, stayed graceful and quick on his feet, landing short, devastating blows to his opponent's face and body.

Rybak stumbled back, and then charged him again and managed to get Esperanza in a headlock. Letting out a nerve-wracking primal scream, Rybak banged the top of Esperanza's head against a kitchen-cabinet door just under the marble ledge. Esperanza saw flashes of light, and for a moment, he started losing consciousness.

Rybak flipped Esperanza over, threw him on the counter, then rammed his forearm into Esperanza's throat and pushed his jaw back.

Fuck. Asshole might not be light on his feet, but he's much stronger than I thought. Gotta stop thinking.

Rybak snatched a huge butcher knife from the wooden knife block, pulled it over his head and brought it down on Esperanza's face. Esperanza whipped his head to the side, and the tip of the knife nicked his ear. Esperanza thrust his thumb into Rybak's right eye, sending him reeling backward.

Coughing and gagging, Esperanza fought to regain his faculties. He could see his reflection in the toaster. *You don't look so good, Nick.* Though Rybak was stunned for a moment, he came after Esperanza once again, expertly waving the knife. His eyeball was filled with blood. Esperanza swiftly pulled the toaster's cord from the wall outlet, swung the heavy toaster like a knight wielding his mace and whacked Rybak right across the temple.

Before Rybak could recover, Esperanza grabbed the handle of the refrigerator's freezer door, swung it open and nailed his opponent square in the face, sending him to the floor. Esperanza kicked the butcher knife away.

Let's finish this.

Blood poured from Rybak's nose. His eye was swollen. Almost shut. *Cabron looks way worse than I do.* Esperanza tried to stomp him, but Rybak rolled out of the way and kicked him in the groin. Esperanza went down. Rybak sat on Esperanza's stomach and proceeded to beat the living daylights out of him.

From the bottom step of the basement stairs, Havelock stepped on the concrete floor. The air was cold and dank. There was the sickening odor of feces and urine, and an unremitting drip-drip of water coming from one of the pipes.

He heard a soft moan.

The beam of light from his flashlight revealed an unconscious teenage girl curled up on a flimsy canvas army cot. Wasn't Alina. *This girl's white. Strawberry blonde.* All she had on was a filthy T-shirt. Her swollen ankle was chained to a water pipe. *Damn. These are some sick muthafuckas.* Havelock kneeled, and checked her pulse. *Still alive.* He'd have to come back for her. Had to find Alina first.

Stairs creaked, and Havelock whirled around. In the glare of the flashlight, there was a middle-aged white man with silver hair aiming a revolver.

He fired twice before Havelock could get off a shot.

*   *   *

Rybak was on the tiled floor, with Esperanza on top of him. Esperanza's back was to Rybak, who had his arm locked around Esperanza's throat. *He's got me like I had Devona.* Esperanza stared at the ceiling, and it started to blur as Rybak choked the life from him.

"Now you die, fucker," Rybak said and squeezed harder. *That's what you think, asshole.*

Esperanza bent his right leg upward, and his hand crawled downward. He stretched, seemingly helping Rybak's strangulation plan. But when his hand reached his ankle, he felt for the mouse gun in the ankle holster.

Enough of this bullshit.

Esperanza snatched the tiny firearm, jammed the barrel against Rybak's temple and squeezed the trigger. The side of Rybak's head exploded, splattering gray, pink and red all over the floor and the cabinet doors.

He sat up, gasping for air. He stumbled to his feet and stared down at Rybak's body. *Two down, one to go.* His own eardrum felt blown out.

"Fuck you."

He kicked Rybak's corpse, retrieved his other weapons and then raced out of the kitchen to find Alina.

Chapter 27

Esperanza methodically searched the upstairs part of the house. Opened a door. It was the master bedroom. Queen-size canopy bed. A chaise lounge and a dresser. Camera on a tripod. *This is Bishop's playground? Not what I expected.* He moved on. Opened another door. Looked like a study. There were several desktop computers and servers and scanners on long tables. Wires all over the floor, like coiled black snakes.

Still there was no sign of Bishop or Alina. Or Havelock. Dead quiet.

Esperanza moved down the hall, gun leveled, making sure he cleared every corner.

Though in pain from his brawl with Rybak, he didn't let it affect him, didn't let it cloud his judgment. Still in the hallway, Esperanza looked up, noticed a pull-down door on the ceiling. *That's gotta lead to the attic.* He grabbed the handle and pulled, and the stairs flipped open, like a giant hand calling to him. *Hope Havelock's okay, wherever he is.* Esperanza carefully made his way up the stairs and into the attic. He adjusted his eyes to the moonlight pouring in through the single, circular window. Methodically, he scanned the room. There were boxes and plastic garbage bags. A soiled mattress propped against the wall. Computers covered in dust and cobwebs.

In the far corner, Esperanza saw Alina. She was nude, hog-tied and blindfolded. Before checking on her, he carefully inspected the attic. Checked behind the mattress, the boxes and the bags. *No surprises.*

He went over to Alina. She heard his footsteps and raised her head as best she could, trying to listen. Esperanza noticed the single light bulb overhead. Pulled the cord. Alina tensed up.

Esperanza stuffed his gun in the back of his pants and squatted down. There were black-and-blue bruises and welts all over her waif-like body. Cigarette burns, too. *Alina doesn't deserve this. Nobody does.* He reached out and touched her matted hair. She started squirming like crazy.

"Shhh." He took the bandanna from her eyes. She squinted, adapting to the light. "It's me. *Tio* Nick." He pulled a saliva-soaked sock from her mouth.

"Oh, my God. Oh, my God," she said hoarsely. "Get me the fuck outta here."

He put a finger to her blistered lips. "Quiet."

Esperanza pulled his switchblade from his back pocket and quickly cut the ropes. Alina moved sluggishly, rubbing her wrists.

His internal alarms suddenly went off. *Somebody's coming.* Alina struggled to stand, but he put his hand out, indicating to her not to move. He threw the knife to the mattress and drew his piece.

In a crab-like crouch, he swiftly moved across the attic. It was like his feet didn't touch the floor, because he didn't make a sound. Esperanza retreated to the back part of the floor opening, with his gun aimed. Someone was coming up the steps.

Due to the bright light emanating from the hallway below, Bishop's head seemed like an apparition emerging through the doorway. There was a nickel-plated .38 in his right hand.

As Bishop turned to look around, the barrel of Esperanza's automatic pressed against his forehead.

"Hello, Bishop," Esperanza said flatly. "Or should I call you Alladice?" A voice kept telling Esperanza to blow the bastard away. But he wanted Bishop alive. "Drop the gun." Bishop obeyed. The revolver dropped to the hallway floor below. "Now put your hands on your head, fingers interlaced, and join us." Esperanza gradually rose, the gun barrel ascending with Bishop as he climbed the steps into the attic. "I should waste you right this second."

"Then bloody do it," Bishop said. His eyes were detached. Ice. Not the affable man Esperanza met two weeks ago. Alladice/Bishop was much more of an impressive actor than Esperanza could've ever imagined. "Just spare me any speeches."

It took every ounce of self-restraint for Esperanza not to pull the trigger. "I think I'd rather see you in prison. You can do a short-eyes version of Shakespeare for the rest of the cons. They love pedophiles in the pen."

"You think you're intimidating me?" Bishop smiled. A strangely confident smile. Like he had something on Esperanza. "You're more of a—"

Bishop jerked forward. His face went white, and his jaw dropped as he let out a guttural moan. *What's he trying to pull? Oh, fuck this.*

Esperanza was about to fire his weapon when Bishop twirled around. Blood spurted from a knife wound in his back.

Alina, both hands over her head, held Esperanza's switchblade as she stood face to face with her tormentor. Any innocence she'd had was long gone. What Esperanza saw in her eyes was an unadulterated thirst for revenge. Something rabid. Something he understood all too well. Alina screamed and lunged, plunging the knife into Bishop's chest.

"Alina, no!" Esperanza yelled.

Too late.

Bishop collapsed to the floor. Though in a weakened condition, Alina moved way faster than Esperanza would've expected her to, leaping on top of Bishop and savagely stabbing him over and over.

Esperanza snatched her up by the waist, and Alina shrieked, legs flailing, as she attempted to break free.

"Muthafucka! Fuck you!" she screamed, and spit at Bishop. "Fuck you!"

"Calm the fuck down."

She kept struggling wildly. Her naked body was so fragile that Esperanza didn't want to squeeze too hard. She might crumble to dust. Alina finally relented. She wept, heaving and shaking. Esperanza released her, and she turned to him, hands covering her face. Blood all over her. Then, she abruptly embraced him. *Such a tiny, frail thing.* He held her and stared at Bishop, the knife handle sticking out of his chest, shirt stained crimson. The body twitched a couple of times, and the life finally drained from those steel-blue eyes.

Payback's a bitch, Bishop.

"It's over, *nenita*. It's over."

Esperanza easily scooped Alina up in his arms, and she wrapped her arms around his neck and buried her tear-covered face in his shoulder. He stepped over Bishop's body and carried the girl down the stairs, and the both of them, finally, walked into the light.

Thankfully, Havelock was fine. He'd taken two hits to his body armor. Might have a couple of fractured ribs. After Esperanza found blankets for Alina and the other girl, he called 911 and then went outside to check on Devona.

When Esperanza returned to the gazebo, the air rushed

out of him. He lost his balance for a moment. He stood there, dumbfounded.

Devona was gone.

On the floor, next to Esperanza's belt and bandanna, written in scarlet lipstick, were the words: "I'll see you in your dreams."

Esperanza got so dizzy, for a second he thought he might pass out.

I don't fuckin' believe it. I know I made those knots tight enough. How the fuck was she able to escape?

He picked up the belt and bandanna. Sniffed the bandanna for a moment. The scent of mangoes. Esperanza closed his eyes for a moment and took a deep breath. This wasn't over yet. He went back to the house to wait for the authorities to arrive.

Bishop's house swarmed with police cars and ambulances and a battalion of uniformed officers, detectives and emergency personnel.

Esperanza, hands cuffed behind his back, his face and clothes caked with dried blood, was escorted from the house by two detectives. One white, one black. The police had already taken Havelock away.

Alina was being strapped onto a gurney. She stared at Esperanza with tearful, grateful eyes. In her hand, she clutched her abuela's rosary beads. Esperanza had handed them to her minutes before. She smiled at him. He was amazed that she was able to smile. He couldn't. Not now. He nodded instead.

As they put Alina in the ambulance, Esperanza wondered about her future. *What kind of woman will she be after what she's suffered? She's already buck-wild. Is it all downhill from here? Will she end up a junkie, like her mom? Or will she turn her life around? Who knows. What-*

ever happens, her abuela will be there for her. Legs will be there for her.

I'll be there for her.

A beige, unmarked police car pulled up. It was Santos and Legs. They hopped out and raced over to him.

"Nick!" Legs called out.

One of the detectives held his hand out, stopping Legs dead in her tracks. Santos flashed his badge and said to the detectives, "Can you give us a minute?"

"No can do. He's a murder suspect," the white detective said. "You won't believe the bloodbath in there. Five corpses."

Legs tugged on her hair.

"Do a brother in blue a favor," Santos said.

The white detective glanced at his partner, who nodded. "Okay. Five minutes."

The detectives stepped away. Legs hugged Esperanza. He stared straight ahead. She was the last person he wanted to see. He was unable to look her in the eye. *I wish she hadn't come. I can't face her.*

"I'm so glad you're okay," Legs said. He watched her from the corner of his eye. She looked burned out. Eyes bloodshot and sunken in. "Alina?"

"She'll be okay. Girl's got a lotta heart," he said.

Legs made the sign of the cross and kissed the tip of her fingers. Just like her abuela. *"Gracia' a Dio'."*

God had nothin' to do with this.

"Go see your niece," Esperanza said, and jutted his chin. "She's in that ambulance over there."

Legs kissed Esperanza on the mouth and then dashed to the ambulance. He watched Alina break out in tears again when she saw Legs. They embraced. Held each other for a long moment as Legs planted soft kisses all over Alina's face. Legs looked over her shoulder at Esperanza. She was also crying. She mouthed the words, "Thank you." The ambulance doors slammed shut. Red lights flashed, the siren wailed and the ambulance pulled out of the winding, gravel driveway.

"You've gotten yourself into one hell of a jam, partner," Santos said, reaching out and squeezing Esperanza's arm, but his eyes were somewhere else. Somewhere far away.

"They're all dead," Esperanza said in a flat voice.

The two detectives returned. "I'll meet you at the precinct," Santos said, and headed for his car.

As the two detectives led Esperanza to their vehicle, the black one read him his rights.

". . . and anything you say *can* and *will* be held against you . . ."

How many times have I read a suspect his rights? More than I can remember.

The white detective put his hand on top of Esperanza's head and helped him climb into the backseat of their car.

The sun rose and smeared the sky with streaks of amber as the police car made its way through the lovely Long Island suburb. On its way to the precinct, where Esperanza would be booked, photographed, fingerprinted and interrogated. Placed in a holding cell.

Esperanza leaned his temple against the smudged window, his battered face bathed in the magical light of dawn.

It was difficult to believe that something so vile was going on in such a lovely neighborhood. But no more. He ended it. Found Alina. Shut down Bishop's child-porn ring. Broke plenty of laws in the process. Even committed murder. Esperanza knew that he could end up doing serious time. End up in the place he'd sent so many others to. *I went way over the line and danced the devil's mambo. Fuck it. I'm glad Rybak, Bishop and all the rest are burning in hell. They won't ever harm another child. And that's worth whatever price I gotta pay. Devona's still out there. I should've finished her off, too. The police will search for her but won't find her. But I'm sure she'll be back. And I'll be waiting . . .*

Esperanza watched the picture-perfect scenery zoom by. Finally, he closed his eyes, and as he drifted off into sleep, he didn't notice the tears running down his cheeks.

Epilogue

Naked and sexually satiated, Devona lounged on the bed of the motel room near John F. Kennedy International airport, sipping a glass of wine and reading the *Daily News*. The headline read: LOTTO COP NOT GUILTY!

A whole year had passed. Damn. She'd left the country for a while and returned a couple of months ago.

Devona sat up, leaned forward and carefully read the article.

Former N.Y.P.D. homicide detective Nicholas Esperanza was found not guilty yesterday morning in Manhattan Criminal Court on charges of assault and manslaughter. Esperanza became famous five years ago after purchasing a winning $30 million Lotto ticket. He affectionately became known as the Lotto Cop.

The criminal charges against Esperanza stemmed from the ex-detective's personal investigation into the kidnapping of his common-law wife, Magaly "Legs" Rivera's, 14-year-old niece. The girl's name is being withheld because of her age. During the course of his investigation, Esperanza inadvertently discovered and then broke up a human-trafficking and child-pornography ring, led by Rupert Alladice. Alladice, who was killed by the teenage girl during a struggle, was the director of

The Sanctuary, a shelter for runaway teens in Midtown Manhattan. Due to Esperanza's efforts, computer records were seized, and the attorney general announced that a major investigation involving the Justice Department, the F.B.I., and Interpol had been launched. Arrests have been made across the United States as well as in several other countries, including Canada, the United Kingdom, and Russia. Those arrested on child-pornography charges include schoolteachers, youth counselors, police officers, prominent businessmen and, in a surprising turn, New York State Court of Appeals judge Roy Tennenbaum. More arrests are expected in the near future.

Manhattan A.D.A. Jackson Thorpe spoke to reporters outside Manhattan Criminal Court after the verdict was announced yesterday.

"It saddens me that a jury has decided to send a message that vigilantism is OK. Though Mr. Esperanza shut down a major organization involving the trafficking of children, his methods were still criminal. The bottom line is, he broke the law. Unfortunately, the jury believed otherwise."

Esperanza's attorney, Ethan Wolvek, who used justifiable homicide as his client's defense, made this statement: "My client should never have been put on trial in the first place. The people of New York see him as a hero, not a criminal. He accomplished what local and federal authorities were unable to and put some very evil people out of business. We're happy that the jury saw through the D.A.'s political posturing and delivered the right verdict. The only verdict. Justice has been served."

Devona tossed the newspaper to the floor and looked up at the television. The eleven o'clock news was on.

Well, hello Nick. She grabbed the remote and turned up the volume.

Esperanza emerged from the courthouse, flanked by friends and family and police officers, and stopped in front of the army of reporters. Devona noticed he'd gained a few pounds, and there were more gray streaks in his hair. He sported a nicely tailored, single-breasted suit. Still looked yummy.

"I'm elated by the verdict," Esperanza said. "Relieved that all of this is over with. Now I just want to get on with my life."

Devona was momentarily distracted by the sounds of moaning. Harry was on the floor, ball gag in his mouth, wrists handcuffed behind his back and ankles tied with a leather belt. He was a pretty boy with strawberry-blond hair and a model's muscular body. She smiled to herself as she admired the welts and bruises decorating his body.

Too bad he was such a wimp. Couldn't take a fraction of the pain Esperanza endured. She was tired of him. Later on, she'd drug him, take him for a ride somewhere and end his miserable life. Devona turned her attention back to the television.

A reporter asked Esperanza how he felt being hailed as a hero by fellow New Yorkers. "I'm not a hero," Esperanza said. "I was just doing what needed to be done to help a family member in trouble."

And you killed my husband in the process.

She aimed her finger at the TV. Esperanza probably believed everything was fine and his life would soon return to normal.

No way, Jose. I'm not done with you yet.

Devona knew that she needed to be patient. Take her sweet time. Be methodical. Come up with the right plan.

Revenge, like sex and pain, should be savored.

She closed her eyes, and as thoughts of torturing Esperanza filled her mind, she began to giggle uncontrollably.

A thumping sound pulled her out of her reverie. She looked down at Harry. He was pounding the back of his head against the floor and whimpering like a baby.

How annoying.

Devona wagged her head, reached out, picked up the sharp knife from the nightstand and climbed out of the bed.

Harry screamed for dear life.

Too bad no one could hear him.

A CONVERSATION WITH
JERRY A. RODRIGUEZ

Q. How did you become a writer?

A. I was actually a pretty talented artist when I was a kid and intended to become a comic-book illustrator. I grew up reading Marvel comics, but I also loved books and watching movies. While attending Long Island University, I changed my major from art to media arts. Doing films and video was like creating comic books with actors, sound and image. An old high school friend who became an actor invited me to join a theater group. I started writing and directing plays, which I did for many years. I also did short films. I didn't start writing fiction until much later, when I decided to try out some short stories. I've worked in a variety of arts, from photography to illustration to theater, and I have to say, fiction writing is tougher then any of them, as far as I'm concerned. As a fiction writer, you're completely alone and your only tools are words. No fancy visual effects, talented actors or suspenseful music scores can save your butt. All you have is your imagination and words to stimulate all five senses. But the special intimacy between author and reader is the ultimate payoff.

Q. How did the idea for the novel come about?

A. Back in the early 1980s, when Times Square was a very dark, volatile and dangerous place, I decided to write a screenplay set in the area. I put the script away for ten years, and when I finally decided to rewrite it, Times Square had transformed into Disneyland. My original protagonist was an ex-con. I decided to make Esperanza an ex-cop instead, and substituted Times Square for New York City's sexual underground, which was thriving. There were some major issues regarding the Esperanza character. I'd read so many mystery novels in which the private investigator is struggling with being an alcoholic, is a loner and doesn't have any kind of personal life. I decided that Esperanza should be happy, successful and in a loving relationship. I also didn't actually want him to be a detective-for-hire. The idea was, what if he gets thrown into an investigation that takes him to such dark places that his life completely unravels? I thought it would make a much more exciting story. I decided to turn the Esperanza screenplay into a novel. I knew that turning the script into a novel would allow me to explore the characters and the settings in a much deeper and vivid way. Screenplays are pretty restrictive. You have to be concerned about visuals, budgets, shooting schedules, ratings and all those kind of things. The novel freed me up to creatively take the story much further than I could've ever done with a film script.

Q. Why do you write crime fiction?
A. I grew up watching crime films. Everything from *The Godfather* to *The French Connection* to *The Maltese Falcon*. I eventually started reading hardboiled authors like Raymond Chandler, Dashiel Hammet, Jim Thompson, Cornell Woolrich and David Goodis, and loved their work. Frank Miller's graphic novel *Sin City* was a huge influence. When I saw David Mamet's *American Buffalo*, a play about petty criminals planning a heist, I was blown away, and it made me decide those were the kinds of stories and characters I wanted to write about. I also like the moral ambiguity of crime fic-

tion and the fact that you can delve into the darker side of human nature. Crime fiction allows you to confront the negative characteristics of society. Whether you're dealing with issues ranging from politics to corruption to drugs to poverty to violence, the genre has no limitations as far as what questions you can raise.

Q. How do you think this book will be different from other mysteries and thrillers?
A. I think the fact that Esperanza is Latino and there haven't been many lead Latino characters in crime fiction gives the novel a distinct style and flavor. As much as crime writers deal with violence, they tend to stay away from sex and eroticism. I wanted to explore both sides of sex—when it's tender and loving and when it's dark and twisted. And it's not just sex for sex's sake; it's a major theme of the novel. I also think that the antagonists, particularly Devona Love, break away from convention. Funny thing is, Rybak and Devona were originally two run-of-the-mill male hitmen. I then decided that a married couple would be much more compelling. What if they were in a very loving relationship and made killing and torture a part of their lifestyle? Devona eventually took on a life of her own, became a force to reckon with, and turned out to be one of the most memorable characters in the novel.

Q. Did you do a lot of research?
A. Yeah, both on the Internet and in real life. One of the things I love about being a writer is people's willingness to open up and tell you all kinds of things. I've spent time in some pretty wild places, and I've interviewed some pretty wild people. I gain their trust because I don't judge them, so most of my subjects have been pretty honest. Over the years, I've interviewed sex workers, pimps, cops, drug dealers and dominatrixes. I've also hung out at different types of under-

ground sex parties. Nothing beats real research. A lot of other information and statistics I got from a variety of international and national law-enforcement Web sites.

Q. What do you hope readers will get out of this book?

A. Most of all that they've been taken on a journey into a world they've never experienced before. I hope that it will raise questions about the darker side of sexual desire and what it means to different people. I also want readers to come away wanting to know more about Esperanza and other characters, and want to follow them on their next journey.

Q. What is your writing process like?

A. I try to be really disciplined and write every day. I'm constantly thinking about stories, whether due to an article I saw in the newspaper, or some incident someone tells me about, or something that I see go down on the street. All of it becomes this constantly evolving mental stew. The writing process is not only about the physical act of writing; it's also about thinking, imagining and even dreaming. It's a process that goes on 24-7. I wouldn't have it any other way.